HEART OF THE STORM

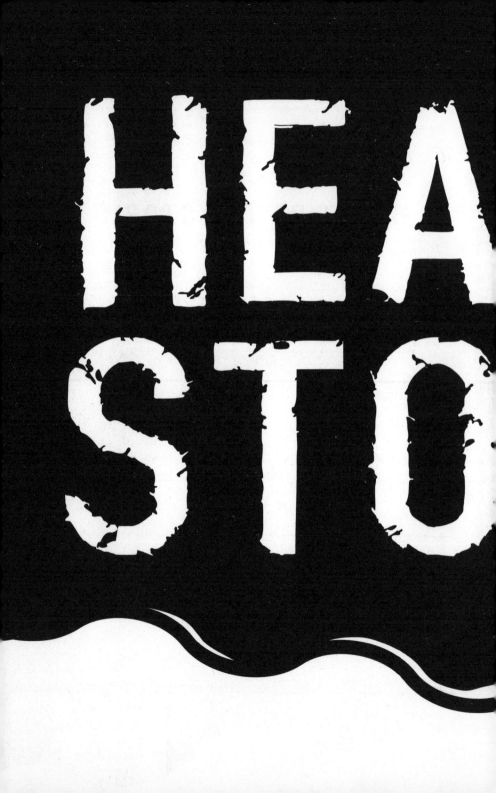

RT OF THE
RM

MICHAEL BUCKLEY

HOUGHTON MIFFLIN HARCOURT

BOSTON NEW YORK

The text was set in Dante MT Std.
Book design by Lisa Vega

Library of Congress Cataloging-in-Publication Data is available.
ISBN 978-0-544-34867-7

Manufactured in the United States of America
DOC 10 9 8 7 6 5 4 3 2 1
4500638918

For Gabi Gualpatin, a little mermaid

HEART OF THE STORM

CHAPTER ONE

I CAN'T MAKE OUT FACES AT FIRST. ALL MY TIME IN THE DARK has made me super sensitive to light, but I'm not worried. My other senses are heightened and helping out. I've learned to depend on the others—smell and sound, the taste of things, the sensations on my fingertips. They've helped me survive and will tell me a lot about the men who have come to rescue me.

From their breathing I count four of them, each wearing pants made from some slick and plastic material that crinkles when they walk. Their footfalls help me guess their height and weight. Each is over six feet tall. Three of them are hovering around two hundred pounds but the fourth is closer to two fifty. They all reek of fish and hard work. They must be fishermen. When they talk, they speak Spanish, a language I barely understand, but their voices give me a sense of their ages. One is an old man, and there are three younger ones. I'm on their ship. Every time the water slaps its side I hear a hollow pound.

"*Te tengo,*" one of the men says as he hoists me out of the water. He has strong arms. He sets me down next to him and when I put my arm on his shoulder I feel a heavy wool sweater. I wish I had a sweater. The wind is nasty and bitingly cold. My jumpsuit is so torn and mangled it no longer insulates much, so the weather pokes at every part.

"Mira su espalda!" one of the men cries. His fear drifts into my nose. He's terrified of me. Perhaps he sees the scales. I reach for my jaw and feel my gills vanishing under my skin.

"Mira a los brazos," another shouts. *"Ella es un demonio."*

Demonio is a word I know all too well from Shadow's mother. She was a very religious person, and whenever anything bad happened, she blamed the *demonio*—i.e., the devil. The man backs away from me, reaching for something long and dark mounted on the wall.

"No se engañen, ella es una sirena," the old one says. My eyes are starting to adjust. I can make out his bushy gray beard.

"Wait? Did you just say Sirena?" I cry.

"She speaks English."

"Where did you come from?"

"I thought they had tails."

"There are all kinds," the old man explains impatiently. "Back up. You're crowding her."

"No! We have to throw her over the side! More will come," the smallest of the group cries. His hands lock on my arms. He's pushing me toward the railing.

Bam! My palm crashes into his jaw. It's a crushing shot, considering I still can't fully see him. My second punch connects as well, and knocks the wind out of him. The oxygen flies out like a rocket launching into space. While he recovers, my foot crashes into his partner's kidney. He backs away, groaning and in pain.

"Girl, you must calm yourself," the old man shouts.

"You calm down. I'm winning."

There's a long moment where only the wind is begging us to relax.

"This is my boat," the old man yells at the others. "She needs help, and we're going to help her. If you have a problem with that, you can start swimming for shore now."

I don't hear any complaints.

"I need a ride," I finally rasp. My voice is weak and cracking from lack of use. It sounds unfamiliar on the surface.

"First you tell me the truth. Are there more of you out there?" the old man demands.

"No. I'm alone, and I'm not a mermaid. I'm American, from New York City. I need to get to land. I have to get back home."

"What's your name?" One of the younger ones demands. He's tall, handsome, a youthful version of the old man. With my sight fully returned, I can see the others have the same features. They must be his sons. I haven't seen a human face in so long. I'd reach out and caress their cheeks if I hadn't just punched them.

"Lyric Walker."

He studies me closely, rubbing the three- or four-day scruff on his face. I'm a square peg, and all he has in front of him are round holes.

"Lyric Walker is dead," he says.

A bitter blossom opens wide in my belly. The world has given me up for dead? If four fishermen in the middle of nowhere think I was killed, then everyone must think the same thing. My mom and dad must be heartbroken. Bex, the Alpha kids—I've caused so much pain. Is that why Fathom didn't come for me? No, that's letting him off easy. He should have come.

"Can you take me to shore?"

"There's a nasty storm coming our way," the old man says as he gestures toward the horizon. Rain pours out of a hole in the clouds and batters a little rock of an island you wouldn't see if you didn't know it was there. Hot lightning slashes the sky, leaving glowing purple scars. "We'll take you, but no more rough stuff."

I throw up my hands in surrender.

"Pop! Are you sure?" The tallest of the three boys is not happy.

"It's my boat," his father roars, again. "Did I raise the three of you to leave a girl stranded out here in the middle of the Atlantic? You wait until your grandmother hears how selfish you have become. She'll disown the whole bunch."

"She's no girl, Pop. She's something else."

The old man waves his sons off with his huge, meaty hands. "You let me do the thinking around here. Keep packing the fish in ice. That's three hundred thousand dollars' worth of mackerel spoiling in the sun."

There are no more complaints from his boys, and the old man seems satisfied. He turns, tilts his head toward a flight of stairs that lead down into the belly of the boat, and then points himself in that direction. His three sons get back to work, turning on a huge machine bolted to the deck. It whines and shakes, crushing ice into tiny cubes. The brothers use hooks to drag monstrous white fish into the hull, and the ice spills down on top.

"Those are good fish," I say.

The youngest son gives me some sideways shade, then puts his eyes back on his job.

The captain helps me manage the steps. We descend into a tight and narrow hallway. The ceiling is too low, and the walls are too close. I have to fight the urge to turn and bolt back up the stairs.

"Something wrong?" the old man asks.

"I'm not used to tight spaces, or having something over my head," I explain.

"Sorry, but it's all close quarters on a boat. Comfort takes a back seat to practicality," he says as he continues onward. We pass three hatches, each dark and cramped. One is a bunkroom with two sets of steel bunk beds mounted to the floor and walls. Footlockers rest beneath them. Everything is neat and tidy. Not a single thing is out of place. He flips on a light, and my eyes squint into it. I can't help but marvel at its glow. Electricity is something I once took for granted. With just a flick of the finger, darkness is dashed. It's such a casual activity, but now it feels like I'm witnessing a miracle.

While I'm gawking like Harry Potter on his first day at Hogwarts, my host bends down, opens a lockbox, and removes a wool sweater just like the one he's wearing. In a flash I'm out of my jumpsuit. It's the first time I've taken it off in months, and it feels good to get the clingy, wet fabric off me. The old sailor stumbles back in surprise. I've shocked the hell out of him with my nakedness. I yank the blanket off the bed and wrap it around me, but he's already seen the whole show.

"Don't get any funny ideas," I say to his tomato-colored face.

"Oh, this old-timer isn't looking for another punch in the face," he says. "Now, what is going on with your back?"

He gently turns me around and pulls the blanket away a little.

"What's this stuff you've got wrapped around you?" he presses. Before I can stop him, he unties the twine that holds a mound of black weeds to my skin. All of it falls to the floor like a wet towel.

"*Dios mío,*" he whispers.

I have no idea what my back looks like. I haven't seen it,

and even though there is a mirror in the cabin, I decide not to look. What do I need to see? I can imagine the crisscrossed collection of scars and welts and fresh lacerations easily enough.

"I've got a first aid kit in the kitchen," he says, darting out of the room like he's seen a ghost. "You're going to need a doctor."

"I'll be fine," I call after him.

I can hear him rummaging around in one of the other rooms. While he's gone, I study a map pinned to the wall. It's of Central America, from Costa Rica all the way up to Haiti. At the top, where the map stops, is the Caribbean Sea.

"Where are we headed?" I shout.

"Panama," he says when he returns with a rusty steel case featuring a big red cross painted on the front. He opens it, sorts through some of the packs, then finds a can of something and gives it a good shake.

Panama. I wasn't too far off in my guesses. I knew they took me south. The water was warmer. I wonder if my geography teacher would be proud. I wonder if she's still alive.

"This is going to sting," he warns, then sprays my skin.

He's no liar. When the icy cold propellant hits my back, it feels like a cowboy is branding it with a sizzling poker. He apologizes, but he doesn't stop.

"It's a miracle that this isn't infected," he hisses, as if my wounds offend him. "The spray will go a long way to keeping it clean."

"What's the date?"

"February twenty-sixth," he says.

Three months. I've been gone for three months.

Next he smears a greasy salve over everything and bandages me the best he can. He helps me into the sweater and a pair of baggy running shorts that threaten to fall down.

"What hurt you like that?"

"It was a who."

He doesn't push me for more information, and I'm grateful. How am I going to explain the last three months of my life? It's just too much, and telling him seems unfair, like I'm dumping a burden on his shoulders.

"Let's get you something to eat." He leads me back into the hall, past a door I guess leads to the engine room. A colossal, boxy machine lives inside, covered in gauges and glowing buttons and a pressure wheel. It rocks back and forth, like it's thinking about breaking through the door and making an escape. The final room is a galley kitchen with stainless-steel cabinets, a microwave, mini fridge, and a padlocked cage full of canned goods. Like the other rooms, everything is bolted to the floors and walls, including the table and chairs. He smiles when he notices my curiosity.

"A big wave could send it all flying," the old man explains. "You can't have furniture soaring through the air when you're trying to survive a hurricane."

He gestures to an empty chair, and I sink into it while he

goes to work removing bowls and a carton of milk from the fridge.

"I haven't sat in a chair in a while," I say out loud, not really to him, but more to myself, a statement of fact, a reminder that I'm back in the land of the living. He's a bit bewildered, but then either accepts that I've been through hell or doesn't want to get wrapped up in any more of me.

"What's your name?" I ask.

"Encardo," he says. "Those are my sons up there, Ricardo, Manuel, and Nicky."

"They're nervous about me."

"They don't see a lot of mermaids," he says.

"I'm not a mermaid."

"That's not what I read. What are you then, Ms. Walker?"

The answer feels trapped at the center of a maze. I wonder if I can steer him in the right directions, help him avoid the dead ends, until he finds the truth, but I can't trust where the path will take him. It's too confusing. Even I get lost on the way to the answer.

"My mother is a Sirena, sort of what people think of when they think mermaid. My dad is human."

"Interesting," he says. I can't tell if it's good interesting or bad interesting. "Are there many like you?"

"No, not a lot," I say. "Your English is very good."

"Thank you. My mother was from Cleveland. How do you find yourself floating more than two hundred miles from any inhabited area?" he asks, keeping his eyes on the stove. He tosses tortillas into a skillet and flips them over using only his bare fingers.

"Oh, you've probably heard this story a million times," I tell him.

He laughs. "Try me."

"I was taken against my will. I escaped, and now I'm trying to get home to find my family."

"It's a miracle you didn't drown out there. That's a nice talent. Any chance you can teach me and the boys how to do it?" he says, scooping refried beans out of a Tupperware bowl and putting them into the pan.

"You'd be better off staying out of the water, Encardo."

He hears the warning in my voice and locks eyes with me for a brief moment. Again, he doesn't press for more information. Maybe he's smart enough to know better.

When the timer goes off, he adds a little cheese and some chopped tomatoes, then slides it all onto a paper plate. I look down into my lunch, feeling the heat on my face, smelling the lovely, spicy aroma, and quietly thanking God that it isn't fish. I haven't eaten anything I didn't kill myself in a long time. The first bite reminds me of home; lunches at the cheap Mexican place on Neptune that served plantains and tacos with red cabbage. The flavors and memories sweep me away, and tears I can't explain dribble down my cheeks.

"Something wrong?"

I shrug, because words feel inadequate to express the rush of memories, and the shocking reminder that I was once a teenage girl. How do I tell him that his kindness is almost too much to take, like having a memory of a past life? Only a crazy person is overcome by a fork and a plate and a table and a napkin, but they are a glorious equation that proves I am human again, and alive. Maybe there are words, but I don't know them. My energy has to stay focused on fighting back sobs and the impulse to pocket the fork because it would make an excellent tool.

Encardo sets his hand on mine and gives it a pat before pulling it away. Maybe he doesn't need any words to understand.

There is a vague recollection of table manners buried in the back of my mind, but I'm too hungry to care, and considering the number of stains on Encardo's sweater, I suspect he doesn't care two shakes about niceties. I gobble everything down with a ferocity that's embarrassing. Encardo scoops up the plate and piles more on top. He hovers until I'm ready for thirds, piles them high, then pulls a chair up across the table from me.

"They say you're a killer, Lyric Walker."

I set the fork down and shake my head. "They say a lot of things, Encardo. Here's what I'm saying. I was a kid when New York was attacked. I did everything I could to stop it. I saved people. You have to believe me. I didn't want my home to be destroyed in a tidal wave, but what could I do? I was a soldier for the second attack. I fought hard, but people still died. Friends of mine died, but I saved the world. Anyone who tells you different doesn't know what they're talking about."

I'm not expecting him to believe me. He's read what he's read, and he's seen what he's seen, and all of it was filtered and edited into whatever sold the most outrage. I shouldn't be surprised that people don't know the truth, but I can't help feeling indignant.

"Does that answer your question?"

He sits back in his chair, studying me until he nods.

"Got any more of those beans?" I ask.

He chuckles to himself and snatches my plate for the third time.

When I'm so full I can barely breathe, I help him clean up and thank him for the meal.

"I had a daughter once," he says, wistfully. I don't press him on it. I guess we're even. "C'mon, I'll get you a place to sleep."

He leads us back through the hall and into the room with the bunks. Under the bed where he got the sweater is another trunk full of blankets and pillows. He snatches a few and throws them on a bottom mattress.

"Sleep if you can. If the storm catches us, there won't be rest for anyone," he warns. "You can lock the hatch from the inside, not that you'll need to, but if there is an emergency, I'll need you on deck helping out. Just letting you know. The ocean is an unpredictable creature."

"Yeah, I've heard."

I flip the lock back and forth, just to try it out.

"I heard Coney Island is gone now," he says. "Where will you go?"

"The most boring place I can find," I reveal.

"If they have rum, I'll come for a visit. I'll wake you before we get into port."

"Encardo, do you have family in Panama?"

"My wife and some grandbabies. Nicky and Ricardo are married. Why?"

For a moment, I consider not telling him the truth. I really want to put it all behind me, get on land, and find my way back to New York. I want to be done with everything, but he's been so nice. He deserves a chance.

"There's something out in that water," I say. "Be ready to take the people you love and leave when it comes onshore. Do you believe I'm telling you the truth?"

He stares at me for a long time, mulling my warning, then he nods and wishes me a good night. When the hatch is pulled close, I lock the door and listen to his boots stomping down the hall and up the steps. I don't take another breath until I hear him above me.

"I think we're okay, now," I whisper to myself, then crawl

onto the bunk and curl myself into an embryo. How decadent it is to lie down, to pull a quilt over me for warmth, to fold the pillow in half to support my head, all the little labors of making myself comfortable. Everything is a miracle, even the yellow light bulb ticking on the ceiling. I'm so excited by the possibility of sleep I can barely lie still.

With a flick of a switch, the room becomes a tomb. In my old room I needed it to be practically pitch-dark before I could sleep, but now I feel like I'm in a crevice at the bottom of the sea where horrible things scurry. My throat constricts. Panic wraps around my lungs and squeezes the air out of me. I open my mouth to scream but nothing exits. I sit up, frantically searching for the switch with clumsy fingers. Click. The room is aglow again, but I'm still shaking, my bones rattling in their joints. The dark is no longer my friend.

Lyric, you cannot abandon us.

"Where I'm going you can't come," I whisper.

The voice wants to argue, but I push it out of my mind. Damn his expectations, his heroic plans to rally the world and prepare for a fight. I'm going to find the people I love, and we're going to Denver, or somewhere else that's high on a mountain where the bogeyman can't ride in on the tide.

Lyric. They will find you. You can't hide.

"I'm sure as hell going to try," I cry, pressing my hands

against my head to block out his pleas. I rock back and forth on the mattress until his voice fades and the creaking ship returns as my only soundtrack.

"I thought I had this room to myself," I whisper to no one. The emptiness feels awfully crowded.

CHAPTER TWO

THREE MONTHS EARLIER

F OR FIVE MINUTES, I WAS A FLAMING GODDESS OF FURY, A total badass powered by magic, science, and a little inner-city swagger. Basically, I was Beyoncé. So, when an invasion of brain-sucking sea monsters attacked, it was hardly a problem at all. A nightmare made out of tentacles and hunger crawled out of the ocean, and I didn't even break a sweat. I was five foot eight inches of atomic power—rocking a shaved head to boot. I saved the frickin' world. I should have been allowed a victory lap or a ride off into the sunset with a dreamy prince or a hot nerd with potential. Instead, the last of the enemy showed up just as I burned out my batteries. I was exhausted, weak, and surrounded.

Typical, right?

Shocking plot twists come fast and furious in Coney Island, like the time I watched a race of sea people walk out of the ocean and set up camp near the boardwalk, or when I found out my mom was one of them and that I'm not 100 percent human, or when I was locked in a prison camp and forced to train a team of children to fight a war. I've learned to dodge some of the punches and absorb the rest, but this wasn't fair. Having to watch those ugly bastards leap out of the ocean to drag me under was all kinds of wrong. If it happened in a book, the reader would be super pissed. People like a happy ending. Trust me, I was in the mood for one myself.

The monsters were everywhere. There must have been dozens of them, behind me, in front, on either side—even if I could have fought back, I doubt it would have made a difference. Hands clamped down on my limbs. Teeth gnashed and chattered in my face. Long black tongues licked greasy mouths. They dragged me toward the water, always back to the water.

But there was one glimmer of hope. I caught a streak of light in the corner of my eye. Its owner was a boy in a black jumpsuit like mine, with dark hair and eyes, his glowing fist encased in a silver metal glove. He streaked toward me like a comet. Riley was ripping the ocean apart. The glove gave him command of the water, and he sculpted it into something bigger and uglier than the monsters trying to kill me. A wave rose up, arrogant and eager to crush those beasts into mud. Riley wasn't going to let them take me. He liked happy endings too. I'm not going to lie—it was kind of sexy.

The creatures knew what was coming. They let loose an indignant howl. None of them could do what Riley could, and they knew the smackdown was coming.

Do it, Riley! Turn them into bags of bones! I thought, and as the swell crested higher and higher until it threatened to blot out the sun, it looked like that was exactly what was going to happen. The wave convulsed and boiled, eager to do its ugly work, but one of the creatures refused to accept its fate. It sprang at Riley, leaping an impossible distance, and caught him in the gut. The punch was so cruel and savage the world winced. Riley's body folded in half and flailed backward. His glove's once blazing power blinked out before he even hit the sand. He lay still and quiet.

"Lyric!" A voice rose above the clamor, one I didn't want to hear. Chloe shouldn't have been there. I didn't want her to see Riley's body or watch what was about to happen to me. *Chloe, run away! Just go!* But she was as stubborn as me.

"Why aren't you fighting them?" she cried. My little freckle-faced friend expected a miracle. She believed I had a well of second winds, an unlimited supply of grit and determination, but she was wrong. Killing a ten-story sea monster and its million babies had taken a lot out of this girl.

"Run!" I shouted, spending all that was left of my strength. She was startled by my tone, but it pierced her brain and she did what I asked. I watched her little feet kick up sand as she raced back toward the camp for help. I told myself the soldiers would take care of her, or the other kids. She'd grow up. She'd be fine. She'd manage. She was the strongest one of us.

I felt a jerk, and I was back in the water, under the salty, gray Atlantic. A bone-chilling cold wrapped its hands around my lungs and squeezed. Swirling sand and pollution blinded me. Bellowing water punched my ears. Every sense was assaulted and overloaded. I felt myself slipping away into a blessed unconsciousness where I would not know when the monsters killed me, or what they would do to me afterward.

Where was Fathom? I wondered. Why wasn't he there to save me?

In the murky soup there was only one face I recognized —Minerva's. She circled me, her eyes burning with a sick joy. Her already fragile mind had been pushed over the edge when Fathom killed her husband. Then she watched me destroy most of her monster army, decimating her plans to conquer humanity. Together, Fathom and I had taken everything from her. Now, it appeared, all she had left was revenge. She pulled back and slapped me with a hand like concrete, and then there was nothing but black.

Let's get something straight—waking up underwater was all kinds of wrong. There was salty liquid invading my nose, swirling down my esophagus, and spilling into my gut. Panic took over, and I screamed. The creatures who had snatched me off the beach barely acknowledged me. They kept swimming and dragging me along.

I'm not drowning, I told myself, over and over again. Intellectually, I understood that I was not fully human and I couldn't drown. Seawater awakens my DNA, and my body adapts. My mother is a Sirena, one of the many tribes of the Alpha nation. My dad is human, so I've got only a few of mom's genetic gifts. Luckily, they were enough to keep me alive. A burning sensation beneath my jawline told me the skin had separated to make room for my gills. The sea filtered through them, oxygen was removed and fed to my bloodstream; water poured down my throat and into my gut, only to be pumped back out.

Whether or not being alive was a good thing remained to be seen. Minerva and her monsters still had me, and I was still not strong enough to break free. I shouted at them, but they ignored me and kept swimming. I took some relief in the belief that they weren't planning to eat me. Why would the Rusalka drag their food miles and miles into the ocean when they could just rip me apart?

Unlike Sirena, the Rusalka are not beautiful. They don't have the fish tails or the pretty faces. Rusalka are freakish, malformed goblins swept off the bottom of the ocean where even the light is afraid to go. Their skin resembles an eggplant with white undersides, and their frames are a collection of stringy limbs and bloated bellies. They've got more fangs than face. Their mouths chomp and gnash endlessly. They crack their own teeth into pieces that fall out like spittle. Their eyes are bulbous, black orbs as vacant as bottomless pools. Looking into them is like standing over an open manhole wondering how deep it goes. But by far their creepiest feature is the snake-like strand of flesh that dangles down from the tops of their heads and ends in front of their mouths. In the dark its shiny lure dances in the dark, beckoning to its prey. *Come closer, just a tiny bit closer.*

Rusalka, however, were not my biggest fear. Their boss struck terror in everyone. Despite being one of the most beautiful people I had ever seen, Minerva couldn't hide the insanity that crept behind her eyes. As her husband's greatest adviser, she was the voice that encouraged his doomed invasion. She was the giggling puppet master who pulled the strings of death and destruction. I couldn't see her in the milky water, but I could hear her, rambling and bellowing, sharing her heartbreak with the entire Atlantic. I should have laughed at her grief. She'd tried to kill everyone I love at least once. She was tasting the tragedy she'd served to so many. My joy at her suffering should have filled tiny silver bubbles with giggles. I was too afraid to laugh at her. Her anguished shrieks felt dangerous, like a high fever, a contagious pathogen bent on invading my bloodstream and infecting my mind. Even the Rusalka kept their distance. They held their hands against their tiny ears, desperate to protect their feeble brains from her sickness.

No, I didn't dare laugh. I was afraid I wouldn't be able to stop.

When the White Tower corporation sent me back to Coney Island with the kids, they put us all in black jumpsuits with their stupid logo on the front. I hated them. It made me feel like a product, something you could pull off the shelf at the grocery store and run across the scanner. I guess that's exactly what the children and I were to them. They sold us to the military as secret weapons against Alpha aggression. Like most people, they didn't understand that the Alpha were not a threat. They were "other" and had to be destroyed.

During those dark hours in the sea, I thanked heaven for that jumpsuit. It was insulated and kept me from freezing to death in those depths, but it didn't protect my fingers, toes, or head. My hands and feet filled with concrete, and I'd lost all feeling in my pinky fingers. I was panicked about frostbite. My father, the cop, used to tell horror stories about homeless people who crawled under the boardwalk during blizzards to escape Coney Island's relentless winter wind. He'd found so many with black and lifeless hands and feet, he started carrying extra hand warmers around and passing them out to anyone in need, but he still had to help countless victims into ambulances.

It was so dark at those depths I couldn't see the telltale sign from his warnings, the purple blossoms that form underneath the skin, and not knowing elevated my fears into something that threatened to strangle me. A choking vine of horror sprouted in my belly and grew up into my throat.

The other symptom of frostbite is sleepiness, and my eyelids were like anchors. My father's voice shouted at me to fight.

Lyric! You have to stay awake. If you go to sleep, the oxygen levels

in your blood will drop and brain damage will occur. You'll go into a
coma. You might never wake up.

Tiny fireworks were popping in my eyes. Dreams were coagulating in my vision. Suddenly, I was at the YMCA pool learning to float on my back, then I was lying on our couch in our apartment staring at a water stain on the ceiling. I was playing Uno with my parents at our rickety kitchen table. I had a green "draw two" card, and I slapped it down on my mom. She scowled, and my father roared with laughter. Then I was on the beach with her and she was correcting my pigeon pose. Seagulls swooped and dove overhead. The sand became a classroom with windows covered in construction paper. I sat on the floor trying to teach a beautiful and difficult Alpha prince how to read *Where the Wild Things Are*. When he pulled me close, it felt as if I'd been waiting for his mouth my whole life. Our kisses were urgent, our breathing frantic.

And then it vanished—all of it. A slap to my face rocked me awake. The pain of the blow sizzled down my cheek and along my neck. Minerva clamped her hand on my jaw, and dug her nails into my skin. I tried to pull away, but she was too strong. She pushed her face into mine. Her corneas erupted. Her mouth twisted and screamed, but I couldn't understand a word. The message, however, was loud and clear. She wasn't going to let me die so easy.

She barked at one of the Rusalka, and it swam to my side, roughly snatched my forearm, and pulled me upward. Higher and higher we went, until the black became gray, then blue, then yellow. We must have risen hundreds of feet in a matter of minutes. A normal person couldn't have survived the sudden changes in pressure. I should have suffered the bends. My brain should have turned to jelly. I had my mother to thank again.

"Why are we here?" I asked when we broke the surface. It was warm there, and the sun was bright and hot. There was nothing in any direction worth looking at, just the bubbling swells and crashes of an anxious sea.

"Can you understand me?" I asked.

It blinked.

"Do you have a name?"

The creature said nothing, only stared at me with its empty eyes and waited for the warm water to melt my frozen body.

The farther we swam, the warmer the ocean grew, so I assumed we were heading south, maybe toward Florida or even beyond to Central America or the Caribbean. We were swimming closer to the surface and moving into waters that were clearer and cleaner. I was seeing things there I've only seen on Discovery Channel—turtles, and multicolored fish, and slowly prowling predators as big as my arm. They streaked past us in every direction, sometimes darting up to my face to inspect me, then shooting off like lightning.

We swam above a coral reef that was alive and unspoiled

by human hands. It was a vast bed of reds and oranges, a sanctuary to fish and flora for miles and miles. Lobsters scurried along its twisting tendrils like squirrels racing across the branches of an oak tree. Tiny blue fish peered out of crevices and stared as we passed by. Anemones waved their magenta tendrils left and right with the current. Everything was vibrant and alive. Back in seventh grade, Bex did a report on coral reefs. She built a model complete with little fish stickers and chunks of a kitchen sponge she cut up into tiny pieces. She was really proud of it before her mother's boyfriend at the time came home drunk and fell asleep on top of the whole thing, crushing it flat. I helped Bex put it back together at the last minute, and I guess some of what she learned stuck with me. Coral reefs grow near coastlines, mostly in tropical areas of the world. It wasn't a lot to go on, but it was a clue to where we were heading.

Despite all the beauty, Minerva's grief poisoned my surroundings. Her voice rang out as fresh and raw as the day her husband fell dead on the beach with his son standing over him. Now it was accompanied by prayer. I'd heard the Alpha version of worship before, back when Arcade, Bex, and I traveled across the country. The Triton girl sat for hours beneath the desert sky, shouting threats and demands at her god, the Great Abyss. There is no humbleness in the Alpha religion. They don't bow their heads and kindly ask for help from heaven. They rail for justice and blood and promise that if it isn't delivered, there will be hell to pay. Arcade was Fathom's fiancée, promised to him as a child, and when she believed he was dead, she dared the Great Abyss to refuse her vengeance. She scared the crap out of Bex and me. We huddled in the car like frightened children while our friend brought down thunder and lighting around us, and Arcade was sane. Well, relatively sane. Minerva, on the other hand, was completely nuts. Her prayers stabbed my ears.

We entered a part of the sea that was hauntingly deep. Massive mountains rose up to meet us. The valleys between them spread wide for miles and dropped into barren, empty bowls of blackness.

The water was thick and metallic. It filtered through my gills, stinging the vulnerable flesh. My throat burned. My tongue swelled. It was a poisonous place, and it grew more toxic the closer we got to a glowing red light in the distance. I begged the Rusalka to turn around. Their gills were as raw as my own, but they didn't listen to me. They dragged me onward, toward the massive mountain ahead of us, and its crown of fire.

Within a day, we cowered at its feet. The red light was a burning furnace that breathed in and out, a greedy inhale that swallowed the entire ocean and an exhale to regurgitate it all. Fish and filth alike were sucked into the broken crater at its very top. No one had to tell me what I was seeing. This was the Great Abyss, but it was no god. I was never a good science student. I was never a good anything student, but I recognized a volcano. The Alpha deity was an active underwater vent. It was the source of light we had followed for days. It was the source of the tremors that rattled my bones.

And I suddenly realized why Minerva brought me there. Both Arcade and Fathom told me criminals were tossed into the Great Abyss and never seen again. Their deaths must have been excruciating, burned alive as they were dragged deeper into the volcano's boiling jaws. Minerva was going to feed me to her god. She was going to toss me in and let the Great Abyss swallow me whole.

I was fucked.

CHAPTER THREE

A HEAVY FIST POUNDS ON THE STEEL HATCH DOOR. ONE of Encardo's sons is outside shouting my name.

"We're coming into the dock," he shouts.

"Thank you," I call back, then listen for his boots to climb the steps. When he's gone, I stand and come face to face with myself. A mirror mounted on the back of the door, something I didn't dare use the night before, can't be avoided. I have always been unapologetically vain. I'm seventeen. I'm young and, well . . . I was hot, once. Now, as I look at my reflection, I feel like I'm staring at a stranger. My skin is markedly pale, almost like a corpse. I'm way too thin. I've lost all the curves that used to make me self-conscious and then some. Now I want them all back. My body is all muscle and tendon, lean and efficient, pure necessity. My eyes are sunken. I look crazed. I play with the mop of hair on my head. It's like hay. Chunks of it come out in my hand. None of this concerns me the way it once would, when I was a wild thing running the streets of my neighborhood and making boys crazy. What concerns me is that my appearance is going to draw attention in ways I don't want, especially if I'm on foot. My plan, once I get off this boat, is to do exactly what Bex, Arcade, and I did in Texas—hitchhike, steal cars, and rob convenience stores until I get back home. It's going to be harder now that I look like the walking dead.

When I unlock the door, I find a cup of coffee waiting for me outside on the floor. It's swirling with creamy milk, and next to it is a plate with two donuts. It's crap coffee, and the treats are about two days past stale, but the sugar will put a little light in my eyes and maybe a little weight on my frame. I gobble them down, shocked at the sugar and buttery flavor.

There's a loud whirring sound outside, one I know very well. I used to hear it back in the Zone on hot summer nights when the Alpha ran the streets and the cops took to the air to hunt them down. Helicopters are flying over this boat.

I charge up the steps and into a pissing rain. The storm Encardo and his sons wanted to outrun is creeping up on us, and the sea is boiling over. The ship rocks back and forth in a herky-jerky motion and forces me to hold on to a railing, while high above and descending fast are two black choppers, both loaded with guns and rocket launchers. Ahead of us, and on either side, are two small military boats with guns and soldiers of their own. When I look back, there are two more, just as heavily armed. We're fast approaching a rocky shoreline. A marina floats alongside it, with a few more fishing boats like this one, all bobbing up and down in the water.

There's a dock as well, packed with people. Most of them are wearing black uniforms covered in pockets and pouches. They wear black berets with golden badges sewn into the fabric and carry assault rifles. Even at this distance, I can see their anxiety, the way their eyes are trained on me, how their fingers tickle the triggers on their guns.

It doesn't take a genius to figure out how they found me. Encardo's boys won't even look at me. They are ashen as they busy themselves preparing to dock. They look physically ill as they tie knots and pull ropes and shout to one another.

Their father is in the bridge just behind me, wrestling with the steering wheel and shouting as well. I throw open the door and stomp inside to confront him.

"I just wanted to go home."

Encardo grimaces. "We found you floating out in the water. You were unconscious. It's basic maritime rules to call in an incident. It happened before we even dragged you onboard. I swear I didn't tell them who you were. I swear."

A boat speeds alongside, forming a wake that pushes against us. On the deck are more of the soldiers in black.

"You know they will kill me," I say. I want him to understand what he's done. "Give me a gun."

Encardo blanches. "This might not be what you think. This is Panama, not the United States. The Alpha didn't attack us. I'll talk to them for you. We'll make them listen to your story."

"Five boats are escorting us into the marina. There are two helicopters flying overhead. The pier is full of armed men. This is exactly what I think," I rage, then push the door open and stomp out onto the deck. I peer over the side, preparing to leap, hoping I'll hit the water before the marksmen on the dock can put a bullet into me. If I make it, they won't be able to catch me. I put one foot over the railing when a voice sledgehammers my brain.

"LYRIC WALKER HAS LED US TO THE BAD CHILDREN."

A stampede of images tramples my mind—the fat, bloated faces, the obese bodies letting go of the volcano walls, flames and waves of heat rising around them as they swim upward, by the tens of thousands. The voice awakens a migraine like I haven't experienced in months, and I stumble back, falling hard onto the deck. I curl up in a ball and press my hands to my head, certain that it will explode if I do not hold back the pressure. My mom and I used to label bad migraines. The worst was an F5. This one makes those feel like a mild inconvenience.

"What's wrong with her?" Ricardo shouts.

"Step back. Give her some air!" Encardo kneels before me. "Lyric, can you hear me?"

"They're coming!" I shout at him. I don't know if he can hear me. The voices are drowning everything out. "They're following me here."

"What is she saying?" Manuel demands.

"Try to get her on her feet," Nicky says.

Hands help me stand, but I shake them off. I lean on the railing, trying not to throw up, and watching the approaching shoreline.

"I've led them here. No one is safe," I say. "I'm sorry."

"She's hallucinating," Encardo says.

I turn to him. "Take your sons and everyone you love and get as far away from the ocean as you can."

Nicky rushes to the bridge and steers the boat into the marina, brushing against the slick, algae-coated wood of the pier. The crowd pushes forward, and I realize it's not just police and soldiers waiting for me. There are reporters with cameras and video equipment. They shout questions in both English and Spanish, wanting to get the first interview with the notorious Lyric Walker.

A dozen serious-faced soldiers point their weapons at me. Every one of them looks like a clone of the soldiers that used to patrol the boardwalk in Coney Island. I've met a hundred men with identical faces, all of them impossible to read. Are they here to arrest me? Kill me? They surround me, shouting in Spanish and then English. They want my hands on my head and me on my knees. I glance at the water. No, that chance is gone. My plan has crumbled. I won't find my family and get them to safety now. I'm probably going back to Trident and Bachman. She said she'd get me back. I hate that she was right.

Encardo tries to put his body between the soldiers and me. His sons shout at him to stop, and the soldiers join them, but he keeps demanding to be heard. He yells in Spanish, but the soldiers act like they don't understand a word he is saying. He tries English, but it's clear they don't care what he has to say.

"She's just a kid, and she's not well," he tries to explain over the din.

They put guns in his face and order him to step back. When he doesn't, one of the soldiers tackles him hard, and he crashes to the pier. He's handcuffed and dragged to his feet. A trail of blood leaks out of a cut on his temple.

"I'm sorry, Lyric," Encardo cries, over and over. "I didn't want this for you."

"SO MANY BAD CHILDREN," the voice booms, pouring acid on the migraine. I fall again. "SO MANY TO CLEANSE. SPACE MUST BE MADE FOR NEW OFFSPRING."

A soldier and his colleague shove me down the steps and off the boat, into the waiting mob. The crowd pushes forward with cameras and microphones, but soldiers are waiting for them. They force everyone back with their plexiglass shields and make a path for me through the crowd. One reporter breaks the line and gets a closed fist to the mouth for his trouble. A man in a dark suit and tie steps into our path but isn't assaulted. He exchanges words with the soldiers in Spanish. I don't understand anything they say except for the words *United States of America,* but whatever is being said puts all the men in black berets into a foul mood.

"Ms. Walker, my name is Miguel DeCosta," the man says when he turns his attention away from the soldiers. "I'm the

United States ambassador to Panama, and I work on behalf of U.S. citizens on Panamanian soil. I am officially taking you into custody on the request of the president of the United States. I'm legally obligated to tell you that you have a choice. The Panamanian government wishes to arrest you, and you can choose to stay here with them, but you will be imprisoned. Tell me, how much do you know about prisons in Central America?"

"Are you sending me to Trident?"

"I'm turning you over to the State Department for questioning," he promises.

I shrug, too exhausted and in too much agony to sort through my options. They both sound equally terrible. "Fine."

"Let's move!" he shouts, bringing several more soldiers to join us. They're wearing camo fatigues with the American flag sewn onto the arms. The Panamanians reluctantly hand me over to DeCosta.

"We will bill you for the handcuffs," one of them says to the American soldiers.

"You do that." DeCosta laughs. "Ms. Walker, do you need medical attention?"

His hand vanishes before me. Suddenly, I am with them —the beasts on their way to find me. I see what they see, the ocean floor below them and their endless army. Sorrow rolls through me, but it is not mine. I feel what they feel. I sense their anguish. The children cannot hear the voice of the parents or one another. The disconnection has terrible consequences. It has made us turn on our brothers and sisters. The peace they hoped would be ours is lost. We are spoiled and ruined. No! Why am I feeling what they feel? I'm trapped inside their minds, or are they inside mine? I fight to keep from melting into their consciousness. I cannot risk returning to the family.

"NO!" I scream, and with everything I have, I shove back at their invasion. I bear down on their voice, fighting back at the tendrils that threaten to wrap around my brain.

"IT IS POINTLESS TO FIGHT THE FAMILY. WORK WITH US TO END THE BAD CHILDREN." I hear my voice repeating their words, just as I make a final push to free myself.

"What did she say?" a soldier asks.

"She needs a doctor. She's in bad shape," DeCosta explains. "Have Lima meet us at the airport. Tell her to hurry, too. We have to try and beat this storm, or we'll never get out tonight."

I fall forward. I can hear my head crack against the wooden pier, and then everything goes black.

CHAPTER FOUR

THREE MONTHS EARLIER

THE RUSALKA PULLED ME UPWARD TO THE LIP OF THE volcano's crater. Minerva was waiting there, her body aglow in blood-red light. She stared down into the hole, seemingly seduced by its churning power, trapped in a mash-up of terror and ecstasy. Part of me wondered if she was considering jumping in herself, but somehow she shook off its spell. She shouted to her grotesque army, and suddenly I was free, completely untethered and drifting over the crater. I tried to right myself and swim for the side, but I got only a few feet before the Great Abyss inhaled, turning me into a bug at the bottom of a bathtub drain. It was useless to struggle. The pull was too strong. How do you defy the very planet? My only hope was to reach one of the rocky outcrops inside the volcano's throat so I could cling to something until the inhale ended. I managed to get to a handhold, but it felt like I'd fallen out of a moving car and was trying to cling to the door. In desperation, I wrapped my whole body around the rocks. *Just hold on!* I shouted at myself. If I wanted to live, I had to fight the pull. I told myself it would stop soon and cough me out, but at that moment, I felt like my arms were being torn out of their sockets.

My handhold crumbled in my grasp, and I once again flailed out of control. I skidded along the wall, slamming hard against porous, volcanic rock. I hit one awkwardly, and it sent me spinning, end over end. I was falling and falling and falling. All the while Minerva raved. Even over the din of a hungry planet, I could hear her ugly prayers. Her monsters, however, watched silently from above, their eyes glowing reflections of the death beneath me.

And then someone took my hand. Fingers wrapped tightly around my palm. They were strong and sure. I was no longer falling. A voice shouted something to me just before the volcano spat us out, but I couldn't make it out over all the noise. We shot higher and higher, spinning and turning inside a zillion hot bubbles. I lost my grip on my hero as I breached the surface and rocketed into the warm, salty air, before crashing painfully back into the rumbling ocean. I had enough strength left to tread water and keep my head above the waves. The light up there was blinding so that when the hand found me again, I couldn't see its owner, only the silhouette of a man with broad shoulders. He pulled me onto land—even though I knew that it wasn't possible out there in the middle of nowhere, still it was there. My gills receded and my lungs took over, always a painful, stressful transformation. I coughed up water and tried to thank him, still unable to decipher his form, but certain I knew him.

"Fathom?"

"Just breathe," he said in a voice strange and alien. I hunched over on hands and knees, looked at the dense, black rock beneath me, and watched his shadow drape over the ground.

"Who are you?"

"I am called Husk."

I forced myself onto my knees then lifted my hands to block the sun. I had to see this guy's face. If he wasn't Fathom, I had to know who had helped me, but when I did, I reared back in horror. He wasn't a man at all. He was a Rusalka.

I scampered on hands and knees, ignoring how the ground tore the soft skin of my wrists. My only goal was to get away from that thing, but it stalked me as I crawled. When I reached the water's edge, his claws dug into the back of my jumpsuit and pulled me to my feet. I surprised him with a punch, striking the side of his jaw with everything I had left. It was wild and weak, a glancing blow that didn't seem to faze him.

"Get away from me!" I screamed, pounding my fists on his chest as he pulled me close.

His answer was a slap so hard I worried he'd broken my cheekbone.

"Calm yourself!"

"You speak English!" I say. "How can you talk?"

"Listen to me. We have little time. The prime will be enraged if I do not report to her at once. I offer you a bargain, human—your life in exchange for your service."

"What are you? Rusalka do not talk. They aren't smart enough to talk."

The Rusalka slapped me again. "Watch your tongue, bottom feeder. Do you agree to my terms, or do I throw you back into the Great Abyss?"

"I don't know what you're talking about! What terms?" I cried.

"You are simple and foolish. I will choose. You will live. I will present the prime with the bargain. Stay here," he said, then leaped into the water and vanished.

It took a second for my brain to reboot, but when it did, I scanned my surroundings, desperate for some way to escape. There was nothing out there. I was trapped on a barren island, a tiny, tiny dot in the middle of nothing. It wasn't even an island. It was a stone pretending to be an island. A few courageous blades of grass defied the rocks, but nothing else grew. I hurried to the edge, straining my eyes to find a boat, another plot of land, anything I could get to that would take me away, but I was utterly alone, and I knew that thing was coming back.

A splash behind me sent me spinning. Husk leaped twenty feet into the sky, riding a spout like Old Faithful. He landed nimbly in front of me, then trained his eyes on mine. At that moment, I wished I had my glove. For most of the time I had worn it, I'd wanted to be free of the damn thing, but now I wished I could feel its cool metal against my hand again. I missed the tingling charge that activated the power, the whispering voice asking me how it could help. I would have made a spear, a giant fist, a tidal wave—anything that might crush Husk out of existence—but the power was gone. All I had was me.

"The prime has reluctantly agreed to the bargain."

"The prime is dead!" I said, taking a big step back from him.

"The former prime is dead. His consort, Minerva, has claimed his title for herself, and her people have accepted. She rules the Alpha and will rebuild our empire. You will play a small, but pivotal part in her efforts."

"I don't understand what you're saying to me. I don't even know how you are possible."

He growled as if I offended him.

"Minerva carries the Alpha heir. Your assistance is required in his birth. You will prepare for his arrival by satisfying her current needs. You will hunt food. You will take all pains to make the prime comfortable. You will prepare a shelter for the heir when—"

"Fuck you."

He stared at me, silently. I think it was the first time he had really looked at me. I don't think he liked what he saw.

"You know what those words mean, smart guy? Minerva tried to kill my mother. She tried to kill my friends. She just threw me into a volcano. I'm not going be her . . . her nanny."

"I will not risk my life for your stubbornness." Without warning he tossed me back into the water. I flailed, trying to get control over my body, but he grabbed my arms and dragged me back down into the deep. All the while, I punched at him, doing as much damage as a kitten might. He continued onward, diving into the dimmest regions while I screamed threats. It was several moments before I realized we were swimming away from the Great Abyss, down toward a hidden valley tucked into the shadows. What waited there was even more impossible than a talking Rusalka. A city revealed itself, an abandoned metropolis of towers and arenas built on a wide, snow-white boulevard, intersected by an intricate maze of short, squat buildings. I'd seen cruder versions of the same layout back home in the tent city the Alpha built on the beach, and like those buildings, these didn't have roofs.

"What is this?" I shouted, but I knew the answer. Fathom used to call it the hunting grounds, the Alpha homeland, built by the Rusalka for the many races of the empire. During our quiet moments, he'd told me about how his father helped settle it after generations of nomadic life. This was the place Alpha had dreamed of for generations, a home to throw off their life of struggle and the ceaseless hunt for food and shelter. This was their promised land.

We drifted down the boulevard, passing architectural wonders made of sand and shells. Elaborate art and sculptures real enough to breathe appeared on every facade. Some were portraits of Alpha, and others portrayed what I guessed were historical events from the empire's past. Stone reliefs of a bloody battle between Selkies and some unknown creatures were so lifelike I could almost hear the violent clash of weapons. Others illuminated hunting packs chasing schools of fleeing swordfish. I saw gelatinous Ceto teachers surrounded by eager students, and scrawny Nix holding radiating spheres above their heads. One tower featured carvings of swaggering Triton, both strong and merciless, standing triumphant over the piled corpses of conquered enemies. One had his foot planted on his victim's head.

Statues stepped out of the walls of a temple at the far end of the road, each an idealized portrait of a different Alpha tribe; Ceto, Feige, Sirena, Triton, Nix, Selkie, and so many more with faces and bodies that boggled my mind. Despite their differences, they stood together, their eyes looking toward the same future. Conspicuously, the Rusalka did not stand with them. In fact, they were absent from all of the imagery scattered about the city they had built. The gloves they wore, like the one I once owned, had made this city a reality. The empire owed every building to them. If their images had been intentionally avoided, it was incredibly cruel.

A massive statue stood high above everything. It was nearly two stories tall, an uncanny depiction of the now-dead prime. The name the Red Cross had given him was Arthur, because his own was unpronounceable on the surface, but he never used it. Anything human, especially our language, was filthy and grotesque. He was Alpha and, more important, Triton, superior to the filth he ruled and the humans he planned to conquer.

The Rusalka artists had done an amazing job depicting the disdain in his eyes. The prime looked out on his feeble subjects with intolerance. His mouth was twisted with arrogance and a touch of his madness. Despite his collapsing mind, the prime's chest was wide and proud, his legs strong and sure. His hands clenched a trident wrapped in octopus tentacles, and the razor-sharp blades all Triton hide in their forearms were extended and ready for battle.

Minerva knelt in the street before him. Her body convulsed as if grief were clawing at her skin. She pulled her hair out in handfuls and shrieks, and after each blistering sob came another bitter vow of revenge that threatened to break the world in half. Husk kept us at a distance. He said nothing to Minerva and offered her no comfort. Instead, he watched patiently, emotionless. Even when Minerva used her tail to slice off the legs of the statue, he did not react. Like all the

Rusalka, he watched as the massive figure toppled and broke apart in the road.

Minerva turned to me suddenly; her eyes flashed even in these dark depths. She was fury personified. Instinctively I tried to back away, but Husk kept me in place. She snarled something at him, and he nodded. Two Rusalka approached and pulled me away from him. They dragged me away from the crowd, toward another temple at the opposite end of the boulevard. Its exterior wasn't as grand. The walls were scratched with graphic symbols, crude depictions of water, the wind, the sun, fish, predators, lightning, so many more. I'd seen them all before, etched into the steel of my glove. Was this building connected to those machines?

The creatures pulled me through an open archway and into a massive room. There was a sense that this place had once been important. A table made out of some unknown substance sat in the corner, and a cage made of wood was rotting to nothing in the corner. There were pieces of metal and odd devices scattered about, as well as an extensive mathematical equation scratched right into the walls. Something had happened there. I could feel a prickly history, but again I was dragged onward without answers. We went through another archway and then up a cylindrical tube that took us to the second floor, and finally into the oddest room I'd seen so far. The walls were high and had no ceiling, but there were slots cut into them that allowed the shimmering red energy of the volcano to permeate, turning everything into a circle of hell. The Rusalka shoved me roughly, like they were tossing out a smelly bag of garbage, then swam back down the shaft and out of sight. When I got control of myself, I studied everything, the walls, the open roof, the floor, and I wondered if the creatures really thought this place could hold me. I was sure I could swim right out through the ceiling, but when I tried, four Rusalka appeared. They perched themselves high on the walls above, like gargoyles crouching on the battlements of an ancient church, and they watched me. I gave them the finger. I don't know if they understood what it meant, but it made me feel better.

Pressing myself against the wall, I peered through one of the thin slots to spy on the city. It was no less a miracle than when I first saw it. I wondered if it was this glorious when my mother lived here, before the prime sent her and nineteen others to spy on the human world. I wondered if having all this majesty was her dream, too, or if the nomadic life was fine. What did Fathom or Arcade or even Ghost think of it? This place had once been theirs to inherit, before they were forced onto the land. It would have been Fathom's to lead if he hadn't given up his claim to protect what he and I had together. It couldn't have been an easy decision. I wondered if he would still have made the choice if he'd known our love wouldn't survive its challenges.

I turned from the peephole, using the walls to move myself

into as comfortable a position as possible. There was a spot in the shadows that partially blocked the Rusalka from spying on me. Once there, I did my best to lie as still as I could, hoping to slip into something that resembled sleep. The real thing had eluded me for days, and I felt tired in every inch of my body. Even my bones felt ragged, but the water refused to let me be. I drifted around the room, carried along by an unseen current. How the hell did Alpha sleep?

Yoga would calm me, but I couldn't wrap my head around how it would work down here. Breathing is at its foundation. Moving oxygen in and out of the mouth and nose, directing it to the limbs and organs, then freeing it back into the universe is central to the practice. How could I do it without lungs? Or air? I wasn't even sure I could do the poses. My whole life I'd depended on them, whether it was to quiet the migraines that used to torment me, to give me some peace in a crisis, or just let me tune out. Now even yoga had been taken from me, and the loss felt heavy and cumbersome. It's silly how upset I got about it, but I was tired of losing things. No, not losing, having things taken from me. I couldn't handle any more of the universe's thievery.

"There's nothing left!" I shouted.

Maybe that was why he wasn't there. Fathom. The boy who'd said he loved me. My memory dragged me back to our last conversation . . . fight, really, when his seeming indifference to my problems in Trident, and the secrets he'd kept from me, broke my heart. I confronted him, demanded to know why he hadn't done more to help me, and his answer blew my mind. He said his love for me had expectations. To fit into his life, I had to fight when necessary. He said I had to learn to save myself and claimed he would never disrespect me by treating me like a damsel in distress. In a nutshell, he expected me to act like a Triton. It was all very inspiring at the time, very girl power, and his unshaking belief in me bulldozed the tall, emotional walls I'd built to protect myself from him. No one had ever spoken to me like that, made me understand my own value and strength, but at that moment, I wanted him to shove his expectations. I needed rescuing. I actually was a damsel in some serious effing distress, and all the pep talks in the world weren't going to help me out of it.

So where was he?

The answer was sharp and cold and harsh. He'd realized he made the wrong choice with me. He'd given up everything for me, and he regretted it. He'd expected me to fight like a warrior for my freedom. He was disappointed.

He wasn't coming.

Fine, I thought, then where was my mom? She was Sirena. She'd lived in the hunting grounds and would know how to find it. There was only one reason why she wouldn't be there that I could think of, and it turned my insides cold. Something terrible must have happened to her. Nothing short of a tragedy would have kept her from saving me.

Maybe the kids would come? They all had gloves. They could get here in no time. Chloe, Maggie, Finn—all the others. No. None of them knew where I was. They might not even know it existed. Even if they did, they couldn't find it.

No one was coming. I couldn't help but cry. My tears mixed with the salty sea. All the while, the gargoyles watched with quiet indifference.

CHAPTER FIVE

BEFORE I EVEN OPEN MY EYES, I KNOW I'M IN TROUBLE. I am not on the dock anymore. The throng of onlookers is gone. Encardo and his sons are nowhere to be found. Now I'm in a tiny room shaped like a cylinder. A curtain divides the space and blocks my view, but I can hear voices coming from the other side. My arms are still handcuffed, and a chain has been looped through, strung to the ceiling, and locked to a pin. It keeps them suspended over my head. There's another chain wrapped around my waist and legs that leads to a similar pin in the floor. Shackles encase my ankles. Someone doesn't want me going anywhere.

That someone has also changed my clothes. I'm no longer in the sweater Encardo loaned me, but a pair of light cotton pajama pants and a matching shirt in soul-sucking gray. The room shakes, and I'm jostled, suddenly realizing I'm not in a room. I'm on a plane. A surprising sting in my back tells me I'm also not alone. Someone is behind me, poking at my wounds.

"Good morning, Lyric. My name is Dr. Lima," she announces in a thick Spanish accent. Her tone is flat, with the air of someone who is both all-business and bored. "I'm examining your injuries."

"How long have we been in the air?"

"Four hours or so," she says. "What did this to you?"

"Fingernails," I say. I pull at the cuffs in some hope of getting a little more comfortable. Having my arms above my head is making my shoulders ache. Unfortunately, the cuffs don't care. I suspect Lima shares their attitude.

"It's best if you stay calm," the woman says.

"I'm calm. Is this how you examine all your patients?" I ask, sarcastically.

She comes around to face me. She's short, standing just over five feet tall, with long, straight brown hair and a strip of sunburn across her nose. "Some of them, unfortunately. Did you say fingernails? Must have been one hell of a manicure."

I nod. "Where are we going?"

"I don't know. I never know. It's not my job to know, and probably not my job to tell you even if I did. I work for the Navy, and jointly with the American embassy in Panama in some special circumstances. They call me when they need me, and I come. Sometimes I'm on a boat. Mostly I'm on planes. Where we land is always different and always a surprise."

"I need to know where—"

Lima frowns and cuts me off. "Now, listen, I know you've got a million questions. I don't have any of the answers unless they have something to do with your health. I'm sure that the ambassador will be back here soon enough. You can ask him then. I'm just a doctor. You're a mess, and I need to know how you got this way so I don't make things worse when I treat you."

The plane jostles again. Lima holds the wall with her hand until it stops.

"I know you're not human," she continues. "But I haven't seen your species before."

"Species?"

She sighs, impatiently. "You're not going to get sensitive on me are you? I don't know the fifty billion different types of Alpha. I've examined Sirena and Selkies and one Triton. I know there are lots more. I've seen pictures of the kind with the spikes. What are you?"

"I'm human, mostly," I snap. "My mother is Sirena."

She nods. "A hybrid. I've heard stories. Do you grow a tail?"

"Nope," I say, trying to fight off a cramp in my back.

"Good, mostly human," she says, jotting something down in a notebook she pulls from her white lab coat. "There are a lot of bruises."

"That's what happens when you find yourself on the food chain," I explain.

"So, you were down there a while?"

"Three months."

She rummages inside a leather bag resting on a countertop.

From it she removes a stethoscope, blood pressure cuff, and that little light doctors use to burn your cornea before shoving it in your ears.

"Are you always this thin? I don't have a scale on the plane, but I'm going to estimate that you are around one hundred and five pounds."

"I'm usually around one forty," I say. She takes more notes.

"There is clear evidence of vitamin deficiency. You have dark circles under your eyes, your nails are brittle, and you're unusually pale. Your hair is falling out, and your skin is dry. What have you been eating?"

"Fish." I feel like an animal.

"I need to take a look in your mouth," she says. I don't fight. "There is some blistering on the gums and tongue, some early signs of periodontal disease, most likely from lack of proper diet and vitamin D deficiency. No sign of infections, which is very good. Do your teeth feel loose?"

"No."

She wraps the stethoscope around her neck and sets the cold steel disk under my shirt and onto my chest, then listens closely as she slides it over my skin.

"Your lungs sound healthy, and your breathing is strong. Your heart rate is high, common for your spec—I mean, for a Sirena."

She wraps the blood pressure cuff around my arm and pumps it up like a balloon, then releases the valve to let the air seep out.

"Blood pressure is high too, but not outside healthy parameters."

She fumbles with her stethoscope, and listens again, this time to my throat and belly. Then she takes more notes, scribbling furiously until she snaps the tip of her pencil. She spits out a curse, then searches her bag until finally finding a replacement. When she's done, she shines the light in my eyes and ears, and up my nose.

"Your eyes are clear and focused. They follow the light, well, but are very sensitive to exposure. Nose is clear, and your ears. Lyric, do you take any medications?"

"When I'm not being held hostage or chained up in a plane? No."

"Are you still hearing voices?"

"No," I snap, defensively. I might as well have shouted it. "I'm not crazy. Is that what you think?"

"I don't know enough about you to make that kind of diagnosis," she says. "DeCosta said you were raving about an invasion and children. You've been through hell, and the mind can play games with us when we are at our lowest."

"My mind is just fine."

"Let's take a closer look at your back," she says.

"Do you examine a lot of crazy people?" I ask.

"I examine a lot of people who are struggling with their sanity. What is this on the back of your scalp?"

"There were staples there from an injury. I pulled them out myself."

"The monsters had staples?"

"The human monsters did," I say. "At the camp where they keep people like me. They beat me up and had to staple me. I don't suppose you've heard of the camp? They call it Trident. I assume that's where we're going."

There's a long, uncomfortable silence. I think I've finally cracked this woman's professional callus.

"I have to suture these cuts. Some of them are wide open and will never close without help," she says as she digs through her bag.

"Stitches?"

"Yes. You really should be in a hospital right now. I'll raise a stink, but they never listen. I'm going to do my best for you," she promises.

Her finger is tapping on something. I turn awkwardly, the chains fighting against my body. In the corner of my eye, I see her priming a hypodermic needle. Flashes of Nurse Amy from the camp slam around my skull—her bored expression as she went about her sadistic work, drugging me, poking at me like I wasn't human, all so routine for her.

"What is that?"

"It's a tetanus shot," she says. "I have no idea what kind of bacteria and viruses you were exposed to. There's also something imbedded in one of your muscles. If you refuse the injection, you could get lockjaw. You don't want lockjaw."

"Don't drug me," I beg, trying to soften the edge in my voice. "Please. I need to keep a clear head."

"This won't make you sleepy, Lyric, but it's not the only injection I need to give you—vitamins, antibiotics, a few vaccines just to be safe. I need blood samples, urine—and that's before I even get to working on your back. You're going to need lidocaine to numb the area, maybe ten injections before I get it all done."

"Can you do it without the shots?"

"You're joking, right? This isn't an action movie where the hero sews up his own wounds. Suturing skin is a violent, painful process, and to be honest, I don't think I could handle it if I knew you were suffering. It's for me as much as it is for you."

"I thought doctors were supposed to be tough," I say.

"I'm not that good of a doctor. I swear, I won't give you anything that will affect your motor functions. Keeping you doped up is not part of my job description," she says, gesturing toward the curtain. "If they want to drug you, they'll have to do it themselves."

She's got her needle poised and ready, waiting for me to give her the okay. This could be a trick, of course, but I nod, and she jabs my shoulder. The plunger pushes the medicine into my muscle. It's like a wasp's sting, but I suck it up.

I feel her hand reach around my shoulder. There's a flask in it. I smell something sweet and woody inside.

"I'll share, but don't hog it," she says. "I'm pretty sure I'm going to need some when this is done."

She lifts it to my lips, and I take a pull, coughing most of it back onto the floor.

She works on me for hours. When the lidocaine wears off, as it does very quickly, she gives me another shot. Lima suggests it may be my half-Alpha genetics that are burning through it. It takes twenty-two shots to finish me. She wraps my torso in clean, white gauze, then sterilizes her equipment and puts it away.

"Hey, I got a souvenir for you," she says, and holds up a hard, white object that looks like a small, flat stone.

"What is it?"

"A fingernail," she says, then slips it into a small pocket in my pajama pants. "Our time together is finished, Ms. Walker. I have to let DeCosta know I've done what I can. I'm going to push for you to go to a hospital, but—"

"Doctor, do you have family in Panama?"

"I have a fiancée, and I take care of my sister's daughter now that she's gone."

"I know you think I'm delusional from starvation and exhaustion. What if I'm not?"

She pauses at the curtain, studying me.

"Call them," I whisper. "Get them to safety."

She crosses the room again, reaches into her bag, and takes out her phone, then she pulls the curtain aside and vanishes into the other half of the plane.

Several minutes later, DeCosta steps into the space. He's flanked on both sides by soldiers in full gear. He's smiling. They aren't.

"Where are you taking me?"

"Norfolk International Airport," he says. "The closest usable airport to Washington, D.C. There you will be turned over to the State Department. I'm told the president is flying in to escort you himself."

"Any chance you might unfasten these chains?"

He smiles.

"I need you to listen to me," I say as calmly as I can. "I don't want to cause any trouble. I just want to find my family and disappear. No one will ever hear from me again."

He smiles at me. It's condescending, like I'm a little girl.

I'm tempted to tell him the truth like I did with the doctor, give him a chance to help some people escape as well, but this guy is not my friend. He says I'm going to the State Department, but there's something in his eyes that's hinting at a lie. If I start shouting about the end of the world to him, I can predict with certainty how it will all end for me. He won't believe me and when we land, he'll hand me over to people who will toss me in a padded room and ask a million questions and fill me full of drugs. Then they will ship me off to Trident anyway. No, I'm going to keep my mouth shut and my head down and look for chances to escape. I have to get to my friends and family before it's too late. I can't let anything get in the way of saving their lives.

The plane starts its descent just as the sun clocks out to go home. I can see it through one of the tiny windows. Dusk cuddles up to Norfolk, lending the little homes below its oranges and reds. There's a lonely skyscraper out there, glowing like a torch. It's too much for me to absorb. I push back at the tears fighting to escape. America. I'm finally home. There were so many days I was sure I would never see it again. Still, even from thousands of feet above the ground, I can tell something is wrong down there. Where are the cars? The lights? There's no evidence of a single living soul.

DeCosta and his soldiers return, pushing the curtain aside. There are three more behind them, each with a handgun drawn and ready. DeCosta holds up a key and grins.

"Time to go," he says, then gets to work unfastening me from the ceiling and floor while the soldiers watch, eagerly hoping I'll make a stupid move. I wonder if they think their guns will expire if they aren't fired every once in a while.

"What's happening down there? It's deserted," I ask.

"They call it the ghostline. The East Coast states that are still in the Union were mandatorily evacuated after the last Rusalka attacks. The president doesn't want to risk more casualties if they return, and this allows troops to move freely without interference. Civilians are not allowed within five miles of any beach, at least civilians in states that still claim to be part of the United States."

"Five miles is not far enough," I mumble.

DeCosta looks out the window and squints into the setting sun. "Millions are still displaced, and that's on top of the people who fled after the first attacks. I've heard they are gathered along the fence. I wonder if we can see them from up here."

"Yes, there's always a fence or a wall. That's how we roll in the U.S.A."

A thin, swarthy man with a beard enters and hands DeCosta a phone.

"What's this?" DeCosta asks.

"Something is happening at the embassy" is all the man says.

DeCosta listens to whoever is on the other end and then he drops his phone. He quickly scoops it back up, his face pale, and his eyes both wide and white. He's staring at me and trembling. I know what has happened in Panama. They have arrived.

He rubs the space between his eyes as he puts the phone back into his colleague's hand.

"I . . . my wife took our son to the beach. Do you have her schedule?"

His assistant nods. "I've already got calls in to them."

"Get them on a plane. Tell everyone at the embassy to do the same. They should abandon the embassy."

He turns and stares at me, his mouth full of questions he can't seem to ask.

The phone rings, and the assistant gives it back to DeCosta.

"We're landing. Yes, yes, I understand. Yes. No, everyone

goes. Dammit. All right, I'll send this plane back as soon as it's fueled . . . Officials and family get priority, then lower staff. My wife's father is . . . yes, if you can. His number is in my contacts."

The soldiers turn their attention from him to me.

"What's going on?" one of them presses me.

I dip my head to avoid their eyes.

"He's four years old," DeCosta continues on his call.

"Sir, what is happening?" one of the soldiers demands. DeCosta looks up at him. There's panic in his face as he looks from one soldier to the next, then over his shoulder at the rest of the plane. In every seat there's a soldier, and they have all turned to listen to his call.

"Did you do this?" DeCosta asks me.

I don't know where the idea comes from or the courage needed to do it, but suddenly my hand reaches out and snatches a gun out of the holster of the closest soldier. I click off the safety like my father taught me, and I point it at DeCosta. The soldiers are too confused, too caught up in their fear that something terrible is happening on the other end of his phone to stop me. They seem trapped in the moment, unsure of what to do next.

"Listen to me. When we land, I want you to arrange it so I can walk away. I have nothing to do with what's happening in Panama. I don't want anything to do with it, either."

I hear soldiers falling out of their seats, shouting at me to drop the gun. They rush down the aisle and into the tiny space just as the wheels touch down on the runway. Everyone falls into one another, and when the brakes lock, we're all knocked to the floor. In the chaos, I drop the pistol. It skitters under a row of seats and disappears.

The pilot's voice crackles on the announcement system as he welcomes us to Norfolk. He asks that everyone please stay seated while military personnel take their positions. He has no idea what is happening on his plane.

DeCosta gathers himself and orders the soldiers to give him the keys to my chains. He unlocks them with one hand while holding the phone to his ear with the other.

"We have to get everyone off this plane now," he shouts. "Tell the pilot to refuel immediately. We're going back to Panama right away."

Sweat pours down his face and rolls into his eyes. He frantically wipes them with his sleeve, then grabs me by the arm and pulls me down the aisle just as Dr. Lima leaps up to block our path.

"You have to be gentle with her," she demands.

"Take your seat, doctor, or I will have you arrested," DeCosta shouts.

She bites her lip, but steps aside. As we pass, she slips something into my hand that's cold and hard.

"Thank you," she says. I turn and watch her as I'm dragged toward the exit. All the while, I squeeze her strange gift, too frightened to open my hand to take a look. It's made of metal. It feels like a key. Has she given me a chance?

DeCosta pushes me through the doorway and out into the mean-spirited winds of Norfolk, Virginia. It's brutally cold here due to a super-frozen chill coming off the water that bellies up to the runway. My pajamas are as thin as paper, and I'm trapped in a shiver that won't go away. Snow is on the ground a foot high, making it hard for airport employees to push a flight of stairs on wheels into place for us to descend. Waiting for me are a hundred more soldiers. Sprinkled among them are police, firefighters, and men in White Tower uniforms like the ones worn by Trident employees. I roll the key in my fist. It doesn't feel much like a chance anymore.

"You lied to me. You're turning me over to White Tower?" I shout over the wind and the plane's humming turbine.

"No, they're here to provide security and to assist in your questioning," DeCosta says.

"You mean torture," I shout. I want to punch him in his face, but I just can't see how it would help.

"Lyric, this isn't about you, at least it wasn't when we got on the plane. They want your family and friends," he shouts over the wind.

"What? Why?"

"They've caused a lot of trouble since you vanished. Your friend Rebecca is on the FBI Most Wanted List. They want to use you to bring them in."

His assistant hurries down the stairs to join us. His phone is in his hand, and his face is terrified.

"Have they found her?" DeCosta begs.

"Not yet," he says. "Electrical power is down across the eastern coastline. Phone lines are failing. All nonmilitary planes have been grounded."

DeCosta turns to me and grabs me roughly. "If you know something about this, you should say it."

"I just want to be left alone," I cry as I pull away.

"I can make that happen, Lyric, I'll talk to them. I'll show them that you are valuable, but you have to stop what's happening."

"I can't stop it," I say.

His assistant hands him the phone again and gives me another opportunity. I shove my shoulder into DeCosta so hard he stumbles forward, down the stairs. I'd love to watch every painful bounce, but he's just my distraction. As he falls, I take the key, bend down, and open my shackles. They slide right off, and my feet are free. I take the steps two at a time, leaping over DeCosta and onto the tarmac before dashing through the confused soldiers. I manage to weave past seven of them before I feel arms wrap around me from behind. Four of my stitches snap, maybe more, and my back becomes a bonfire. Two more hands grab my legs, others my shoulders, and we all crash down on the hard black ground. A knee presses down on my neck, and everyone is shouting at me to stop resisting.

"Let her up," a voice says. It's one I haven't heard in a long time. Samuel Lir is standing over me. The last time I saw him, he was taking his first steps out of a wheelchair he had been trapped in for nearly three years. Gangs attacked him back home when they discovered his father was an Alpha. My dad found him stuffed under the boardwalk like a sack of garbage and got him to a hospital, but they could only do so much to help. He couldn't walk, couldn't take care of himself, couldn't even speak. He needed a feeding tube and a ventilator. They shipped him to Trident, along with his parents, and gave him a glove. It changed him in unexpected ways. I saw the results not long before I left. Now he's standing unassisted with the confidence of a man. He's strong and lean, the boy he would have become if he hadn't been victimized. He's wearing a White Tower jumpsuit, and wrapped around his palm is the same metal glove, now glowing like a star.

"Lyric, don't make this harder than it has to be," Samuel says.

He doesn't have to tell me whose side he's on. It's obvious, and it breaks my heart. I grew up with this kid. We had play-dates and sleepovers and took baths together when we were four. He was like a brother to me, and he's just like me, half human, half Sirena. It makes the betrayal sting all the more.

"Sorry, I can't help it. It's always the hard way with me," I say. "I think it has to do with where we grew up, Samuel. Why are you here?"

"I've been sent to secure your transfer to a safe location."

"You mean Trident, right? Did she send you?" I ask him,

referring to Pauline Bachman, the woman who now runs the camp. "How did you manage to avoid being one of her experiments, Sammy?"

"You've got her wrong, Lyric. She helped me out of my wheelchair and off the feeding tubes and the catheters. She hired people to help me learn to talk again. I can do all the things I did before the Alpha came," he brags, though the word *Alpha* has a particularly angry sound in his mouth.

"And she taught you who to blame? Right?"

"You think she brainwashed me? Lyric, I might have been trapped inside a broken body, but I could see everything that was happening around me. Monsters invaded our neighborhood!" He turns his attention to the soldiers. "I said let her up!"

They do as they're told and get me on my feet.

"You can't blame the Alpha for what happened to you. Human beings hurt you, Samuel."

"Frightened human beings, Lyric. Those things came without an invitation. They camped on our land and ran through the streets terrorizing people. They were spying on us too. They're all criminals. I can't blame people for being afraid when they found out what I was."

"Samuel, you can't believe that. Our parents are not criminals. They loved us. They turned their backs on what they were sent to do. All of them did. Where are they now, Sammy? Where are your parents?"

He lowers his eyes to avoid mine.

"Samuel? Tell me!"

"She told me you would do this," Samuel says. "You're play-ing games with my head, trying to confuse me. I'm not going to let you!"

There's a sound behind me followed by shouts from the soldiers. They open fire on something I can't see, but there's water everywhere, coming across the tarmac like a flash flood. I look to Samuel, seeing his glove fully ignited, but his face is as surprised as mine. He's not responsible for this.

A wall of ocean water smashes into the soldiers around me, knocking them down and dragging them across the ground. A second attack takes out nearly twenty-five heavily armed men. Suddenly, my odds of escape are looking a little better, but who is making it happen?

I turn toward the waterline and see a figure with jet-black hair rising out of the waves. Next to him is a young girl, then another boy. Soon, there are nine of them in all, each riding a spout that shoots into the air. I know all their faces; Chloe, Maggie, Finn, Sienna, Harrison, Brady, Renee, Jane, and the boy with black hair, Riley—all kids from Trident, each with a glove just like the one on Samuel's hand.

"Open fire!" one of the men shouts, but he's drowned by a tidal wave that sweeps him into the sea. When the other sol-diers start firing, a wall of liquid slams into them, knocking them about and breaking their guns. The massive army that met me when I landed is dwindling by the second.

"No!" Samuel shouts, and he raises his hand. Water rises up, eager to be commanded. He launches it at the children, missing Chloe by inches. He fires half a dozen shots more, but they all miss. He doesn't seem to have the control I would expect. His aim is way off.

Riley rides a wave until it eases him to the ground in front of me. With a flick of his wrist, he whips liquid at some approaching soldiers, sending them flying across the tarmac; spouts smack into more of them with crippling strength. Riley gives me a smile and extends his free hand.

"Want to get out of here?" he says. I am so ready to go, but water on the ground rises up, swirls into the shape of a fist, and comes down hard on his chest. Samuel limps to his feet, his glove a supernova of light and heat. He sends an unending torrent at Riley that keeps him from defending himself.

"Leave him alone, Samuel," I beg.

He's so caught up in his anger he doesn't even turn to face me.

"He's like us, Samuel," I shout. "We should stick together. We need each other more now than ever. There's something terrible coming this way, and you have to help us fight it."

"You probably sent it, traitor," he growls.

"Fine, Sammy. I tried." I kick him on the side of his knee. It's a dirty trick, but it has always worked in the past, and to be honest, growing up where we did, he should have seen it coming. He screams and falls to the ground, cradling his leg to ease the pain. He lifts his gloved hand and aims it at my face, but Riley is there, pointing right back at my former friend.

"We are trying to save the world, Lyric," Samuel shouts.

"I don't want to live in a world that she's trying to save," I say, then turn to Riley. "Do you have a plan?"

He looks out at the hundreds of fresh soldiers rushing to stop us, then gives me the cocky smile I have been dying to see for months.

"Run."

I throw Samuel one last look, hoping to see a change of heart, but he's still bitter and determined. I take Riley's hand and we sprint toward the shore.

"I'm coming for you," Samuel shouts at me.

"That wouldn't be a good idea," I shout back.

Running is hard with handcuffs, and a few more stitches pop in my back, but Riley helps the best he can. He shouts to the other children, and they follow, shooting torpedoes of water toward the approaching army.

"Can you swim?" Riley asks as we near the water's edge.

I hold up my hands so he can see the shackles, then take the key still pressed into my palm and unlock them. They clink when they hit the ground.

"Don't worry. I've got you," he says, then wraps his arm around my waist. Together, we leap as bullets zing past, then splash down into the frozen water. I've never been this cold in my life, but my gills appear and the webbing between my fingers returns. My scales shine like silver, the same color they make when I am happy. Riley presses his body close to mine, and when I look over, I see his gills just under his jawline. His scales are bright red. His glove rockets us forward, pushing the ocean out of our way. I can't help but feel safe. I have found my tribe again.

It's difficult to tell how far we travel, or even in which direction. All I know is Riley is here, alive, bathed in the light of his glove, which turns him into the moon on a clear night. He holds me tight. It might be hours, days, years. I can't honestly say. I'm in no hurry.

Eventually his glove dims, as do those of the other children, and using his own strength, Riley pulls me out of the water and onto a rocky beach. If I thought it was cold in the water, the open air helps me redefine the meaning. The temperature has to be hovering around twenty-five degrees, and the wind is a swift kick in the ass.

Chloe rushes forward and hugs me tight. My back screams, but I suffer through the pain. She looks up at me with her big green eyes and freckled nose. "I knew you weren't dead. I told everyone you'd come back."

"Thanks for believing in me," I whisper, but I'm shaking so much I wonder if my bones aren't drowning out my words.

"Just a second," Riley says, then lights up his glove once

more. A minute later, the water trapped in my pajamas seeps out, and I am completely dry, even my hair. It's better, not much, but better. The rest of the kids do the same to themselves.

"We need to get her to the house, quickly," Maggie says. "I'm freezing, and she's dressed for bed."

"Where's this house?"

Harrison points toward the dunes. They're stacked high to fight back the tides and keep the line of million-dollar homes beyond them safe. They are dark and quiet structures, sentries made of wood and glass watching for what might come out of the sea. Riley takes my hand and leads me in their direction.

"Where are we?" I say.

Sienna grins. "The Jersey Shore."

We climb the hill of sand to a wooden staircase that takes us to street level. A lonely four-lane road lies ahead, lined with more two- and three-story homes on tiny lots with pebbled driveways. There isn't a soul in sight, the streetlights are out, and not even a cat or a stray dog comes to investigate our arrival. Parked cars sit stranded with flat tires, each painted in dust and bird feces. A block away, a tree has fallen into the street. It pulled electric lines down with it. A kite is tangled in its limbs.

"Why here?" I ask.

"It's completely deserted and ours for the taking," Harrison crows. "The evacuation made for a great hiding place.

Aside from the occasional drone and National Guard sweep, we haven't seen a living person since we found it."

"And it's a great place to do our work," Finn says.

"Our work?" I ask Riley.

He smiles. "You'll find out soon enough."

We cross the road and make a turn down a street inhabited by soft blue and pastel pink homes. On the corner is a little shop that invites you in to see its robot donut maker. On the opposite corner is a bar with a sign that shouts they have the best margaritas on the shore. I see crab shacks and skateboard stores, ice cream parlors and places to buy hats and boogie boards. There are bars and restaurants as far as the eye can see, but they are all empty, patiently waiting for the people to return.

"My dad used to come here when he was growing up," I tell the children. He told me he and his buddies used to raise hell here, but it's hard to imagine. As long as he's been my dad, he's been straight-edge. He doesn't even drink. I have a feeling it was more like "raising heck." He promised to bring me here someday, but then the Alpha came and the fences went up and vacations were a little out of the question.

We stop in front of a three-story home with a two-car garage and a weathervane shaped like the sun on the very top. Riley points to the front porch where three dark figures wait.

"Surprise," he says with a grin.

"Lyric?"

"Dad?"

My father is the first one to leap off the porch. He's in a Navy peacoat and heavy work boots. My mother is right behind him in jeans and Ugg boots, a down coat, and mittens. Their arms wrap around me so fast it takes my breath away. Predictably, I break down crying. They join me, and the three of us sob.

My father holds me at arm's length and gives me a full up-and-down examination. He's not happy with what he sees.

"You haven't been eating," my father says.

"What do we have in the pantry?" my mom cries.

"Peanut butter," Brady says as he runs into the house. "I'll get it!"

My mother reaches up and caresses my face. She's delicate and loving. I really don't know how to process kindness anymore. I haven't been touched in so long. I lean into her hand the way a flower leans into a sunbeam.

"How did you all escape?" I ask.

"It's a long story," she says.

"Not really," Riley laughs. "They rescued us."

"Did you know your mother is, like, crazy strong?" someone says from the porch. I got so caught up in my reunion I completely forgot there was someone else waiting, but now that I'm looking, I know the outline of her body. Bex steps into the moonlight. Her hair blazes like a torch. She is tall like an Amazon, smiling and crying at the same time. I race up the steps and knock her over with a hug. We fall to the floor, laughing and blubbering. I don't care that it strains my stitches.

"You ready to get to work?" Bex asks.

"Work?"

"Yeah, you know, being a pain in the ass?"

CHAPTER SIX

THREE MONTHS EARLIER

ROUGH HANDS RATTLED ME AWAKE. TWO TOWERING Rusalka hovered above with their ugly clown faces and those glowing strands dangling in front of their mouths. One of them was holding a long wooden spear with a carved, pointy end. He forced it into my hands, while the other lifted me upright. I swam back the best I could, certain he was challenging me to a fight. I'd seen how the Alpha settled their disputes—blood sports that often turned into fights to the death, usually over the tiniest slight. I searched my brain, trying to figure out how I'd insulted this dumb beast. What did I do that pissed him off? The answer was probably nothing more than I was Lyric Walker and a filthy human being.

"I'm not going to fight you," I shouted, but I didn't drop the spear. I was smart enough to know I probably didn't have much say in the matter.

"*Groola,*" one of them grunted. It was the closest thing to a word I had heard one of them say, unless you counted Husk, a reminder of how different he was from the rest of those things. From what I could tell, their language was made up of barks and grunts, yet Husk seemed to have a better vocabulary than me.

"Get Husk. I don't know what you're trying to tell me."

The creature snatched the spear out of my hands and just as quickly shoved it back.

"*Groola!*"

"I don't understand! What the hell does *groola* mean?"

He made a waving gesture with his hand, swishing it through the water. "*Groola!*"

"Waves?"

"*Groola,*" his partner growled. Now they were both making the motion. Frustrated, he snatched the spear too and used it to mime himself stabbing something.

"Hunt? Do you want me to hunt for food?"

"*Groola.*"

Without another word, they dragged me out of the room, down the tunnel, through the immense hall with the markings, and out into the street, where the metals and poisons filled my mouth and gills. It dawned on me that the little slots in the walls of my room were somehow filtering out the crap that was in the water, though I had no idea how. Out in the open, my throat itched and my eyes burned like I was sitting too close to a fireplace. Why had the prime picked this lousy spot to build a city? It was a stupid, toxic place to live. Coney

Island wasn't exactly a nature preserve, but at least most of the garbage was on the ground or in the hot dogs, not swirling around in the air.

I knew I'd get no answers from the ugly twins. They pulled me along, down the white boulevard, which I quickly realized was paved with shells and bones. Most looked like they belonged to fish or other small sea life, but more than a few were from animals as big as a man. Could these be the victims I'd seen in the reliefs scattered about the town —the art I saw on every building glorifying war and slaughter? Fathom once told me there were other races of Alpha living in the ocean who had turned their backs on the empire. He hinted that some of them were conquered. Would the Alpha just leave their bodies in the road to be picked apart by fish?

We swam until we were at the farthest edge of the city, as far from the Great Abyss as we could get, where the taste in the water was a bit more tolerable.

"*Groola!*"

"You want me to hunt fish? I don't know how," I said, staring down at the spear. "You have to show me."

Even with their blank expressions, I could see they were confused. Maybe it was because nothing I said sounded the way I intended. My words came out as bubbles, or maybe they just didn't understand English, or maybe they were nothing more than animals.

"*Groola!*" They beat on their chests like apes and bared their fangs.

"Screw you!" I said, though I quickly regretted it. One of them lunged at me, his fists pumping with anger. His speed startled me, but my training sessions in the desert with Arcade were already in motion. She'd taught me that anger led to mistakes, and I was an attentive pupil. I like to think Arcade would have been proud of me when I stabbed the sharp end of my spear into the Rusalka's gut. He shrieked and jerked away, wrenching the weapon out of my hands so that it floated down to the ground. Black blood oozed out of his wound. I'd seen these creatures take a bullet and thought they were nearly invincible, but it appeared they did have vulnerabilities.

"*Charchar!*" the healthy one shouted. I was sure he was egging on his friend to get some revenge, but he didn't attack me. Instead he held his wound with one oversize hand and nervously scanned our surroundings. He sniffed, then spun around, peering into the darkness as if there was something out there only he could see.

"I warned Husk!" I shouted at them. "I'm not your slave, and if you try to force me, I will kill you all. Tell the others to let me go."

They completely ignored me, too busy watching and waiting.

"What is it?" I demanded. "What are you looking for?"

"Charchar!"

Whatever a *charchar* was, they both sensed it now, and it sent them into a panic. They seized me by the arms and dragged me back toward the city, pulling me down the boulevard toward the temple while I fought and scratched. All the way, they took turns shouting, *"Charchar, charchar,"* to the rest of their brood. When they passed one of their brothers or sisters, he or she joined the chant.

"Charchar! Charchar!"

When we reached Minerva's temple, all of the Rusalka were in the street and joined in the alarm. She and Husk emerged through the doorway. He left her there and charged through the gathering crowd just as a shadow passed overhead. I craned my neck to get a better look, only to see something massive and sleek gliding above the city. It was easily fifteen feet long with a white underbelly and a body like a torpedo. It was a great white shark. I'd seen one before, on the Discovery Channel and in a creepy movie my dad made me watch when I was seven. The panic around me suddenly made sense. Husk, however, swam straight for it and slashed at its belly with his claws, shredding the predator's armor. Blood poured into the water and the Rusalka pounced on it, as if the shark were a broken piñata spilling candy at a child's birthday party. They shoved Husk out of the way while they tore at the creature's flesh and ate while its heart was still beating. Husk did not join the frenzy. He swam back to his queen's side and silently watched. She shouted at him, and his attention turned to me. In a flash, he was by my side, forcing me to bow before her. Minerva's vicious tail swished back and forth mere inches from my face. It was the same tail she'd used to slice the huge statue in half. I was certain the next cut would take off my head.

Husk grunted and growled at her. I heard the words *groola* and then *charchar* again. Minerva flashed him a disapproving look, then turned back to me and screeched in my face.

"I don't understand you!" I shouted.

Suddenly, all eyes were on me. I had disrespected the prime, and the Rusalka stopped their feeding frenzy to watch how she would react. Husk pleaded with Minerva, but she shook her head in defiance. Whatever he was saying was not going to be considered. She gestured to me, and he nodded. Before I knew it, he had me in his hands. Once I was on my feet, he spun me around so that my back was to Minerva, but his face told me nothing. There was no hint of what was about to happen, no word of warning, not even a subtle hint to brace myself.

"What's going on, Husk?"

The pain didn't come right away. The surprise of the tearing fabric and the pressure on my back jarred me most. Instead of agony, I felt ice cubes racing along my skin until they were replaced with a red-hot acid that seared my spine from the top of my neck to the base of my rib cage. My knees buckled, and if Husk hadn't been holding me up, I would have fallen forward, but even he couldn't prevent my collapse when the second slash came. I cried out, and my screams echoed back into my ears, frightening me. I fell into a blossom of swirling water and blood that enveloped my head and torso. I tasted copper in my gills and mouth. I smelled the metallic tang of my life all around me.

Husk said something to her, but she growled angrily.

"*Charchar,*" he persisted.

Minerva pouted like a little girl who wants to keep playing with her doll even though it's past her bedtime. She waved us off, and Husk dragged me away, down the boulevard, with stars exploding in my eyes and my nerves screaming. Up we went toward the surface until we broke into the air. He wrapped his arms around me, and we sprang out of the water, landing on the lonely black island. The open air only intensified my agony. The wind felt like steel mesh on my exposed flesh, and the hot sun dried the salty seawater inside the wounds. When my lungs took over from my gills, I tried to push past the pain with the breathing exercises my mother taught me for when my migraines were crippling, but this pain was so different. It was so much worse than anything I had ever experienced.

"The rumors of human stupidity are true," Husk said to me stiffly. "Are you trying to get yourself killed?"

I couldn't speak. I could only rock gently back and forth on the stones, watching my blood paint them red. I was sure I was going to bleed to death. The birds would pick at me until I was nothing but bones, and the winds would blow them away. No one would ever know what happened to me.

Husk leaped into the water. I was sure he was giving up on me. Maybe he'd alerted the others that they could finally eat me. I knew I needed to get away before they came back. I didn't want the last thing I saw to be Rusalka teeth. I tried to stand, but the slightest movement caused my back to shriek. I fell down onto my belly, helpless, as the warm sun turned everything to steam.

Husk was there, then he was gone, then he was back, kneeling over me with handfuls of a murky black weed. He squeezed the moisture out of the leaves, then twisted some into long strands of twine. With this homemade rope finished, he piled the rest of the mound directly onto my wounds, then tied them tightly around my chest. He was rough with me, and when I cried out, he shouted impatiently, demanding that I shut my mouth.

Whatever his medicine was, it had an immediate effect. Numbness swept over my wounds, hushing roaring agony into a whispering ache. It seemed to be having a similar effect on my mood. My anger and fear melted like ice cream on the pavement. Even my fists were unclenching.

"Your suffering is your own doing, human," he shouted as he pulled the twine tight. "I thought you'd understand the delight the prime will take in your failures. She will not pass up an opportunity to be cruel, no matter how important your role. I suppose you are the type that must learn the hard way."

"I'm not going to help her," I croaked. Even talking hurt. "I told you, but you wouldn't listen."

"Then I doubt you'll survive her next disappointment," he shouted.

"Why would she even want my help? I'm her enemy!"

"She has no choice," he explained. "Many of my people have suffered a great sickness of the mind. Right now it is impossible to tell which of them are healthy enough to be trusted to assist her."

"Sickness of the mind?"

He looked out toward the sun, squinting into the light. The waves crashed against the rocks. The wind howled into his face, but he was somewhere else.

"You think Minerva is safer with me than with a Rusalka? There's an ugly troll down there with a hole in his belly who might disagree," I say.

"You brag about your stupidity? You drew blood today, luring the *charchar* to our borders."

"You mean the shark?"

"Those with the endless hunger. They can smell a drop of blood from a great distance. Today you were lucky there was only one. They often hunt in a pack. It was a foolish thing to do."

"You're changing the subject," I said. "What's wrong with the others? It's the Great Abyss, right? You know that's not a god down there. It's a volcano, and it's blasting poisons into your precious kingdom. There's lead and mercury, I bet. It's probably what has caused the sickness of the mind, you know. It can mess with your brain. Can't you feel it?"

"This is a holy place, heretic. Our god speaks to us here. He gives us visions and insights. The giver and the taker ignites our blood and makes us strong," he said.

"Yeah? Did he tell your people to slaughter the rest of the Alpha and eat their bodies?"

Husk picked up my spear, and I flinched, certain I'd pushed him too far, but instead of impaling me, he sharpened the tip against a rock until he was satisfied with the point.

"You know I'm telling the truth, don't you?"

He nodded.

"Then why don't you urge everyone to leave?" I cried.

"Because this is our home."

"It's making you sick!"

"Minerva will never abandon the hunting grounds. It would be the ultimate defeat to be forced to return to our nomadic ways. Abandoning her husband's city would lead to challenges from the others. As long as she wants to be here, the others will stay. She is the prime. Her wishes will be carried out."

"Even if it kills you?"

He waved me off. "Keep our bargain, human. Hunt for her. That is all that is asked of you until the baby is born. In return, I will keep you alive."

"I don't know how to fish."

"Then learn," he said, then turned to jump into the water.

"Wait! How do you know English?" I begged.

"The Great Abyss gave me a blessing."

"A blessing?"

He shook his head, clearly frustrated by me. "That's what Tarooh called it."

"Tarooh?"

He growled. "It's like talking to a jellyfish! Tarooh was the High Thinker of the Alpha empire, a Nix of great intelligence and imagination. I was one of a few of my people he gave a device. It changed all of us, but I alone became something new."

"He gave you a glove, right?"

His black orbs peer at me suspiciously.

"It's made out of metal? Covered in little symbols? You wear it on your hand? I used to have one too," I explain. "I used it to fight off the prime's invasions—that is, until I put on the second one. I was amazing for a couple minutes and then the power just fizzled out."

"This is not possible!" he shouted. His frustration and impatience with me turned to shock and fear. He backed away as if I were the horrible monster instead of him. I hadn't seen a lot of emotions on a Rusalka aside from "kill, kill, kill" and "eat, eat, eat," but at that moment I knew he was bewildered. "The voice told me of another like me, but I assumed it was one of my brothers and sisters, not a human."

"Wait? You heard a voice too? When I wore one of the gloves, I could hear a whispering, but when I put on the second one, I actually saw an old friend who told me I was going to change. I guess the gloves cause hallucinations in all of us."

Husk stepped forward and clamped his heavy hands onto the sides of my head. "The voice is not in your head, human. It is real!"

Lyric, can you hear me?

I stumbled back, pulling myself away from him and falling onto the unforgiving ground. He stalked me, his face crazed and alight, his hands reaching out for me. I crawled backward, desperate to get away.

"You heard the voice. Tell me now, human!" With an incredible leap, he was over me, falling to the ground and snatching my head once more. This time everything changed. Husk's hands, the little island, the clear blue sky—they all melted away, and when my vision cleared, I was home, back in the Coney, popping a squat on one of the weather-worn benches lining the abandoned boardwalk. I had sat there many times, smoked cigarettes on it, kissed a boy or two on it, but that bench doesn't exist anymore. It was demolished to make room for the fence that separated the Alpha camp from the Zone. Still, it felt real. The Wonder Wheel slowly turned behind me. Rudy's Bar was open for business, too. The jukebox played Sinatra's "The Summer Wind." I could smell corn on the cob. I heard popcorn popping. There was a bell ringing somewhere, announcing to some lucky kid that he had won a teddy bear. Everything was just the way it was before the Alpha arrived, and Shadow was sitting next to me shoving his phone into my face.

"I'm taping this. Say something interesting."

"You're dead," I said.

He frowned. "Way to start on a down note."

He looked like he always did, brown-skinned, wide-eyed, and with a mop of unruly hair he couldn't have cared less about. His round baby face was losing the baby, and he was growing into a man, and a handsome one, too. This was the boy who followed Bex around until he earned his nickname.

"You're in the light," he complained as he squinted into the sun behind my head. "Can we switch?"

"This is breaking my heart," I said, because it was.

"I'm sorry. This is just easier," he said.

"Easier?"

"For you."

"Is this a dream?" I scanned the boardwalk in both directions. Everything was remarkably clean. There should have been beer bottles, used hypodermic needles, and discarded lottery tickets up to my ankles. There should have been a sunburned junkie drifting around aimlessly waiting for the methadone clinic to open.

"In a way," he said. "It's hard to explain. If you want to be picky about it, I am not your friend, but I am made of the parts you find dearest about him. You need a familiar face to help explain what's happening to you."

I turned and saw Husk lingering by the funnel cake stand.

"Does he see you too?"

"Husk sees his father. He was a very important figure in his life. It's actually quite sweet."

"So, we're sharing a daydream?"

"Yes . . . no. You know what? I'm hungry. C'mon!"

In a flash, he was up and trotting along the boardwalk. Before I could stop him, he was down the ramp that led to Nathan's. The restaurant was deserted, another unlikely occurrence, but everything else was exactly like I remembered it—the grimy floors, the murky yellow and muddy orange linoleum, the five wobbly tables standing in the center of the room without a chair in sight, the busted ketchup caddy, even the messy glob of pickle relish on the floor. Like the beach, it felt authentic down to the scratch graffiti someone had carved into the tabletops. It even had the stinging smell of barbecued pork, but it was also completely wrong. Where were the panhandlers begging for change and the middle-aged Russian guys whistling at young girls? Where were the tired, crying children, the young Puerto Rican boys keyed up and looking for a fight, the sunburned tourists try-ing not to make eye contact with the locals? Where were the seagulls? Coney Island was lousy with seagulls swooping up and down, dive-bombing for pretzels right out of your hand. Where the hell were the rats?

"These are so amazing," Shadow confessed as he popped a Tater Tot into his mouth. I looked down and found a red tray had materialized in front of us. Along with the Tots were two chili dogs and a couple of lime rickeys. Shadow reached for more, but I pulled the tray away.

"Answers first. Food second."

"Fine," he said, and threw his hands up in surrender. "Do you remember when the Undine came onshore and you put on the second glove? Do you remember talking to me?"

"You said my brain was getting a software update."

He rolled his eyes. "The real Shadow was kind of a nerd, huh? It's as good a description as any, I guess. Husk calls it the blessing, but it's more like your mind is being overwritten with a new operating system, just like when you upgrade a com-puter or your phone, and when it's done, things will be differ-ent for you."

"Husk got super smart? Is that what's going to happen to me?"

"I have no idea how you will be changed," he confessed.

"Any idea when it's going to happen? I'm in a lot of trouble at the moment."

He shrugged.

"That's all you've got for me?"

"Sorry, kid," he said.

"Well, that sucks, Shadow! It's no help at all," I grumble. "Can you explain how he and I are having the same hallucination?"

"First, this is not a hallucination. Second, you're linked," he said as he pointed to his head.

"I'm lost," I confessed.

"C'mon, Walker. You've got to keep up. My Tots are getting cold," he complained.

I pushed the tray back toward him. He forced three of them into his mouth, then took a huge bite of his hot dog. Chili rolled down his chin and landed on his Sugar Hill Gang T-shirt.

"Haven't you ever wondered how the gloves work?" he asked with his mouth still full.

"No. I've been trying to stay alive, so that's kept me busy," I snapped.

Husk entered the restaurant and stood next to Shadow.

"She's not ready to understand," he growled.

"You weren't ready at first either," Shadow scolded. "Don't you remember how afraid you were when I told you this? Help her."

"What the hell are you two talking about?" I demanded.

"The gloves have a power source unlike anything else in

the world. It's a living energy," Husk said. "We both heard a whispering voice that helped us master the water, correct? That voice was not conjured inside our minds. It's the power inside the glove talking, and it comes from a much larger consciousness."

"Yes, I've heard this before," I said. "Ghost and Luna thought the voice belonged to the Great Abyss, but—"

"She's not ready for this part either," Husk said.

"Fine, tell her what she needs to know and save the rest for later," Shadow replied.

"Putting on the second glove awakened an ancient ability that all intelligent creatures once shared—a link to the voice, and to one another."

"The two of you sound like my mom's yoga buddies. Can you cut all the hippie-dippy stuff and just tell me what has happened to us?"

"We are bound, our minds are connected," Husk said.

"You've entered a hive mind," Shadow explained.

"A hive mind."

Shadow sighed impatiently. "Some groups of animals think and act as a single organism, like a beehive, with one goal and one voice. Let me make this simple, Lyric. Your brain and Husk's brain are like a swirl cone from the Mister Softee truck."

"We can hear each other's thoughts?"

"No," Shadow said. "But you can speak to each other that

way. You'll share information and knowledge. But that's not the important part. This hive you are in—you didn't create it. You joined it. It's big, and there are others in it with you. You are sharing everything you know with them, as well. It's important to—" Shadow raised his finger to his lips. "Shhh."

Nathan's vanished, along with Coney Island, and I was dragged back to the little island in the middle of the ocean. When my eyes focused, I found Husk pacing by the edge of the water.

"Where did he go?" I asked.

"They were listening," he said, peering over the side of the island as if the eavesdroppers were out in the water.

"Take me back. I have questions!" I felt an odd sensation wash over me, like my spirit was reaching out to Husk—no, more like I was following in his footsteps, breathing on the back of his neck, even though we were several yards apart. I could sense his heartbeat, the way the sun hurt his eyes, his anxiety about being on the surface too long and making Minerva grow paranoid that he and I were plotting against her. His emotions were mine. I felt the same fears. I was in his head and under his skin. I was tethered.

"Get out of my thoughts," he bellowed.

"I am not doing this on purpose," I cried defensively. "This is not something I want. Tell me how to turn it off, and I will."

"We don't have time for this. The prime will be expecting her dinner," he growled.

"Forget her dinner. This is more important," I said.

He shook his head. "No. We should go. Learn to fish, human. It will keep you alive."

He leaped into the water and vanished beneath the waves.

CHAPTER SEVEN

MY MOTHER FINDS A BOX OF MAC AND CHEESE, THE good kind with the sauce instead of the powder. Luckily, the house they are squatting in runs on electricity, and with the help of a couple of generators, Riley and Maggie stole from a Home Depot, they've got enough power to cook, keep the lights on, and even make hot water for showers. We gather in the fancy kitchen, with the farmer's sink and the marble-topped island, and everyone takes turns assembling the last three months for me. The group has been hiding in different houses in the area since they arrived, moving from time to time to avoid attracting attention from drones and the occasional door-to-door search by soldiers checking for squatters and burglars.

"I still don't understand how you all got together," I say, between bites. Along with the mac and cheese, there are canned peaches, Ritz crackers, and chewable vitamins my father found in an upstairs bathroom. I have been instructed to eat everything on my plate.

"Remember Jackson?" my father asks.

I do. He was one of the soldiers who helped us fight when Minerva sent the Undine to kill us. I learned to trust him.

"The soldier he ordered to take us to safety turned out to be working for White Tower," he explains.

"Do you think Jackson knew?" I ask. I hate to think he did.

"I don't know for sure," Dad says. "I'm leaning toward no. He had a million opportunities to sell us out to White Tower if he wanted. I think a lot of the military is working for Bachman on the side, but Jackson felt solid to me. Anyway, this kid—'cause he wasn't older than eighteen—he took us to a jeep, and we started driving away from the battle zone, but the dummy kept his radio on, and all the while, we're hearing people shouting for him, telling him that White Tower guards will meet him on the other side of the Verrazano for the exchange."

Bex laughs.

"Why is that funny?" I cry.

"You have to picture this. So your dad is in the front seat. I'm in the back with your mom, and she's sitting right behind the driver. His radio is in the back with us, and we look at each other, and I just couldn't believe it, right? After all that craziness, they're still screwing with us. So your mother reaches up, grabs the soldier by the back of the collar and tosses him up and out of the jeep. He let out this crazy scream and landed in a tree. Aaarghhh! It was hilarious."

"I was angry," my mother says, as if she's ashamed a little.

I marvel at the story. My mother is a yoga instructor. I have a hard time imagining her as an Alpha warrior, even though I've heard stories about her from other Alpha. To me, she's Summer Walker, on the beach in her cutoff shorts and flip-flops.

"Next time I could use a little warning," my father says. "Luckily, I got into the driver's seat before we crashed."

"We didn't even stop driving," Bex says. "But that's not the best part. You can't imagine what we found in the jeep—guns, flashlights, radios, and a state-of-the-art, untraceable laptop computer with built in Wi-Fi. Private Stupid taped his password to the keyboard so he wouldn't forget it. You have no idea how valuable it has been for us."

"But I don't know how you found the kids, and what happened to the others." Half of them are not here—McKenna, Geno, Dallas, Alexa, Cole—there are at least fourteen missing from my team.

The good feelings around me seep away. Everyone's eyes look to the floor. Chloe seems like she might cry.

"When you killed the Undine, White Tower came in and captured all of us," Maggie explained. "They used the EMP device the lady in the wheelchair gave the soldiers when we arrived. When they turned it on, our gloves were useless. We fought back, but they had guns and Tasers."

"Still, we tried," Brady bragged. "I knocked at least a dozen people out."

"They arrested us and put us on buses," Riley explains.

"And the buses headed right toward us," Bex says.

"We waited for them to show up, blocked the road with the jeep, and Momma Bear hulked out again! Your mom ripped the door right off the first bus," Bex said.

"The driver peed his pants," Finn says. He and Harrison break into giggles.

"But helicopters came and soldiers, and we were just outnumbered," my father says. "We couldn't rescue the kids on the other bus. If we had stayed, we would all be dead."

I share a look with Bex, then Riley. No one needs to ask where the rest of the team is right now. They're back at the camp, most likely locked in tiny cells while Bachman pokes and prods at them.

"And then you came here?" I ask.

"Well, after a couple problems, yes," my mother says.

"Why didn't you come for me?"

The question wraps around everyone like a straitjacket. No amount of squirming loosens its stranglehold. It's a brutal question to throw out into this reunion. I understand, but I've needed an answer to it for a long time. My mother flinches like I've punched her in the face. She stands, her face awash in grief, and hurries out of the room and through the back door.

"She knew were I was. She could have found me," I say defensively.

"She wanted to, Lyric," Bex says.

"What stopped her?" I cry.

"She's been hobbled," my father says.

"What?"

"The government forcibly evacuated the eastern seaboard. People were put on buses and driven away to camps. People who fought back were arrested. Some were shot. Families were separated. It was out of control. We camped out at an abandoned motel in Elizabeth for a few days to stay off the roads. We needed to get our bearings and figure out what to do next.

"One night a group of soldiers raided the motel and found us. Before we knew what was happening, a guard locked this thing on her leg."

"What thing?"

Bex reaches across the counter to where a thick, heavy-duty laptop computer has been sitting. She starts it up and types a few words on the keyboard, then spins it so I can see the screen. On the screen is an image of someone's leg encased in a metal band. The skin around it is raw and red.

"It's an iron cuff," my father explains. "They lock it onto an Alpha's leg or arm to prevent them from transforming in the water or, in the case of the Triton, to stop them from releasing their arm blades. If your mother goes into the water, she'll die. Her transformation to her true form begins automatically. It would tear her legs apart. Not that it mattered much. I had to chain her to a post a few times to make sure she didn't just leap into the ocean to find you."

"She couldn't come," I whisper to myself.

"I tried too," Riley says, quietly. "I was hurt for a while, but I tried. I just didn't know where to look. Even following your mother's directions, the ocean is just too big to search. I'm sorry. I wish I—"

I reach under the table and take his hand. It's warm. I give it a squeeze.

"No one gave up on you," my father says. "We haven't given up on the other kids, either. We'll rescue them, too, but right now it's just not possible."

"I'll be right back."

Maggie tosses me her hoodie, and I put it on as I open the back door. My mother is sitting on the steps, crying quietly. I sit down next to her and wrap my arm around her shoulders and pull her close to me.

"Does it hurt?" I ask.

She sniffs and nods. "Sometimes. I prayed for you every day."

I lean my head against her shoulder. It feels like home, and we sit quietly for a long time.

"I have to tell you what happened to me," I say, finally breaking the silence, but before I can start, the back door opens and my father steps out to join us. He's got my bowl of mac and cheese in his hand.

"Bex is about to go live," he says to me. "I thought you might want to see it."

"Go live?"

"Yeah, but be quiet. She's very picky about the broadcasts. Oh, and please finish your dinner. I don't like how thin you are."

I stand and take the bowl, shoving an overpacked spoonful into my mouth like a petulant child. I get the desired result when he laughs.

"Three months underwater and still as sassy as ever," he says. "C'mon."

He leads us through the kitchen and down a hallway littered with extension cords. They snake into a family room, though most of the furniture has been pushed aside to make room for a tripod, a gray sheet hanging from the ceiling, and a chair. There are boom mics and lights on stands. Maggie is busy adjusting the camera and peering into its viewfinder while Jane angles a light to bounce off the wall. The windows are covered in black construction paper, and there are maps tacked to the walls, all of which have big circles and lines scribbled in bold red ink. Chloe has a bottle of water in her hand.

"Pretty cool, huh?" she says, gesturing to the setup.

"About what? What is this?"

"It's the broadcast center," Bex says as she enters and sits down in the chair.

"We call it the Batcave," Riley says as he creeps in next to me. His hand brushes against mine. I reach out and take it, sliding my fingers into his, intertwined. He smiles, and I realize how much I've missed it.

"Nerd," Bex says, poking Riley in the ribs as she pushes past us. "If anything, it's the Bexcave. How is my look?"

"Foxy revolutionary," Renee crows.

"You're learning, kid," Bex says, then sits in the chair in front of the camera. "So, I'm thinking we're going to just tease that Lyric is here. I assume that photos of her return are out there, but I'd like to get those people living under a rock a reason to go looking for them. Plus, no offense, Walker, but you look like hell. A bath is in your future. Anyone want to volunteer to help her? Riley?"

Riley's cocky grin slides off his face when my father lets out a low growl behind us.

Bex laughs at her own joke. "Are we almost ready, darlings?"

Maggie flips a switch on the camera, and a red light glows just above the lens. "In three, two, one. You're live."

"Hello, party people, I want to give a big shout-out to all of the protestors who are standing up to soldiers and cops today, and one to the peace marches that continue to sprout up across the country, including the one yesterday that faced down National Guardsmen in West Texas. There were also huge rallies in Los Angeles, Cleveland, and Portland, Maine.

Good work, everyone. Getting in faces and getting things done is how we roll. Don't be intimidated by the arrests. It's vital to our cause to show up and shout loud. Getting arrested isn't the worst thing that can happen to you. Martin Luther King got arrested, and it didn't hurt his reputation at all, so keep causing trouble, keep supporting our brothers and sisters who are looking down guns and brutality. I'd like to remind you to check out the video from January fifteenth that explains how to handle tear gas and pepper spray, and to remind you not to wear cotton and wool if you plan to get into a cop's face. Pepper spray and mace are designed to stick to those materials. I know it ain't exactly sexy, but polyester is your friend during a protest, and remember, be careful, be smart, and most of all, wild things, stay together. I can't stress how important it is to stay together. Remember, peace is the word. Don't fight back, just resist.

"I'm so proud of all you're doing out there, folks. You're demanding serious change in this country, and people are listening. And because I'm so proud of you, I have a special treat. If you haven't seen the news, a little starfish just crawled out of the sea. I'm talking about you know who, the one the president likes to call a terrorist and a threat to humanity, the one he swears is dead. He doesn't like it much when I contradict him with facts, no, sirree, Bob. He's really going to blow his top when he hears what Public Enemy Number One has to say, because she's back. Stay tuned. Soon she'll get her say. Don't blame me if minds are blown."

Maggie turns off the camera. "You nailed it."

"Thanks, Mags," Bex says, then points to me. "Let's go."

"Where?"

Without another word, she leads me up a flight of carpeted stairs. On the landing is a vintage pinball machine and a wooden sailing wheel mounted on the wall. There are framed photos of a family that look as if they all stepped out of a Lands' End catalog. They're athletic, outdoorsy, hiking and surfing folk who wear Tevas and lots of T-shirts from 5K runs.

"Whose house is this?" I ask.

"It belongs to the Douglas family—Manny and Luanne; their teen daughter, Katherine; and spunky son, Nicholas. They have a teenager named Dylan, but he's been in some trouble with drugs so they Photoshopped him out of most of the family pictures."

"Really?"

She chuckles. "No. I have no idea who owns this house."

She opens a door to the bathroom and turns on the shower, running her hand under the spray for a few moments. On the floor, stacked against the wall, are clean towels. There's a trash can in the corner filled with even more, all wet and dirty.

"Give the shower a minute. The generators are great, but getting warm water takes a little time," she says.

She opens a linen closet and digs around on the top shelf. Hidden by a pack of toilet paper is a bottle of fancy shampoo and some conditioner, as well as a jar of apricot salt scrub from a swanky spa in Manhattan.

"I've got a secret stash. Chloe uses up all the good stuff with her bubble baths, so I have to hide the essentials. Get undressed. I should have mentioned that when the hot water comes, it doesn't stick around long."

"Bex, I . . ."

"What?"

I don't want her to see what has happened to my body. I don't want her to cringe at the bruises and cuts, or gasp at the state of my back. I take a step back, defensive, and she takes my hand and kisses me on the forehead.

"It's gonna be all right," she promises, then she carefully helps me out of the pajamas DeCosta and his men made me wear. I cry when the shirt comes off. She shushes me the way one does a child who has woken from a nightmare. "It's all right. It's all right. It's all right."

"No, it's not," I whisper. "It's bad. I haven't seen it, but I know it's bad."

She removes the bandages Lima wrapped around me. I'm expecting her to gasp, some kind of pity, sympathy, shock, something that will make me cry even harder, but she says nothing and acts as if I'm perfectly healthy. She wads the old dressings up and tosses them into a waste bin, then helps me into the shower. Blood circles into the drain. I turn my back to the spray and bear down on the pain until the water is clear.

"Some of the stitches broke in the rescue," I explain.

"I'd hate to see the person who did this to you," she whispers to me. She giggles a little, and then I laugh. I don't know why it's funny. Maybe it's just so horrible I have to laugh, but my life has been so free of joy for so long that giggles are desperate for release.

Bex helps me clean the places I can't reach, then busies herself rummaging through cabinets, leaving the room for a few minutes to return with packages of fresh bandages. I squirt shampoo into my hand and try to run it through my coarse, dry hair. I wash it again, then use some of Katherine's bubblegum-scented conditioner. I repeat the whole process three times before my hair feels like something approaching soft.

By the time the hot water is gone, I'm clean and pruny and feeling considerably more human. Bex hands me a dry towel, lets me do my thing, then takes it to dab at my back. When she's satisfied, she smears on some antibacterial ointment she found in the medicine cabinet and then redresses my back.

"You're good at this," I say, acknowledging the obvious.

"Lots of practice," she admits. She's been in the role of caregiver more than once. Her mom, Tammy, was in a steady stream of abusive relationships before she met the king of all pricks, Russell. One loser after another tossed her down flights of stairs, put cigarettes out on her arms, choked her, and slapped her. Russell once shoved her through a window in a restaurant when she teased him about his singing. Bex was her nurse, and their bathroom an emergency room. My friend might have made a good doctor if the world hadn't imploded.

She wraps me up in the towel, and leads me into another room. There, she snaps on a lamp with an exposed bulb and closes the door behind us. I find myself in what must be Katherine's room. It's decorated in pink. There are posters of a boy band I don't know from South Korea and a shelf with every one of the Twilight and Harry Potter books. A little white dresser with crystal knobs is in the corner, next to a full-size four-poster bed. The room is big and comfortable, but sparsely decorated. A half dozen sleeping bags litter the floor.

"There's not much left in Katherine's closet," Bex apologizes. "The other girls have gone through most of it, and there wasn't anything warm to begin with. I'd take you to Luanne's closet, but it's almost entirely Jimmy Buffett T-shirts and weird country bands. We're gonna have to go on a run for some clothes, I think, but we can find something to get you through the night."

I fall into the bed and marvel at how comfortable everything is here. The mattress is a pillow top. The sheets are flannel. The comforter is thick and downy. The pillows are made of clouds. I stare up at the popcorn ceiling, trying to relate to this luxury, not just the wealth this family has, but the easy quality of their lives. This was a beach house. They used it on the occasional weekend and in the summertime. Their real lives were somewhere else and were probably no less fancy. I feel so removed from this experience. My family never had a beach house. We didn't even own our cramped, two-bedroom apartment, but there's more than luxury to envy about Katherine's life. She's normal. Her greatest privilege was not having to consider much, a steady roll of days and weeks and months passing by without complications and obstacles.

"Katherine was lucky," I say.

Bex shrugs.

"Did that sound bitter?"

She shrugs again.

We share a look and call Katherine a bitch at the same time, then we laugh.

"I wonder where she is right now."

"Probably in a refugee camp," she admits.

The stark truth makes me sick to my stomach.

"Things have gotten pretty messy since you disappeared," Bex continues. "Hopefully she's with her family. Lots of people were separated. I've let people use the site to find one another. You know, a wife can post where she is in hopes of finding her husband. We've had a few successes. Not that they can leave the camp they're in to get back together, but at least they know where their loved ones are."

"So, this site . . . Bex, they wanted to use me to get to you. What have you been doing?"

"That's flattering. Usually you're the criminal at large," she says, then crosses the room to give me a pink Juicy hoodie and a skirt. She sits down while I get dressed. "I hijacked Shadow's webpage."

"Really?"

"Yeah. We've been posting videos on it."

"About?"

"You." She smiles big, her eyes full of pride. "There was so much crap out there, Lyric. The news just repeated whatever the government wanted them to say about you. Everyone knows they're censoring things, but after a while, people just accept it as the truth because that's all there is out there. I wanted to say what really happened. I wanted them to know you weren't a terrorist. You didn't stage the invasions. You fought to save us all on more than one occasion, and people needed to know it. The second we got settled, I broke into Shadow's page. After all the time that had passed, and everything that has happened, people were still visiting it—hundreds of thousands of people. His videos were still some of the most viewed things on the entire Internet. People are fascinated by what happened in our neighborhood. So I had a captive audience, and a fancy, top-of-the-line military laptop, so the kids and I made a video and posted it. The next day I went back in, just to double-check that we did it right, and fifty million people had watched it. Can you even believe that? Fifty million! The comments section was insane."

"Haters."

"Yeah, but you know, that's the Internet. There were lots of people supporting you too, but to be honest, it didn't matter. They wanted more! So, we posted another video, this time about you and the hell we went through at Trident. Seventy-five million people watched it. Every time I posted something new, the number of views grew. Soon we had a hundred million people visiting the site every day, and they weren't just here in the U.S.—they were watching all over the world. People wanted to hear your side of the story. They wanted to know the truth about what really happened. Lyric, in three months, I've flipped the script on your entire life. You're no longer the terrorist from Coney Island. You're, like . . . well, I'll put it this way. People are starting to get tattoos of your face."

"That's ridiculous," I sputter.

"You're a hero, and our audience is helping you stay that way. They're posting their own videos on the site. People had images of you from the first attack. A soldier posted one of you fighting the Undine. People we met in Texas came forward to talk about Trident and what you were trying to do. Others organized protests all on their own, so we started announcing the dates and times, and it grew and grew. If I said there should be a protest in San Francisco, one happened the next day. People were so excited to stir shit up. There's, like, a massive protest along the fence near Coney Island. They show up every day and give the soldiers crap. They post videos. They wear T-shirts with your name on them. There are, like, thousands of teenage girls who try to dress like you."

I look down at my pink hoodie and skirt, with my bruised legs and chalky skin. Any kid dressing like me is a sad creature.

"Now you're back from the dead. You have to talk to them. You have to tell them what we're going to do next."

"What we're going to do?"

"Yeah, you know, help the Alpha, unite everyone, get things back to some sense of normal. Everything is a disaster, and you have the influence to fix—"

"You think I'm a peacemaker."

She nods. "Yeah, a hot seventeen-year-old Gandhi from Coney Island who just happens to be white and female and part fish, but yeah. Don't worry! I know you suck at public speaking. Riley is a genius with words. He'll write something for you to say; we'll videotape it and upload it to the site. It's going to be huge. With the right words, we could force the government to close the detention center and lift the travel bans. People won't stand for it any longer if you say so."

"Bex, no."

She looks at me in stunned silence.

"I can't help you start some revolution. We have to leave here and get as far away as we can. There's something in the water. It followed me to Panama and killed a lot of people. It's probably on the news or—"

"The news is censored now," she interrupts. "Nobody watches it."

"Then ask one of your viewers if they have a tape. People need to see these things. They're coming here to kill us. It's not an invasion like the Rusalka. They don't have any plans to take over. They just want to erase us. When they get here, we have to be long gone."

"You want to tell everyone to fight?"

"No, Bex, I want to tell them to run. We need to take my parents and the kids somewhere safe. Denver was always my dad's idea, and it's in the mountains. It might work."

She gets up and crosses the room to rummage through the closet again.

"Bex? Are you listening? Do you understand?"

"Gawd, all of Katherine's stuff is so Old Navy. This will fit Jane," she mumbles as she snatches a shirt off a hanger. "I miss your closet. All that stuff you used to find. Stella McCartney would have been so jealous."

"Bex? Don't stiff arm me. You need to listen."

"Why don't you take a nap? I'll keep everyone away for a while, though you're gonna be pretty popular, especially with Chloe. She never gave up on you, you know. No one did. If you need me, I'll be in the studio. Nothing gets done if I disappear. Sweet dreams."

And then she's gone.

I lie down in the center of Katherine's bed and stare up at the ceiling pressing down on me. My heart races, and I can't breathe. I jump up and hurry to the window, forcing it open, and letting a frigid breeze invade the room. I can hear the distant waves in my ears and the faint voice of death growing louder and louder.

"CLEANSE THE BAD CHILDREN," they say, over and over and over.

CHAPTER EIGHT

THE HUNTING GROUNDS

WEEKS PASSED, LONELY DESPERATE WEEKS WITH no one to talk to and no hope of escape. Husk kept his distance after our meeting on the island, but I could feel his presence skirting the edges of my mind. Sometimes, his emotions swam with mine so that I could not separate what he was feeling from my own experience.

I spent my days doing as he demanded—learning to fish. It was a frustrating suckfest, chasing the fish with the staff, throwing the staff, watching the fish swim away unharmed. If I was lucky to catch anything, it was a minor miracle, but to feed Minerva I needed to bring back four or five good-size fish, and she liked specific kinds—the white and pink ones, the brown ones, the ones the color of steel. Every day I returned with my measly offering, only to have Husk put several more in my bag. I feared the day when I came up short and he wasn't there to help me. I could still feel the prime's raking fingers on my skin, even though the wounds were almost healed.

One day he joined me on my hunt while my two Rusalka guards looked on. He didn't speak to me, just sat down cross-legged with his spear in hand and closed his eyes. Silent and motionless, he was a statue on the ocean floor, and then when a fat fish flitted by, he shot the spear like lightning and impaled it. In one quick and fluid motion, he yanked it off the tip, buried it in the sand, and sat on it, only to return to his zenlike stance. I watched in stunned amazement. Later I realized he was teaching me without saying a word. I repeated everything I'd seen, even going so far as to bury the fish, which I eventually learned kept them safe from other predators while I was hunting. With practice, I was soon bringing back six, seven, sometimes even ten fish for Minerva. She never thanked me. Her eyes were consistently disgusted with me, but she kept me alive.

One afternoon I watched a fish circling me. It was gray and fat, maybe twenty pounds, and one of Minerva's favorites. It paid me little notice until I tensed in preparation to strike, and then as if it could read my mind, it darted away to one of the black cracks in the earth, the deep crevices so empty I was afraid to even look into one. Maybe it could hear the spike in my breathing or smell the eagerness on me? I tried to force my gills to hold themselves still. I didn't want any noises to startle the skittish thing. *Just a few more seconds*, I thought, maybe another pass, and I could take my shot. I just needed to get the right angle so the spear would sink into the meat and not bounce off the hard, thick skin on its head and back. Closer . . . closer . . . I told myself I wouldn't miss. I visualized the tip shooting through the water with perfect and deadly aim. Imagining it happening seemed to help for some reason, and when I was certain I couldn't fail, I let the weapon fly. *Wham!* I got it with a perfect shot! I swam to pull it off my spear and bury it, just as Husk had taught me, but the damn thing was heavy and still stubbornly alive. Its tail caught my hand and sliced it open enough so that blood escaped. I pulled away, angrily and in pain, then stabbed the fish over and over in my rage, like some deranged aquatic serial killer. Finally, it stopped fighting me and died. I put my foot on its head to wrench the weapon free, then got down on my hands and knees, scooped sand away to make a hole, and buried the beast. It was a sloppy effort, but I did it. I was proud of myself. That fish was the biggest one I had managed to catch. I raised my hands in triumph to an audience of two Rusalka, one of whom still held a grudge from when I put a hole in him.

"I am awesome!" I shouted to them.

That was when I noticed the shadow. I looked up and gasped. A shark drifted over my head. It looked huge, as long as a taxicab, and fast. It was another great white, and it was hunting me, slowly circling, descending to my level.

I turned to the guards, but they were gone. After attacking them, I had to guess that this was their revenge, and they left me with nothing to defend myself but a stupid spear. I nestled it under my armpit and pointed the tip in the beast's direction. The shark immediately bolted to the right, abandoning its attack, but circled back and steered its nose right at me again. I was hoping it would see I planned to defend myself, but this one must have been hungry. It suddenly turned on the speed, rocketed at me, and cut the ocean in half. I barely got the spear up in time, though little good it did me. The shark chomped down on the end, yanking it from my hands, then turned it to splinters. There was one sizeable piece with a freshly jagged point near my feet, but trying to retrieve it would have left me vulnerable. Still, if I was going to have any chance of surviving, I had to have it. I dove and swam frantically while the great white circled again, picking up speed for a fresh assault. I snatched the broken spear, now no bigger than a dagger, and stood my ground. My only chance was to jam it into the shark's eye and try to blind it. I'd seen that in movies. I'd also seen people fly and shoot webs out of their hands in movies, so I had no idea if it would work.

Hey, Shadow, remember when you said I was going to get some kind of special ability? It would really be useful right now.

The shark bore down on me and closed the gap between us quicker than seemed possible. I had only one chance, so just as it crashed into me, I stabbed at its eye. The shark's nose hit me right in the rib cage. The impact felt like a subway train had slammed into my side. My only weapon floated downward, then swirled into one of the bottomless crevices and vanished. The impact screwed with my equilibrium, threw me off balance, and caused me to drift out of control. I couldn't right myself. My legs were up, and my head was down. I bounced in every direction. I had made myself the easiest target in *Shark Week* history. What a stupid way to die.

I tasted blood in the water, unsure if it belonged to me. It swirled in front of my face in leaky curlicues. Had the shark bitten me? I hadn't felt its teeth when it crashed into my ribs. There was no pain other than the dull ache in my muscles. I wondered if that was death—fast and furious, so shocking and efficient, I was saved the agony. When the shark sailed past again, I learned the origin of the blood. There was a jagged cut in its belly. Tiny fish that might normally tremble in the face of a predator that large raced from every direction to feast on its dying body. They were followed by a swarm of bigger fish, all digging into the shark's vulnerable wound, pulling out strands of pink flesh. A pack of smaller sharks joined the buffet, feasting on their dying cousin. Before I knew it, there were thirty of them chomping down on the still-warm carcass. One swam close to me, its eyes glued to my body as if I was on the dessert cart. My fight to live wasn't over yet. I started swimming toward the city, frantic to escape, but my sudden movements drew the smaller sharks' attention. They abandoned their meal for something different.

Husk appeared and grabbed me by the arm. He dragged me toward the surface and we exploded out of the water, sending a spray into the air that came down like rain. I scampered up onto the island just as a fin rose near my feet. The sharks swam along the shoreline of the black island, hoping we'd come back in, then sank below and disappeared. I stared at slapping waves until a nervous breakdown seized me, shook me hard, and let loose every tear in my body.

"Foolish girl. You barrel through life with less sense than a guppy," he bellowed. "Not only did you attract those creatures, you lost your catch."

"I almost died," I shouted, then curled up in a ball, doing what I could to stop the involuntary shakes tearing me apart. Husk stood over me. I could see his neck muscles tighten as he prepared a torrent of insults, but something held him back. He took a long, deep breath, leaned down, and helped me to my feet. "How did you know I was in trouble?"

"I sensed it. I cannot be present at all times to keep you safe. Minerva is ill. She requires my attention, and I must be at her side, but I am out here with you! I do not hold favor with her. She will kill me when she grows tired of your nonsense."

Husk swam with me back to the strange temple where I slept. He stopped at the archway and, without a word, swam off down the boulevard.

I went through the halls and up the tunnel, to the room

with the strange markings on the walls, and somehow found a way to fall asleep. Maybe my body just couldn't take any more of the terror I'd experienced that day and had decided to shut me down. It was a welcome escape, but it led nowhere. My brain wouldn't let me slip away. My thoughts led me back to Husk.

I could feel him and knew he could feel me. He was agitated by my presence. He felt I was intruding, or maybe it was just how I felt at first. Regardless, I didn't want to trespass. I would have rather turned back, but when I tried, there was nowhere to go. I was stuck there, peering at his greatest fears and vulnerabilities. It suddenly dawned on me how ridiculous it was to care what he felt. He'd captured me. He'd turned me into a slave for a woman I despised. He wouldn't let me leave. Did he deserve my respect?

A step forward led me to a familiar site. I was back in the same room I'd been locked in for weeks, but it wasn't the barren, lonely cell I knew. Instead it was a bustling space filled with Nix scientists. They buzzed around working on projects, unaware that I was walking among them, which at first was unsettling, until I remembered I was in one of Husk's memories.

Nix look very similar to me, thin bodies with tight skin, long, bony arms, heads like pumpkins and fleshy mouths. Underwater, their bodies were more serpentine, almost eel-like without the legs they grew when they came on land.

Ghost was the first one I met, when he and a few other Alpha were forced into my school. Honestly, he was always a prickly jerk, but he was responsible for putting the glove on my hand. He probably saved my life the day the tidal wave came. He often bragged about his grandfather, who he claimed invented the gloves. Was Tarooh Ghost's grandfather? It was impossible to know. Any one of those creatures could have been Ghost's identical twin, but there was one who attracted my attention more than all the others. He was scratching an elaborate mathematical equation on the walls in a frantic hand, all the while muttering to himself feverishly. I was sure he was Tarooh. These were Husk's memories, and what he knew I seemed to understand as well. Husk called him the High Thinker — a scientist, and an important one.

I guessed the other Nix were his assistants. Each labored on the same project, though they were busy on different aspects of it. I had no idea what they were building. All I knew for certain was they appeared to be worried about their boss. Tarooh was crazed, talking to shadows, and not sleeping. It had started shortly after he returned from an expedition to the Great Abyss. He told the others of the wisdom he acquired inside the crater. He told them he believed the Great Abyss spoke directly to him. The others feared him.

Husk threw up walls, but they were easy to steer around. *What's the matter? Does it suck when someone else controls you?*

You can push back all you want but it won't slow me down. All your secrets are laid out for me to rummage through.

I was eager to learn more. Something terrible happened in that room, and Husk was desperate to keep it from me. I scanned every corner while his mind bellowed at me. At first there was nothing, but then I noticed a figure huddling in the shadows. It was too dark to see his face but I knew he was important. The closer I got to him, the less I could see his face. He was little more than an outline, empty and nondescript, until we were suddenly face to face. It was him! Husk was chained to a wall, exhausted and frightened, but he was not the intelligent creature who now held me prisoner, but rather a howling beast. The revelation came with another surprise. I understood the noises he made. They weren't just grunts. They were a language, a crude one, but a language, nonetheless. The snapping teeth were his way of saying he was confused. The whines were calls for mercy. I knew Fathom could speak to Rusalka, but he'd told me that they were barely smarter than a dog. He was wrong. Rusalka were intelligent —not rocket scientists, but not animals, either.

The Nix ignored his cries. Nothing he said or did got their attention, because they didn't think he was smart either. Husk, like all of his kind, was below all others in the Alpha hierarchy, at the very bottom of a list of life forms that mattered to the empire. He was beneath consideration. I suspect it was how the Nix avoided the guilt of making him their guinea pig. It was the same willful ignorance that allowed the rest to turn his kind into slaves.

Get out of my head, human!

I could feel his embarrassment with this version of himself. He was humiliated by who he was before the "blessing." His shame was suffocating, or perhaps it was my own. I had gone too far. I pulled back, trying to find my way out of his memory, but there was nowhere to go. I was trapped. I turned back to the bustling lab, and more history unfolded. I suddenly understood that Tarooh had brought the Alpha to this place. He'd settled the empire in the shadow of the volcano after going into it and coming back changed. Alpha made pilgrimages here throughout their history, receiving visions from their god, but Tarooh claimed the Great Abyss wanted his children near. He convinced the others to make the holy site their home.

Each time he entered the volcano, and each time he returned, he came back as if possessed by some mad spirit. He no longer slept. He carved symbols and numbers on everything, night and day, and he swore he had been given instructions for a machine that would change his people's lives.

I could see a glass container with a cork top. Inside the container was a viscous black liquid. It swirled and spun, flipped onto itself, and shot upward at the cork as if it were alive. Husk feared it right away. It was something beyond his understanding, and the hunger in the High Thinker's eyes when he looked at it frightened him.

The High Thinker's actions hinted at madness, but he held the ear of the prime, so the others did as they were told. They worked tirelessly on his invention. When the pieces were complete, Tarooh assembled them himself. A small compartment in the palm flipped open and he poured his holy treasure inside. His assistants cried out when the machine glowed as blue as the moon. They knew they were people of science, and this was something they should not have been tampering with at all. They raced out of the room, leaving him alone with Husk.

Tarooh slid his glove onto his long, stringy hand, and even though it was a perfect fit, the latch would not close around his wrist. Husk watched him try to force it on, but it would not stay.

Enraged, the scientist turned over tables and smashed his equipment. The Great Abyss's gift had rejected him, and he felt betrayed. He railed for hours, and there were many times it seemed he might take his own life, but then Tarooh was struck with an idea. He leaped to his feet, retrieved the glove, and forced it onto Husk's hand.

I felt dread crawl up my throat, sour and hot and full of hopelessness. Husk instinctively knew something was going to happen to him, and he was terrified. He pulled at his chains, but the truth was unavoidable: he was disposable. He trembled with both sorrow and fury, and when the glove clicked shut around his wrist, I felt his dread. I wished I could have consoled him. I wished I could have told him that he would be all right.

The glove glowed blue once again, and the same rush of power that swept me away when my glove locked around my fingers came over him. There was a brightness inside as beautiful and yellow as the orb he watched ride the sky above the waves. Now he had an orb all his own, living in his chest, and it had a voice. It offered him favors. It told him he could have anything he wanted; all he had to do was ask.

Tarooh couldn't hear the voice. Husk knew, because if he could, Tarooh would have been afraid. Instead, his master's eyes were wide with wonder. Even when the water broke the clamps around Husk's feet, he clapped and cheered. He celebrated when Husk turned the power on the lab, sending metal and tools flying in every direction, some piercing the very walls and letting in the red light of the volcano. When he turned the glove on the High Thinker, Tarooh smiled. He told Husk that he was special, and that if they worked together, they could make all the Rusalka special. Husk lowered his hand and listened.

The lab shimmered into nothing before my eyes, and I found myself somewhere new, a place I had never seen. Here, in this sandy, dark valley beneath the raging volcano, a line of Alpha waited patiently while Tarooh and his assistants locked gloves onto their hands. The power rejected many, especially from the other races, but it embraced hundreds of Rusalka. I watched them glow, then build a kingdom out of nothing. Roads snaked through the sand, towers sprang up like weeds, great works of art were brought to the very edge of life. Husk stood in the street, working on a massive sculpture of the prime. It was the same one I watched Minerva destroy.

Again, I was taken somewhere new. I found myself on the edge of the crater, looking down into the volcano. Tarooh was next to me, as were hundreds of Rusalka wearing their gloves. The prime was with us, his long blond hair swirling behind him as he peered into the unknown. Minerva stood by, though she kept a respectful distance. The prime was with another woman, a Triton with gorgeous features and eyes like hurricanes. I knew she was Fathom's mother. She was pregnant and terrified, begging her husband to stay with her, pleading with the priestess dressed in sealskins to make him listen to reason. He didn't seem to hear either of them; he was too hypnotized by the swirling horror below.

Tarooh leaped into the volcano and the Rusalka followed. Despite his wife's pleading, the prime went as well. Minerva followed without hesitation. Husk swam along the side, too frightened to follow. Two Selkies snatched him by the arms and tossed him in against his will.

He was sure his end waited for him, but there was no death inside the Great Abyss. There was something else, something that frightened him more than anything in his miserable life. What it was I couldn't know. Husk found a way to push me out of his mind and slammed the door shut.

CHAPTER NINE

MY FATHER IS LYING NEXT TO ME, HIS ARM DRAPED over my shoulders. He's curled his enormous frame around my body, like the oyster shell protects its pearl. At first I can't trust that he's real. I reach out and jab my finger into his arm. He's solid.

"I'm here," he whispers.

I smile.

"I've got good news and bad news, kid," he continues. "The good news is you came back to us safe and sound. The bad news is I made a deal, and we're all going to start going to church on a regular basis."

I chuckle. "Sucker."

He gives my arm a poke too.

"There were nights when I thought I heard your voice," he says, soft and low, as if he's worried someone is listening. "It was as clear as anything. I'd leap up and hurry downstairs to throw open the door, then walk around the yard and search the neighborhood. I got everyone up to help me. I made them crazy. I couldn't accept that you were out there and I couldn't help you. My brain started screwing with me."

"I heard your voice too," I say. "I actually hear it all the time. You're very bossy."

I wrap my arms around his huge torso and kiss him on the shoulder.

"You've been down for a while. Bex will be waiting."

I sit up and rub my eyes and look to the window. The sun is still up, but a cricket is working his back legs on the windowsill. I hear the crash of waves. Despite it all, it's quiet here, not like the endless hollering of water in my ears.

"There's spaghetti and rice cakes downstairs," he whispers. It's layered with an apology. "Tough to get fresh food right now."

"I'll take anything but fish," I say.

"I can imagine. Riley went to one of the shops up on the strip and got you some warmer clothes." He points to a bag on the dresser. "Can I just say I'm confused? I thought Fathom—"

"Fathom and I are done," I say, a little too sharply.

He gives me one of his knowing looks, the kind he uses when he knows I am exaggerating a story or telling an out-and-out lie. It just makes me angrier.

"He and I, as a couple, as a 'we,' are so stupid it's hilarious. It can't work, and it never was going to work—"

My father cringes.

"I'm sorry. Maybe this is a Mom conversation."

He takes a deep breath. What I'm saying is hard for him to swallow, but he's going to hold his nose and get it down. "No, go on. I'm listening."

"We're just insanely different. What seems like common sense to me—kindness, compassion—they're weaknesses and failures to him. They say opposites attract, but we're not opposites. A person can predict the opposite of something. The opposite of white is black. Up is down. Left is right. With Fathom, there's no way to guess. If I say 'near,' he might say . . . well, hell if I know. I don't have a clue what would come out of his mouth, and that's a huge problem. I've been in this state of denial because when I'm with him, I can't breathe and I've got the feels and I hyperventilate at my imagination."

"Yeah, this is a Mom conversation," my father grumbles.

"I'm sorry. I'm seventeen."

"I have managed to maintain a willful ignorance about what happened when you left the house," he admits. "Keep going, but can you do a little editing for my sake?"

"Sorry. I think I haven't been able to share anything with anyone for so long that you're getting three months of backed-up girl talk. What I'm trying to say is when you're growing up, there are all these pretty songs about true love being predestined by the universe itself, and they brainwash you into believing that real love isn't real unless it is a struggle, and, well, it's stupid. So, if the only way to prove I love him is to spend every day defying the odds against us, then I don't love him. It wasn't meant to be; maybe there's no such thing as 'meant to be,' anyway. I mean, really, he and I were fire and gasoline, you know, just burning until all the oxygen in the room was exhausted and everyone around us was scorched with third-degree burns. That's not what I need or want. So, basically, what I'm saying is Riley is sweet and he's here for me, so don't give him a hard time, all right?"

My father looks like he's been through a war. I throw my arms around him and giggle, knowing I may have broken him.

"Are you done?" he asks.

"Well, there's more, but I don't think you can handle it." I laugh even harder until he smiles.

"Listen, I can't believe I'm going to intervene on his behalf, but you know why Fathom didn't come for you, right? I mean, if that's why you are done with him," he says.

"What's wrong with Fathom?"

"Lyric, all of the Alpha were captured after the last invasion. They were hobbled like your mother and put in a detention camp on the beach. That's part of what Bex and the kids are trying to do—get them released. The protests are about pressuring the government to free them."

My stomach does a flip-flop, and the mac and cheese in my belly is put on the blend cycle. I leap out of bed and into the hall, and throw open the bathroom door, falling to my knees just in time to let go into the toilet. It's a painful retch, mostly dry heaves, but it comes with some vicious cramps. My father sits on the tub and pours water from a plastic bottle sitting on the sink into a Dixie cup.

"I've got to get you healthy."

I nod, but my head is spinning like a top careening against a wall. Fathom is in a prison. It's the one thing I never considered when I was sitting in the hunting grounds, simmering with rage that he hadn't tried to rescue me. He couldn't.

There's a knock on the door.

"Bex is ready," Renee calls out from the other side.

"We need a few minutes," my father calls back, then helps me stand. "Are you up for this?"

"No, but what choice do I have. It's Bex."

Riley is furiously scribbling notes into a spiral-bound notebook while Jane connects extension cords and adjusts light stands.

"Is it nice wherever you are?"

I force myself to focus on him. He's teasing me.

"Sorry," I say. He's opening himself up if I want to talk, but I don't. I can't. He doesn't want to hear that my head is filled with Fathom right now, and I don't want to tell him because the truth is, it shouldn't matter to me that he's locked up. It doesn't change what I've come to understand about us.

I take his hand and intertwine my fingers into his. It's warm and strong, a hand I can count on every time. I admit I am conflicted about this boy, but I don't have to be. He and I could have a future if there is a future to have. He's like me in so many ways. He's the hot nerd with potential, so why do I feel like I'm trying to move him into an apartment that is already too small, with Fathom's memory hogging all the space?

I kiss him — really kiss him. His mouth is warm and soft. It feels safe, and our lips feel like jigsaw puzzle pieces sliding into one another. This kiss makes total sense.

It's not me, Fathom whispers.

"I wish I had found you," Riley says, his eyes sparkling under the lights.

"You get points for trying," I whisper, flirting, luring him. If he's wrapped up in me, deep and tight, I won't lose him while I'm clearing my head. Yes, that will work. When Fathom is finally evicted, Riley can move right in. He'll never even know I was confused.

"Um, I'm in the room," Jane complains.

"We're grossing out the young'uns," I say.

We giggle conspiratorially.

"I didn't have a lot of time, but I wrote you something," he says, handing me his notebook.

I scan his words briefly. Bex wasn't exaggerating. He's put together something powerful for me, but it still feels like the wrong message to send right now.

"Thanks," I say. "I hope you don't expect me to turn into Obama."

"You'll be great."

Renee snaps her fingers. "We're ready, people!"

"Good luck," he says, but he doesn't let me go. His fingers have found a home between mine.

Bex hurries into the room and hops into her seat. Someone has brought another chair from the kitchen and set it next to her. Three lights are shining on her, and she sparkles like a diamond.

"Let's do this," she says stiffly. "Did you write something for her to say?"

"Right here," I say, waving it so she can see.

"Just try to get through it. If you make mistakes, we can always start over," Jane says.

I sit down in the empty seat. Bex smiles, but she's not happy with me. She's worried I'm about to wreck all her hard work, contradict months of her telling the world that I was just a girl from Brooklyn who stood and fought when I had no other choice. I'm her creation now, a folk hero, a beacon of unity, but that's not someone I am allowed to be right now, not even for her. The world is about to end, and it's every person for themselves. I hate having to ruin this for her, but I don't have any other choice.

Maggie hunches over the camera, again. She raises her finger to her lips to shush everyone and then points to Bex.

"What's up, party people? I assume everyone has seen the footage from the skirmish at the airport. I've watched it myself, mainly because we were responsible for much of it. Don't be fooled by what the president's press secretary said.

The girl in the videos is Lyric Walker. For months they've been telling you she's dead, but hey, sad trombone, Mr. President. She's alive and well, and I've got the real McCoy right here. She has a fascinating story to tell us about her missing days and her plans for the future.

"But first, I need your help. There are rumors of creatures coming on shore in Panama and attacking the locals. I'm told they're like nothing we've seen so far. I can't find any video of the event, and the Internet looks like it's being scrubbed of reports. That's no big surprise now that Big Brother manages what's good for us to see. In the past you have sent me some pretty important clips, and I've come to count on you. If anyone out there witnessed what happened and has some visual proof, please send it our way. I'll take anything you have. It's important. All right, I've kept everyone waiting long enough."

Renee hurries to connect a microphone to my shirt while Brady adjusts a light. I marvel at what they do here. I have no idea where they got all this equipment, or even how they learned to use it, but what they have done is important. When I'm ready, Bex takes my hand and gives it a squeeze.

For a long moment, I am hypnotized by the lights and the lens, but the spell breaks when the kids file into the room. They watch me from behind the camera. My mother and father hover, leaning in to hear every word, and then Maggie raises her hand and waves for my attention. I look at Riley's speech, but it feels wrong. I have to tell the world the truth.

I drop the script to the floor and look into the camera lens.

"My name is Lyric Walker. I'm from Brooklyn, New York, from a neighborhood called Coney Island, which was destroyed by a tidal wave not long ago. Some people blame me for it. They call me a terrorist. They're wrong. I'm no hero, but I'm not a killer, either. Everything I have done has been to save my friends and family.

"You have probably heard about Texas and the camp where the Alpha were held and experimented on, and even about the children, the ones like me, who were trained as soldiers to fight the Rusalka invasion. For the record, we saved this world."

"Lyric—"

"I hope this isn't coming off as bitter. I don't have the strength to carry that weight around anymore. I know many of you hate me, and people like me, but I don't hate you. In fact, that's why I've decided to send you this message. What happened to me over the last three months is not important, what is important is that while I was gone, I discovered another race of creatures living in the ocean. They are worse than the Rusalka, worse than the Undine, and they are on their way to the United States. Their plans are terrible. They believe both humanity and the Alpha must be destroyed to make room for a new race of people. They'll attack the eastern coastline soon, killing everyone they encounter, and then they will move farther inland.

"I'm telling you this because this time you can't count on

me. Nothing I can do will stop them. The Alpha are in cages on the beach in Brooklyn. The country is torn apart by hate. We are at our most vulnerable, so I want you to listen closely to my advice. Every single person who hears this message should—"

Suddenly, I am not in the room with Bex and her crew. I am lumbering onto a beach at dusk. People are walking hand in hand along the sand. A small crowd has built a bonfire, and wine is flowing into glasses. There's music in the air. I look around, trying to find a sign, some clue to where I've been transported, but before I can, screams rise up and drown out the celebration. I rush forward against my will, charging toward a restaurant. The people inside look out the windows at me, and they shriek in terror. In the glass's reflection, I see myself. I am not Lyric. I am one of them. The glass breaks. There is blood and crunching bones. I have to kill them all. I have to CLEANSE the world to MAKE ROOM for my NEW FAMILY. The people run, but there's no place for them to go. WE will FIND THEM all and END them quickly. There is nowhere they can hide.

"Lyric," Bex says. I look down and find her hand on mine. I'm back. "Are you all right?"

"No," I say. "I'm being a fool. I was wrong, completely, stupidly wrong. Bex, I know you want me to give peace a chance. What you've done here, what all of you have done, well, it's amazing and brave. But peace is going to have to wait.

Trust me, I'm not getting my way either. I wanted to tell everyone to run for their lives, but I now realize running is not an option."

I turn to the camera. "People, I have to prepare you for war. These things I found—I can't fight them by myself. The handful of children who are like me will not be enough either. I'm going to Brooklyn. The Alpha are being held in detention there, and I'm going to free them so they can help me fight, but even they won't be enough. I need you. Everyone has to fight. Anyone who can shoot a gun, swing a bat, or throw a punch. Whether you're a cop or military or making lattes at Starbucks, I need you to come to Coney Island. There, we will make our last stand. If we fail, we won't get another chance. It's your turn to fight. Now turn off the camera. We've got work to do."

Maggie peers from behind the camera. Her face is tight and irritated. She turns off the power, then the lights, so that Bex and I are sitting in the dark. My best friend leaps up from her seat and storms out of the room.

"Wow," Riley whispers.

In the dark I can see sympathetic looks on my parents' faces, but they've got nothing to offer.

"I guess I better go talk to her," I say.

I find her pacing in the street, smoking a cigarette.

"Got another?"

The pack flies at me, and I catch it. I sit on the stoop and fumble with the wrapping. Inside, are three from the original twenty. I take one and light it with the pack of matches tucked into the plastic sleeve, and immediately regret it. The first drag burns my throat. I haven't smoked in maybe a year and only did it at parties. My body has changed a lot in that time. I don't think I'm built for tobacco any longer, but I'm already walking on thin ice with my bestie. She's not going to be happy if I waste one.

"I never expected you to treat this like a joke," she says. "It's a slap in the face to everyone who supported us. I've been preaching nonviolence, common sense, civil disobedience. You just told the world to start loading their guns. Do you think the government is going to let you walk into the detention center and start unlocking the cages? You've declared war on the United States."

"I know you were hoping I'd be Martin Luther King, but—"

"You had the potential. Now, you're . . . I don't know. Name a sexy terrorist."

"Taylor Swift?"

"Don't make me laugh. I'm angry at you. If I post that speech, you will look like some blood-crazed maniac. All the goodwill, all the organizing—down the toilet. You'll go back to being a villain, Lyric."

"Or, she could be the badass a lot of people need," Riley says, joining us on the porch. "Bex, if she says we have to fight, we have to fight. If she can get people to do it, then that's a good thing. One of the reasons everything sucks is because people expected someone else to come in and be the hero."

"Aren't you tired of fighting, Lyric? I'm really tired of fighting," Bex says.

I tap the cigarette out on the porch steps and slide the unused part back into the pack.

"You have no idea how tired I am. I'd love to disappear, get as far away from the ocean as I can, and grow a garden. I want to move somewhere boring and get a house full of dogs, but I can't. Not yet."

Bex walks over to me and takes her cigarettes, then shoves them in her pocket.

"How the hell do you think you're going to free the Alpha? We've been working on it for months. The government has refused."

I shrug. "Bex, I don't have a clue. I've got a few kids with superpowers, a crazy-strong warrior mom, and a cop for a dad. And I've got you. I'm just doing this a day at a time. To be honest, my only goal right now is to find a store that has some underwear."

She laughs, despite her anger.

Maggie appears in the doorway. "So what's the plan?"

"Post it," I say.

"No!" Bex cries stubbornly, then turns her back to me. Her

face points to the sky as if the answers are written in the day's last rays. I walk up behind her and wrap her in a hug.

"Mags, you and Riley, more than all the others, believed in this the most. You get a vote," Bex says to the others.

Riley looks to Maggie, then to me, then to Bex. "Do you even have to ask? Post it."

"I'll have it up in about ten minutes," Maggie says, turning and disappearing into the house. Riley smiles at us and follows her.

"Unless I look fat!" Bex shouts after her.

"I'm sorry, Bex," I whisper.

"I know," she says. We're going to be okay. She points to where Riley was just standing.

"That one's hot. You might have actually found a keeper."

I laugh. "Don't get too excited. I'll screw it up."

"If you do, I call dibs."

My father and mother appear on the porch.

"What do we do now?" he asks.

I point to Bex. "Teach this one how to fight."

"Bitch, please," Bex says.

CHAPTER TEN

After stomping through Husk's mind, I couldn't tell the difference between his troubles and my own. He must have felt my despair just as strongly, the loneliness, the uncertainty of every dangerous day, the terror of falling victim to a shark's hunger or Minerva's rage. Managing all that hurt was almost more than I could handle, and I found myself weeping at times.

My Rusalka guards ignored my suffering for the most part. They took me out on my fishing trips and kept their distance. The one I'd stabbed was still angry. The other was bored. They never guessed that I understood every word they said. The lifetime of information I'd gleaned from Husk explained a myriad of mysteries about the Alpha. I had a firm grasp of all of their different dialects and customs. The Rusalka dialect was the most interesting to me, primarily because I hadn't thought of it as a language before. It burrowed like a worm into my mind, squirming and making paths of understanding until I knew every grunt, groan, and gnash of teeth. Of course, knowing the language and using it were two totally different things, and as crude as the Rusalka tongue sounded, it was deceptively complex. Rusalka used more than their lips and tongues to form words. The water helped with their pronunciation, as well as the bubbles released into the sea. There was some echolocation going on, like dolphins, and the difference between meanings could be extreme, depending on whether the words bounced off sand, rocks, or even fish.

In some ways, it allowed me to feel connected to the guards, even though they spent nearly all of our time together insulting me. I considered speaking to them but worried they might attack me, especially in light of how hostile they could be toward Husk, whom they considered an abomination. They weren't shy about their disgust, even when he was present. It was just another reason to feel sympathy for him. His was a lonely life.

I was achingly lonely, too, but there was one silver lining to having guards who wanted nothing to do with me. When I was done fishing and had delivered my catch to Minerva, they didn't seem to care what I did. They didn't seem to fear that I might try to escape. I was in the middle of nowhere, after all, so they didn't get in my way when I started making daily trips to the island above.

Every day I rose into the dazzling light and scampered onto the black rocks. The tides had polished an almost perfect square about seven feet across into a smooth, comfortable patch. I spent hours meditating and doing as much yoga as my back would allow. I watched the clouds chase one another across the sky and searched the horizon for boats. It was peaceful there, and the more time I spent on that rock, the better I felt.

I felt close to my mother there. She was an amateur guru who had taught me every pose. I moved into sun salutation, then warrior two, then attempted a handstand. I let out a little cheer when it finally happened. Battling currents to right myself had strengthened me. My balance was incredible. My arms and legs were starting to resemble a Triton's. I was getting lean like Arcade and Fathom. Mom would have been proud.

But the solitude had a downside. In those quiet hours Fathom came to me. I tried not to think about him, but some days he sat down in the front row of my thoughts and wouldn't go away. Even when I slept, he came prowling around, popping up in bizarre cameos. His smile waited in ambush around every corner. I felt haunted by his kisses and hands, but when I woke, a blanket of bitterness covered me.

He isn't coming. He's not even going to try. He expects me to do this on my own. I closed my eyes tight to squeeze out the angry tears.

There was a splash and a thump, and Husk was standing over me, blocking the sun with his body and turning himself into a black hole with flaming edges. He reached down and jerked me to my feet.

"You will come with me."

"What's going on?" I said just before we hit the water. He dragged me toward the city, with the volcano raging nearby. The city's buildings grew close until we were gliding between them, following the boulevard of bones toward Minerva's temple. Husk dismissed her guards, then clamped down on me with his cruel strength.

"Will you please talk to me?" I pleaded, trying both my mouth and my mind.

"The prime is ill. You must go to her and provide comfort. She is in a great deal of pain," he finally explained.

"Pain?"

He led me inside Minerva's royal home and through a labyrinth of hallways.

"What am I supposed to do for her?" I argued. "I don't know how to help a sick person, and forget a half-fish, half-human person."

Husk shook me harshly. "Shut your mouth, fool," he growled, then looked around to see if anyone was spying on us. "Do you want the others to hear? No one can know she is ill. If they believe the heir is in jeopardy, they may try to kill her."

"And that's a bad thing why?"

"There are seventy of my kind left alive. If one of them

steps forward to challenge for her title, the others will do the same. They will turn on one another. I cannot risk the handful that remain to a senseless power struggle."

"You don't really expect me to be sympathetic, do you?"

He growled in response.

"She needs a doctor," I continued.

"The Alpha do not have doctors."

"Which is why there are only seventy of you left," I mumbled. "In the sane world, when people get sick, they go see a very smart person who knows how to take care of them. I'm not one of those very smart people. I don't know what to do about her pain. I have never had a baby. I couldn't even get babysitting jobs in our apartment building because I am irresponsible and undependable. You have picked the wrong person for this job."

"Part of the bargain—"

"A bargain I never agreed to," I reminded him.

"All you must do right now is tell her that everything is going to be all right. That will suffice."

"What if she's not all right, Husk?"

We moved into a room lit by the volcano's crimson glow. Everything appeared sinister there, like we'd stumbled upon a devil worshipper's tomb. It was filled with statues of the dead prime, each looking toward the center of the room. There Minerva hovered, her body convulsing in pain and her tail slashing violently back and forth. She thundered in both agony and anger. The pain must have been intense. Every Alpha I'd ever met refused to acknowledge suffering. Spangler cut Arcade's hand off when we were locked in Trident, and she treated it like a minor inconvenience. Fathom often came to class covered in fresh cuts and bruises, even broken ribs, and he wouldn't accept as much as a Band-Aid.

Two Rusalka swam past us, one with a face disfigured by vicious cuts. Blood spiraled out of the wounds like delicate ribbon. His eyes had been raked, and he was probably blind. I wondered what he'd done to cause Minerva to attack him so cruelly, or even if he'd done anything wrong at all. Husk spotted him as well, and I could sense he shared my concern. What I knew of these people was that if one was blinded or maimed in a way that made him or her unable to fight, they were usually killed or tossed into the volcano. Minerva had put the guard's life in question with just a slash of her nails. It dawned on me that the attack was calculated. She needed to let everyone know she was still dangerous. It was then that I realized just how explosive her illness could be for all of us. If Husk was right and the rest of the Rusalka attacked Minerva, they would certainly turn on each other once she was dead. It could help my escape, but more than likely, I'd just get caught up in the killing and die first. No, it was best to try to help Husk keep things calm if I could. I just hoped he didn't expect me to perform miracles.

I looked over her convulsing body. I didn't have a single

instinct. How was I going to make that lunatic feel better? I didn't know anything about pregnancies. I didn't even know how it worked for her. Sirena have a humanlike upper body, but the bottom half is like a giant fish tail. Her round belly shared both parts, so the baby was growing in the middle. It boggled my mind. Her anatomy wasn't built for giving birth to a human-shaped child. It dawned on me that she might lay eggs, like a real fish. Maybe there wouldn't be one child inside, but millions, all waiting to be hatched.

He gave me a shove, and I crept inch by inch toward the prime like I was sneaking up on an angry pit bull. When I was close, but still safely out of her reach, I stopped and cleared my throat to let her know I was there.

"This foul thing is attacking me," she said when she saw me. She clawed at her pregnant belly, threatening to cut her own flesh the way she had her servant's face, and my back. Did she really think that shouting threats at an unborn child would cause it to obey? I could almost taste her mental illness seeping into the water.

"Tell me how you're feeling." I used the Sirena dialect I'd hijacked from Husk's brain, taking a chance it wouldn't enrage her. She didn't seem to notice.

"There is a stabbing pain in my belly," she growled. "No doubt the heir is extending his blades."

The heir was, like his father, Triton. His race of people had weapons that grew inside their arms, sharp and dangerous. If the baby let them pop out while in the womb, he could kill his mother.

"How long have you felt this pain?" I nudged a little closer, hoping it wasn't a mistake.

"This beast has been fighting me for five days," she said. "I swear he will be born with a trident."

I looked to Husk, hoping he understood what my eyes were saying. Sharp pains for five days didn't sound good. *She's losing the baby*, I thought, doing my best to shoot it into Husk's mind. I didn't like fooling around with his thoughts, but this was something he needed to understand, and I was terrified to say it in front of her.

"Are you tired? Do you feel weak?" I asked.

She roared at me and her fingernails flew out, nearly stripping the skin off my face. I fell back, horrified and desperate to save myself. Husk helped me right myself, but my heart was beating so fast I could barely hear my own thoughts.

"The prime is never weak!"

"Your Majesty, I believe the girl is asking you if you feel anything unusual, only she is doing it in her ignorant and human way," Husk said, moving between us. "Please, be patient. She is a topsider, after all. Respect is not part of her society. Your strength is beyond question, but the growth of an heir can be a taxing process for a mother, even one as strong as you. Remember the story of Zeir, the mother who birthed a hundred warriors."

"Yes, yes, she opened her womb and her babies marched out and off to war. When her children returned after conquering foreign lands, they found their mother had died of exhaustion. I know the story," Minerva said bitterly.

"Has there been any bleeding?" I asked.

"Yes," she growled, but it turned into a wince when another wave of agony rolled over her.

"How long?"

"Five days. Is the heir in peril?" Minerva demanded, and for the first time, I saw something close to concern in her face. Maybe it was self-motivated. Perhaps she realized her future could come to an end, or maybe under the meanness and mental illness was a mother who worried for her baby. It was just a flicker, but I suddenly couldn't be callous to her.

"The baby will be fine," I lied.

"Of course, he will be," Husk asserted. His tone made her fears sound ridiculous. It was almost patronizing, but it seemed to calm her. He turned to me abruptly, his eyes worried and frightened, but he still played along, waving at me like I was some kind of flying pest. "Tell Our Majesty that pain is to be expected when giving birth to a great warrior."

"He's going to be fierce," I said, but I couldn't look her in the eyes.

Minerva studied me, peering closely as if my lies were scribbled on my face.

"His blood runs hot," she said, proudly. She caressed the

same belly she had just tried to slice open. "Stay put, little one. Your empire will be here when you arrive."

She winced against a new jolt of pain.

"Your Majesty, I have an unorthodox idea," Husk said. "And I mean no disrespect, but if the child is already full of fight, perhaps it would be best to calm him if we can. Would you permit me to retrieve something that will ease his passions?"

Minerva's face flared just as quickly as it calmed itself. She lunged at Husk with her hands curled into claws, but the pain forced her to give up her attack.

"Your Majesty, I am not suggesting you are so weak as to need assistance, but the heir does not know his own strength and limitations. His lust for conquering is clear, but he puts you in jeopardy. If he kills you, the empire could lose him as well. Naturally, he will most likely live, but then he will lack his mother's wisdom, and if you are not here, he will be placed in the counsel of Rusalka," Husk continued. "My people will be forced to steer his future."

Minerva contemplated Husk, and her angry face twisted into disgust. It was ridiculous how simple it was to change her opinions. Husk was a master manipulator. He should have been the prime, not Minerva.

"That cannot happen. Retrieve your medicine and take your human with you, Husk. I can't bear to look at her grotesque face another moment," she said. Her hand flipped dismissively, and Husk nodded. He grabbed me roughly and dragged me back through the halls and out into the boulevard. All of the Rusalka were there, some hovering above, watching and waiting.

One growled at him, and Husk barked back, swimming up into his face and pounding on his chest. They wanted to know if Minerva was sick. They could hear her cries and knew something was wrong, but Husk denied it. He told them the heir was healthy and strong and that when he was born, he would hear about how his people crouched around his mother's door, waiting for a chance to kill her. He told them they were parasites, eating off the bottoms of whales, surviving on filth and feces. The Rusalka watched him for a moment, then without a word, they swam away, back to whatever lives they led.

Once we were alone, Husk continued pulling me along until we were out of the city and headed toward the place where I fished.

"Tell me what's going on," I demanded.

"Minerva has lost the baby," he said.

"How do you know?"

"It just happened. Death seeps from her skin," he said.

"Then it's too late? What are you going to do?"

"She doesn't know, yet," he said. "And it allows us a little more time."

"More time for what?"

"Your escape," he said.

"What?"

"The empire dies today. The others will turn on one another to seize power. You should flee. There is no need for you to die. I will distract my people as long as I can. Go to the edge of the fishing grounds. I have left tools for you that will give you a chance at survival."

He reached over and touched the top of my scalp, and images flashed in my head. He had prepared for this day. Despite his seeming lack of empathy, he wanted me to escape the chaos before it rolled over me. What he planned for me was insane, but it was the only chance he could give.

"They'll kill you, too," I said. Minerva's begrudging respect for him was the only thing that kept the others from killing him. Now they would have nothing standing in their way.

"They may try. Now, go," he shouted.

"Husk—"

"GO!"

I didn't say goodbye. I didn't thank him. I just swam, as hard and fast as I could. I looked out on that strange world and realized it was the last time I would ever see it. It was my prison, but I had witnessed beauty there. When the yellow light from above blended with the red of the volcano, everything became an orange cream soda. Silver fish danced from left to right, and turtles as big as dogs dipped and dived inside their tangerine shells. I'd played with curious manatees, who reminded me of

Selkies, and pods of dolphins, who never got tired of games of hide-and-seek. There were brief moments when my despair slipped away, and I felt like some kind of underwater Disney princess who, at any moment, might break into song with a backing chorus of dancing stingrays. But, I reminded myself, even a well-decorated cage was still a cage.

Husk's visions steered me to a tiny cave, and soon it came into view. I searched it frantically and found a spear buried in the sand. There were shells and jagged rocks as well, but I left them behind. I wanted to stay light, keep a hand free in case I needed it. The spear was the weapon I knew the best anyway. Buried beneath it was a woven bag, something Husk made from seaweed. It was full of pieces of dead fish he had collected over several days. When I lifted it, bones and skin and guts dripped out, along with blood and fat. It seemed like an odd thing to help me escape, but I instinctively understood its purpose.

I pulled myself out of the cave with the spear and bag, only to find two familiar faces. My Rusalka guards were waiting. They demanded to know what I was doing. They thumped chests and bared their fangs and threatened with talons. And then, everything stopped, and both of their eyes landed on my bag of fish. Their tiny slit noses smelled the disgusting scent, but how could they not? The contents were so foul I realized they could probably be smelled miles away. And they realized it too.

I swung the chum bag as hard as I could before they could

react. Its contents slammed into their chests. Fish and blood exploded everywhere, coating them in bones and gore. The rest drifted into the water, spreading out like a fan, farther and farther, seeping into the current.

"*Charchar,*" I said.

They took off toward the city, but they didn't get far before a great white appeared. It was joined by another, then another, then another—all cruising silently through the water until there were so many they blotted out the light streaming from above. The first strike took a Rusalka's arm clean off. A second shark went for a leg. Black blood gushed in every direction. It was fresh and would attract even more sharks. It was time to get the hell out of there.

I tossed the sack into their midst, grasped my spear, and swam as fast as I ever had, desperate to get away from the feeding frenzy below. Upward I went, stretching every muscle as the milky yellow sun grew closer and closer. Something brushed against my foot, but I tried not to panic. I knew a shark might spot me, but there was no way to prepare my nerves. I was suddenly on the food chain.

Still, I hadn't survived so long to die like that. When the shark brushed my hip, my instincts took over. I stabbed at the great white's eyes with my spear, missing but knocking several of its teeth out in the effort. It veered off and circled back, but I stabbed at it again, and it gave up, or at least that's what it wanted me to think.

I resumed swimming, hungry for the surface, desperate to

get to the safety of my island. When I broke out of the water, it was with enough force that I nearly breached. I bobbed several times as my lungs took over, then freestyled toward the island, lifting my head up to take a breath every few strokes. It wasn't far, but with hungry predators below, it felt millions of miles away.

You're almost there, Lyric. It's only a little bit farther.

A thin gray fin rose up between the island and me—another shark, maybe the first one, maybe the one who'd been following me, I couldn't tell. I pivoted, forcing the spear out in front of me just as the shark veered into my path. It slammed into the tip and gored itself in its pink gills. The end of the spear broke off inside it, and blood shot out like a fire hydrant. The shark flailed as if trying to eject the weapon from inside its body, then sank. I didn't wait to see if it was going to come back. I swam like the devil and finally scampered onto land. Once there, I lay on my back, breathing hard. My jumpsuit's pant leg was shredded. In a panic, I searched my skin for a bite, bracing to find an enormous chunk missing from my calf, but there was nothing. It had missed me by an inch. I lay back down, trembling like a flower in a storm, and I sobbed. I couldn't help myself; I cried until I couldn't make another tear.

The sky sat like an ugly purple bruise across the world. A storm was coming, but I had nowhere to go. A light rain fell, then quickly turned violent, falling in sheets and soaking me to my core. Being wet wasn't a problem, but the wind that whipped up threatened to knock me off the island. There was nothing out there to slow the storm's aggression. One blast caught me off guard and sent me spinning off the side. I climbed back on, desperate and terrified.

"C'mon!" I shouted at the sky.

A loud howl rang out of the sea, followed by a familiar sound I hadn't heard since Coney Island—a thrum. It grew and grew, vibrating the air and water around the island and jostling my bones. It was a call for war, but who was fighting?

There was a terrible crash behind me. I spun around to find something that should not have been possible. A dead shark lay there, gutted and bleeding. How the hell did it get there? Another splash, and a crunching collision brought a second dead shark carcass shooting out of the water onto the island. Like the other, it had been clawed open, its insides spilled out onto the porous rocks. A third shark crashed so close I had to leap out of the way, only to dive again when a fourth shark slammed nearby. They fell like rain until there were fifteen of them, and then the horror stopped. All was silent. I crouched down, terrified by what new monster was lurking below, when a Rusalka leaped out and planted itself in front of me. Ten others joined him, forming a line. Splashes in the water told me I was surrounded. There was nowhere to go, so I stopped, dead in the middle of my island. It was over. They had me.

Minerva rocketed out of the sea. I watched her body morph as it trailed across the sky. When she landed, her tail was gone and she was on two legs, wearing armor like I'd seen before when the Alpha arrived in Brooklyn. It hung midthigh, like a summer dress, but it was made of claws and teeth. She stood over me. Blood splashed down on her feet. Her hands held her belly. They were crimson and wet.

"Murderer!" she shrieked.

"No," I said.

"How did you do it? Magic? Did you conspire with your filthy human gods?"

"Minerva, I—"

"You took the last piece of my beloved husband from me. How hateful you are to destroy the greatest bloodline in the history of my people."

"I didn't do it," I cried.

"An attack on the heir is an attack on all. It is a challenge to my rule. Let my people hear me. I will show you now what I do to any who are so bold as to stand in my way!"

Her hands were on my collar before I could stop her, and she dragged me to my feet with little effort. She was so damn strong, it took my breath away. I must have felt like a doll to her. I'd seen my mother do incredible things too. She pushed a police car aside once, and could lift our couch over her head, but Minerva's strength made my mom seem like a weakling.

"I should have dismissed Husk's bargain. The Great

Abyss called for your blood, and I denied it," she raged until a choked sob freed itself from her chest. "This is my punishment."

She slapped me in the chest, and my body heaved backward, ten, fifteen, maybe twenty yards. When I landed, the sharp rocks tore my jumpsuit and drew blood on my thigh.

"The heir had a great destiny," she bellowed as she charged at me. I tried to stand, hoping to run, but everything ached. The best I could do was roll, but there was nowhere to go, nowhere to hide. I could fall off the island into the water and vanish into the dark, but the Rusalka would find me, or the sharks.

She stomped forward, preparing another attack. Somehow I stood, and when she was close, I took a desperate leap forward and caught her in the jaw with my fist. I can't say she fell from my sheer strength—it was probably from surprise—but there was satisfaction in seeing blood dribbling out of her mouth.

"Stay back," I shouted.

She moved so fast my eyes couldn't follow, but I felt her for sure. My chest absorbed her fist, almost wrapped around it, then my face was next. When I hunched over, she kicked me in the belly so hard my body left the ground. I saw stars. I was about to pass out, my brain's way of protecting me from the beating, but I fought to stay conscious. If I blacked out, I was dead for sure.

"At least have the dignity to die on your feet, bottom feeder," she said.

"I'm working on it," I grunted as I struggled to stand.

Minerva laughed at me, and the Rusalka cheered and pounded on their chests, eager for the killing blow. I should have probably stayed down, curled up in a ball, and done my best to fend off her attack, but there was too much Brooklyn in me to give up. I got it from my mother, the secret warrior, and my father, the professional hero. But most of it came from Bex, the strongest person I had ever met, who faced down the world with a smile and an extended middle finger. It dawned on me that I had always been surrounded by fighters, even before Fathom and his people walked into my life. I came from a long line of people with clenched fists, and I had two of them at that very moment.

I gave her everything I had, a punch in the face so mean the blood from her nose splattered on me. I landed a kick in her belly, and when she leaned over, my knee crushed some more bones in her face. Blood rained down on the black stones as a stunned Minerva staggered back and forth, swaying on her feet. I'd seen enough fights on the beach and after school to know that when the bully is hurt, you don't let up. You hurt the punk more, so he or she doesn't come at you the next day. I charged at her, firing one punch after another, putting what Fathom taught me in the pool at Trident to work. This was the fighter Doyle wanted me to be. This was why Arcade pushed me so hard in the desert. I had felt small and helpless for so long but no more. I had finally found my secret stash of second winds.

I slammed my elbow into her eye. Punch after punch landed, until she tumbled to the ground. She looked up at me, exhausted and stunned.

"You should never have brought your tired ass to Brooklyn!" Admittedly, I know I sounded pretty cool in my head and probably like a maniac in real life. The wind was screaming, and the rain fell like hammers, but I was the heart of the storm. I lifted my leg, ready to stomp it down on her face, but Husk leaped out of the water and landed between us.

"Are you here to tell me to stop, Husk?"

"No," he said. "I am here to make certain you kill her. She is not fit to rule the Alpha."

Minerva shrieked with betrayal.

I stared down into her bloody face. If I didn't do it, she would never stop trying to hurt me and the people I loved. She would make it her life's mission to hunt us down and kill us one by one, but I just didn't know how to do it.

I took a step back and turned to the gathered Rusalka. I could see they wanted death. This was how conflicts were remedied. Spilling blood was the way things were settled, but they would have to get their satisfaction somewhere else. I talked a big game, but murder was a skill I wasn't willing to learn.

"I just want to go home," I said to them in their language.

"You take the ocean, and I'll take the land. I won't even go swimming at the YMCA. Just say this is over."

They watched me and waited, confused that I had not taken the killing blow.

"I'm leaving here. This place is death. The Great Abyss is not what you think it is. It's not a god. It's poison. You should leave too. You don't have to follow her any longer. You can go and rule yourselves, but leave the city. Get away from the volcano. Husk can help you if you let him."

My body buckled from behind when Minerva slammed into me. The two of us tumbled into the water, kicking and punching as we fell. Her hand found my ankles, and she dragged me downward, despite my thrashing. Nothing I did to break free worked. She was too strong, and too determined. One look into her eyes was all I needed to know her plan. The fire of the volcano was mirrored in her pupils. She was going to throw me in again, and this time nothing would stop her.

"A gift for the Great Abyss," Minerva shouted, pulling me directly over the opening of the crater. When the volcano started its hungry inhale, she let me go, and I spun out of control. I reached for her in hopes of trying to stop my descent, but when I missed, she raked my back again with her nails. A howl erupted from the deepest part of me. Pain cooked my skin, but somehow I managed to grab her by the tail. If I was going in, she was going with me.

Deeper and deeper we were pulled, with the water getting hotter and hotter. She tried to kick me off, but we were in it together. I was hoping she'd see I meant business and that she'd rescue us both to save her own life, but when her struggling ceased, I started to panic. Was she really going to sacrifice herself to make sure I died?

No, unbelievably, her attention was somewhere else. I craned my neck to look at what had her so hypnotized and realized that she and I were not alone inside the Great Abyss.

Clinging to the interior walls of the volcano, like an outbreak of blisters, were tens of thousands of huge, grotesque creatures. Each was like a massive tick, fat and bulbous, only with skull-white skin. Their faces were eerily alien, cut into geometric shapes—triangles, squares, ovals—with only tiny black eyes to hint at awareness. Each had a terrible mouth, a jagged crisscross of open wounds, and the four corners peeled back to reveal a cone of teeth that descended into a spiral.

"CHILDREN HAVE COME FOR A VISIT."

The voice rumbled in my head, under my skin and fingernails, inside my veins, and beneath my teeth. It was loud and crushing. It sparked an F2 on my migraine scale, a shocking return to a pain I'd been sure was behind me. Most troubling of all was that this voice seemed to belong to all of them, joined together in a single chorus.

Minerva brushed too close to one, and it turned its massive

head toward her. In a slow, almost sleepy gesture, it reached out to her with a paw covered in sickly pink suction cups. It clamped down on her arm, and once it had her locked in, it yanked her with frightening speed right up to its face. Because her hand was clasped tightly on my wrist, I felt the pull as dramatically as she.

"THE MINERVA CHILD RETURNS."

"Yes! It's me. Minerva, Daughter of Sirena, prime of the Alpha empire. You remember." Minerva wept with joy as if the horrid thing were a heavenly angel, and I realized that to her, it was divine. These things, combined, were the Great Abyss. They were her god.

The creature tilted its head left and right as it examined her.

"THE VOICE IS SILENCED. THE LINK IS SEVERED. THE BROKEN ONES HAVE DESTROYED OUR GIFT."

The creature leaned forward and let its mouth curl open.

"Yes, my lord," Minerva said in a panic. "I have brought the one responsible here for your judgment. Allow me to make her pay for her crimes against you."

I had no idea what they were talking about, but I understood she was going to try to kill me. I tried to pull away, but Minerva's grip on me was unbreakable.

"THE BROKEN CHILDREN CANNOT HEAR THE VOICE THAT OFFERS PEACE AND SERENITY. THEY ARE DISCONNECTED AND ADRIFT. THE GIFT DID

NOT RECONNECT THEM AS WE HAD HOPED. THEY REMAIN BROKEN AND MUST BE DESTROYED. ROOM MUST BE MADE FOR A NEW FAMILY."

With a speed and viciousness I could hardly understand, the creature wrapped its jaws around her head and bit it off her shoulders. Her torso fell backward, down toward the bubbling lava below. A flowing sheet of blood followed behind us, like a banner in a parade. All the while, I pulled and kicked, still locked in her grip as we sank. Finally her dead hand released me. Exhausted and still suffering from the fresh wounds to my back, I swam upward in that brief moment between the volcano's breaths and watched as Minerva's body hit the surface of the molten lake. Her corpse blackened before disappearing into the deadly soup.

Swim, human! Husk was in my head. I looked up and saw him once again swimming down to save me. He was lightning fast and had his hand wrapped around mine in no time. Together, we shot upward, as the monsters lifted their lazy heads to study us.

"THESE TWO ARE CONNECTED. THEY HEAR THE VOICE AND HAVE JOINED IT," the voice bellowed. "THEY WILL LEAD US TO THE BROKEN ONES."

Husk and I kept swimming, but both of our minds were assaulted by visions. I saw these creatures lumbering onto shore, tearing into innocent people, bent on the destruction of everyone. Rivers of blood roared through my mind. Killing was natural and orderly. It was a necessity, a chore they had put off long enough.

When the volcano exhaled, Husk and I rode its power out of the crater. I looked down one last time to see the horrible beasts tilting their heads to watch us.

"WE WILL FOLLOW," they promised.

Husk pulled me out of the volcano, and we swam back to the surface. Together we dragged each other onto the island amid the waiting Rusalka. One of them growled, not a word really, more an exclamation of surprise. I braced myself for another attack, but nothing happened.

Husk bared his fangs. He grunted a few words at them, which I understood as "accept her claim."

"What are they doing?" I asked Husk when the Rusalka huddled together to talk.

"Deciding," he said.

"Deciding what?"

He lifted my hand above my head and growled in their language. "The prime is dead. Lyric Walker's rule begins. Bend your knee to the new prime. Long live the Alpha empire."

The Rusalka turned to me and stared for a long, aching moment and then, together, they knelt.

"I don't want this," I said.

"You are the rightful owner of the Alpha throne."

"I didn't kill her. Those things down there did."

"Weaker claims to the throne have been made and

respected," he said, leaning in conspiratorially. "You must do this or chaos will erupt. You alone can save my people."

"Why don't you be the prime?" I cried. "You're more Alpha than me. You care about their future."

He shook his head. "They will not accept me. I am other."

"I am other, too!"

"They do not fear your presence the way they do mine," he said. "I am an abomination."

"You're the Charlie Gordon of the underwater world," I said, and knew immediately he had no idea what I was talking about. "There's a story I read in the eleventh grade for school. It's about a guy who is mentally handicapped but goes through an experiment that makes him super smart. In fact, he gets so smart that he can't relate to any of the people around him. Everyone he thought was his friend is afraid of him."

He nodded and silently contemplated my comparison.

"Charlie Gordon and I share a similar experience. What happened to him?"

"It's depressing. The operation wears off, and he goes back to how he was, but he remembers. It's sad. I hated the ending."

"My people do not want Charlie Gordon. They want you."

"I really don't understand them. This morning they would have killed me if Minerva ordered it, and now they're all in the Lyric Walker fan club."

"Fan club? I do not know this term."

I waved him off, too irritated to explain. "Fine, I'm the boss. I command you to take them someplace where the water is not poisonous. You can rebuild the empire on your own! You can make it what you want!"

"I cannot do that."

"I thought you said I was in charge!"

We stayed on the island for days, taking the full force of a brutal storm. It blasted us mercilessly, and without trees, the wind and rain hammered our bodies. Thunder boomed. Lightning zapped the sea. My ears were battered by the endless howl, and I was nearly blind from the downpour.

Eventually, the storm lost its fury, only to be replaced by a cruel sun. It cooked us all day long, until I wished the storm would return. Then the winds came up off the ocean. They cooled us, but acted like a sumo wrestler, trying to push us off the rock.

"I said you were the prime, which is a responsibility to lead. You cannot lead if you are not present."

I looked out at "my empire." They were seventy strong —no, sixty-eight after I fed two of them to the sharks. Even if I had wanted this responsibility I had to admit how pathetic it seemed. Sixty-eight individuals do not make an empire. You could get more people on the Wonder Wheel.

"I'm going home," I said. "You can't follow me."

"You will need us in your war with the Tardigrade."

"Tardigrade?"

"Those that live inside the Great Abyss. They have declared war on us all. You heard their plans. They want to destroy anyone who is disconnected from their hive mind. Only the two of us are safe from the slaughter. We will have to fight them."

"I haven't even graduated from high school," I shouted into the sky. "I can't lead a war, and with what army, Husk? We should run from this—"

"Forgive me for contradicting you, Your Majesty—"

"Oh, don't give me that *Your Majesty* crap."

"Running is not an option. We will go to your people and rally them. They must be prepared to defend the surface world. It would be wise of us to assemble the remaining Alpha who live among them as well."

"Husk, you don't get it. I can't rally my people. I'm the most hated person on the planet. No one is going to listen to me. They're going to shoot me. What am I supposed to say to them? *Hey, everybody, we need to work together, oh, and here's my little army of monsters who were killing and eating people a few months ago, but that's just water under the bridge.*"

Husk bristled. "Only those who visited the Great Abyss many times went mad enough to eat flesh."

"You went in."

"Twice, once to save your life," he said. "Not exactly something a monster might do."

"I'm sorry," I said. "That wasn't kind of me, but you have to understand, to the rest of the world, you and I are monsters. Husk, you and your people should do exactly what I plan to do after I find my family and friends. Find some boring-ass place in the middle of nowhere and stay as far away from the beach as you possibly can."

"With all due respect, Your Majesty, your plan is naive," he said, his voice rising with anger. "The Tardigrade will march across your world until it is cleansed. There will be no boring-ass places in which to hide. They will slaughter your loved ones. You must know this. You can sense their plans as well as I can. We can't turn our backs on the Alpha, or the billions of people on the surface. When your people see how former enemies can work together for a noble cause, they will be inspired to fight. When your blessing arrives—"

"There's no blessing, Husk. It's been three months."

"I can smell the change occurring inside you."

"Okay, that's gross. Honestly, I think you're smelling dead sharks," I said.

"I believe it would be wise to rest here, Your Majesty. This storm will not last forever. We can rebuild our strength and fill our bellies, and then depart with you. In the meantime, perhaps you could teach my people the dance."

"The dance?"

"Yes, the movements that you use to help calm your heartbeat. We have all observed the peacefulness it creates in you, and I have experienced the serenity now that you and I are linked. I believe it could be a great asset to all."

"You want me to teach all of you yoga."

Husk turned to the others, then back to me. "How do we begin?"

During the rare moments of peace that the weather granted, I did my best to show them what my mother taught me about the practice. It wasn't easy for them. Being mindful was just not natural for these creatures. They didn't know how to relax. Husk told me that their lives in the empire were so difficult, so oppressive, that even sleep was a luxury. Their lives were servitude and abuse. Relaxation was completely foreign. Even Husk struggled.

"Who invented this yoga?" he asked me one day, after braving the water for some of the numbing weeds he used on my wounds. He tied them to my back, easing days of agony.

"I don't know. My mother never talked about its history. I think it comes from India, but different cultures have learned it and made it their own. Believe it or not, there's a lot of fighting in the yoga world. Everyone thinks their version is the right one."

"Your mother taught you these techniques?"

I nodded. "She is Sirena."

"I know who she is," he said. "She comes from a proud family. She was considered a great fighter among the empire. How did she gain this knowledge?"

"She took some classes when I was little. She loved it, but I think in the beginning she saw teaching it as an easy way for her to make a little extra money. My dad is a cop, and they don't make a lot. She had a class on the beach a few times a week. It was really popular, but that could have been because she's hot. There were a lot of dudes in that class."

I laughed to myself. I could see how some of what I had said confused him, which made me laugh harder.

"It eases me," he confessed.

"I don't know if it's helping the others."

"They have learned a great deal from you. It is a great gift to them. I would not be surprised if they taught this yoga to their children."

They aren't going to have children if you decide to attack the Tardigrade, I thought to myself.

I lay on a flat part of the rocks and looked up at the night sky. It was a cool one, a lot like those Bex, Arcade, and I experienced driving across the country. When we weren't arguing, we sprawled out on the hood of that day's stolen car, feeling the fading heat of the engine radiating up through the metal, and we talked until we couldn't keep our eyes open any longer. We were impatient and eager, determined to rescue our friends and family, and certain we'd destroy anyone who tried to stop us.

What happened to that Lyric Walker? What happened to the wild thing I used to be? She was so far behind me I could barely remember her at all. The impulsiveness, the hardheaded stubbornness, the eagerness to stand my ground—she seemed like a different person. I liked to think that I couldn't avoid trouble, that it found me, but I was starting to think I'd been looking for drama. Now it didn't seem so cute to charge head-first. It got a lot of people hurt. Look where it got me.

Now Husk wanted me to be that girl all over again.

I turned on my side and gazed out at the horizon. There was a light out there that I assumed was a star at first glance. The universe was bright and flashy, but something about this particular light kept my attention. It was red, and yes . . . it blinked. Stars didn't blink.

I stood up and strained my eyes, wondering if maybe it was a hallucination, like Shadow. It was sitting out there blinking at me. *Hello. Hello. Hello.* Suddenly, it was joined by another light, a white one that glowed brightly for several minutes and then vanished.

"It's a boat," I whispered. After a couple more minutes, I spotted the white light again. Now I was certain it was a boat, and probably only a few miles away. I didn't really know, but something was out there, something that could take me home.

I looked back at "my people" slumbering in the night air. Husk was nearby, his lungs rattling with every breath. If I took them with me, they'd be slaughtered or, worse, taken to Trident to be chopped up and used in experiments. I couldn't let that happen.

Husk is smart. He can lead these people. He should. You're an outsider, I said to myself.

"Good luck," I whispered to him, then crept to the island's edge and slipped into the water. I let myself sink until my gills took over and my scales rose up to paint my shoulders. Webbing grew between my fingers. I pointed myself toward the light, and swam.

CHAPTER ELEVEN

NEARLY EVERYONE IS ASLEEP, BUT I CAN'T GET THERE. Maybe it's too dark. I'm jumpy and flipping on lights. Maybe this day was too exhausting to sleep. When I marvel at where it started, on a plane from Panama, I feel like it was a thousand days disguised as one. There's too much to process. I can't calm down.

I head toward the stairs. Katherine's room will be nice, with that huge bed of hers, only I find Chloe asleep on the steps. I want to pick her up and carry her to a bed, but I'm sure the rest of my stitches will pop if I try. I'm forced to wake her.

"Will you read to me?" she says sleepily.

"Sure, but we have to keep it quiet," I whisper.

"C'mon," she says, and leads me down a flight of stairs to a huge finished basement I didn't know existed. It's what my grandpa would call a rumpus room, complete with a pullout couch, beanbag chairs, a chaise longue covered in a blanket, and a Ping-Pong table. There are kids in sleeping bags every-where.

"Story time," Chloe sings, and sleepy eyes open.

"You were supposed to be quiet," I scold her. "Why are all of you down here? This house has, like, five bedrooms."

"We like to be together," Harrison says. His hair is sticking up in so many places I can't help but smile.

Chloe puts a book into my hand—*Superfudge* by Judy Blume.

"I read this when I was in elementary school," I announce, then find an empty beanbag and gingerly ease into it. Chloe sits next to me and rests her little head on my thigh.

The story is silly in the best ways. Some of the kids laugh, but most of the jokes fly right over the little ones' heads. Chloe doesn't care. My voice is a lazy river, and she's in an inner tube, drifting along with the current. Eventually, her breathing slows and her eyes close. Harrison and Finn carry her to the chaise longue and tuck her in with a blanket.

"Stay with us?" Harrison begs.

I shrug. Katherine's bedroom would be more comfortable, but right now it feels like a million miles away.

"Are we going to fight the same monsters?" Brady asks.

"No, I'm afraid they are all new monsters," I say.

Finn shrugs and lays his head on his pillow. A second later, he's passed out as well.

I nestle into my beanbag. It's probably the best thing for

my back. I sit watching the light from the upstairs hall shining down the steps. It's enough to fight back a panic attack. To stay calm, I focus on the sound of children sleeping effortlessly all around me.

Get your rest. The war starts soon.

I close my eyes for just a moment, no more than a blink, really, until I feel someone sit down next to me. Shadow is waiting, and he smiles when I see him.

"Why are you here? What exactly is your purpose?" I'm annoyed with this dream.

"I'm here to answer questions," he says. "And prepare you for the upgrade."

"Yeah, still waiting on that *upgrade* you promised," I snarl. "Three months late."

"Is that what you think?"

"It's what I know. Oh, wait! It's one of those bogus powers little girls get in movies, you know, the kind where they learn the greatest magic of all is family, or friendship, or was in their hearts all along."

He laughs. "I promise it's real."

"Can it help us win?" I ask.

The smile fades. "I hope so, or I'm out of a job. The truth is, I don't know. Maybe."

"Maybe? The real Shadow wasn't so noncommittal."

"What do you want from me?"

"Answers! Directions! Something that sounds like advice."

"Lyric, I'm not your fairy godmother. You already know what needs to be done."

"And that is?"

"Call your buddy. Tell him to bring his friends. You need all the help you can get."

"And if I get him killed too?"

"He doesn't have to come. Besides, everyone dies, Lyric, even you. There's no twist ending. Everyone goes, no exceptions. A few people get to decide how that's going to happen, though. If he wants to choose, who are you to stop him?"

"Most people want to put it off a little," I say, lying back into the beanbag.

"They're under an illusion that they get a say, Lyric."

"You're depressing as hell."

"Fine, you want some advice? You're worrying about your tiny little army, but you should start trusting in yourself."

"So this is one of those movies after all," I say.

"This is serious, Walker. They're following you. Those things can hear your thoughts. They went to Panama. That vision you just had—looked an awful lot like Florida to me. This house will be next. Don't you see your advantage?"

I sit up and stare him in the face.

"I can hear them, too," I say.

"Someone wins a prize!" he says. "Now, it's time to call him."

I open my eyes, but I'm no longer in my beanbag chair. I'm

standing on the beach in the cold night air. At first, I think it's more of Shadow's hallucinations, but it's too uncomfortable. It's real. It unnerves me to think I walked here in my sleep.

The water bites at my bare feet, and I feel the icy shock in my toes. I know why I'm here and what I have to do. Shadow is right. I need all the help I can get.

I close my eyes and call out to him. "Can you find me?" I call out to the ocean.

We are on our way.

When I get back to the house, I find Maggie sitting on the porch. She looks troubled.

"Where have you been? Your mom is freaking out," she says. "You can't do that to her. You don't know what she's been through."

"I'm sorry. I . . . What's wrong?"

"You have a call," she says.

It takes me a second to understand what she's saying.

"What?"

"C'mon." She leads me back into the house. Bex and Riley are waiting for me in the kitchen. Their eyes are huge and white, like they've just seen a ghost.

"Where have you been?"

"I needed some air," I lie. "What's wrong? Why is everyone awake?"

Bex points to the closed laptop sitting on the counter in front of her.

"What the hell is going on?" my father says when he enters the room. He looks sleepy and confused.

"It started ringing about an hour ago," Bex explains. "I didn't really know what to do."

"We ignored it for a while, but finally the curiosity was too much," Riley says.

"Who is it?"

"He says he works for White Tower."

"He? Is it Samuel?" I ask, shuddering from our last encounter, but hopeful he's had a change of heart.

"No," Bex says, then turns to face my father. "He's some guy in a suit. He wants to talk to Lyric. I thought this computer was impossible to track."

"I thought so, too," he says. "We had five of them at the precinct. No one could trace them."

I sit down on a stool next to the counter. "What does he want?"

Riley shrugs. "He didn't say. I told him to screw himself, but he just keeps calling."

I slowly open the laptop and cringe when a video screen becomes active. Inside it is a dark-skinned man with a black mustache and short, neatly coiffed hair. There are dark circles under his eyes that make the white parts glow like silver. He's in some kind of office, with huge floor-to-ceiling windows behind him; subdued, milky art in white and gray; and industrial touches like the steel desk. For a minute, he doesn't seem to know I'm looking at him.

"What do you want?" I ask.

He jumps in surprise, runs his hand through his hair, and licks his lips.

"Hello, Ms. Walker."

I say nothing. The awkwardness seems to be dictating this conversation. He clears his throat and takes a quick sip out of a fancy glass.

"I am pleased to see you are well. The incident at the airport had many people worried."

"Oh, I bet."

"How did you track this computer?" my father demands. "It's supposed to be untraceable."

"Oh, hello, Mr. Walker. Technically the computer is untraceable to everyone but the manufacturer."

"And you manufactured it," Riley groans.

He nods. "Military contract. We built a back door. You never know when you might need one."

"What do you want?"

"Straight and to the point. Very well, my name is Thomas Johar. I am a member of the board of directors for White Tower. I have a business opportunity for you and your organization."

"A what?" I stand up out of anger, and my chair tips back, clanking on the floor so loud it startles him.

"Please, Ms. Walker, I understand that you have no reason to trust my sincerity, but I promise you this is legitimate."

"Yes, who can question the word of a White Tower employee? So you work for Bachman?" my father growls.

"Actually, she works for us, or rather, she did until a day ago. Her position has been terminated. We wish her luck with her future endeavors."

"Oh, did the kidnapping attempt fail to impress?"

"Unfortunately, Ms. Bachman took the liberty to pursue many unauthorized . . . projects, so she has been relieved of her duties. Unfortunately, she managed to acquire the loyalty of a few employees in her short stay. Yesterday's unpleasantness is just an example. She was always at odds with the company's long-term plans, but we overlooked it until . . . But it's all under control now. It was a mistake to hire her in the first place, a point I made strongly when Mr. Spangler was killed."

Just hearing Spangler's name drowns me in a flood of black memories.

"Great to hear. Thanks for calling," I say as I reach up to close the laptop.

"Whoa! Whoa! Ms. Walker, all I ask is that you hear my offer," Johar begs. He takes another swallow of his drink, swirls the glass so the ice cubes spin and crash against one another, then sets it down. "I understand how threatening this conversation must seem. I'll get straight to the point. We want to help you with your plans."

"My plans?"

"Yes. Freeing the Alpha citizens and preparing for the invasion, of course. We watch Ms. Conrad's videos too."

"And why would you want to help us?" my father demands.

"Well, Mr. Walker, the obvious reason is not to die in a monster invasion."

"You didn't seem to care about the last monster invasion," Bex says.

"I can solve one of your biggest problems. You need proof that these creatures are real, or no one will help you fight. I'm sending you something right now."

The video changes, and a new image appears. It's shaky and moving around in every direction because the person shooting it is running. In the background, I can hear people screaming. He turns, for just a moment, and behind him I see something I'd hoped never to see again. A beast nearly four times his size is chasing him across a sandy beach. Hundreds, maybe thousands more of the monsters are scattered everywhere the camera lands. They lumber forward on all fours, roaring like mutated grizzly bears, only they're albino white with grotesque faces and paws stained with blood. They slam into everything that gets in their way. Cars flip over; a huge moving truck tips and lands on its side; telephone poles snap in two.

A man with a rifle steps into the frame and fires at one. The beast comes to a halt. I can't tell if it's wounded or just irritated. I hold my breath while I watch, waiting, hoping for it to collapse and die, but then it bounds forward, knocking the man over and putting a massive foot on his chest.

The man screams as the monster opens its horrible mouth to release a cylindrical spike of spiraling teeth that stabs him in the belly. Just as quickly, the spike reels itself back into the beast's jaws. This is something I haven't seen before. I didn't know they did this, but as horrible as it is to watch, it's nothing compared to what happens next. The man staggers to stand, his body already convulsing. His torso expands like a balloon, growing larger and larger as he screams in agony, until his chest cracks open and a massive white slug spills out onto the ground. People scream as it turns its formless head from left to right, then in one incredible burst of speed, it burrows into the ground, digging furiously, and disappears into a hole.

The man holding the camera collapses in the road, then scampers behind a parked car. His breathing is panicked, but he keeps trying to capture the terrible event on his phone. "They're everywhere," he says. "Everywhere. They came up on the beach and started slaughtering people."

A moment later, the ground explodes in front of him. A woman who was running by is suddenly swallowed from below as a slug-like creature pops out of the ground beneath her. It swallows her whole. There's no blood. No scream. She's just gone. The creature scans the surface while it chews on her body, like a dog taking a moment to enjoy some table scraps. When it is satisfied with its meal, it digs a new hole and vanishes down it.

The video stops on the face of a little boy, frozen by panic in the midst of all the screams. He's confused and frightened and on the verge of tears. I fear the woman who just died might have been his mother.

The image fades, and Johar reappears.

"This is a different kind of monster," he says.

"That's what you were talking about?" Bex asks me. "That's what happened in Panama?"

"Yes," I say.

Johar shakes his head. "No, that video was shot this morning in Coral Gables, Florida. It happened an hour ago."

"I thought the coastline was quarantined," I cry.

"Most of it," my father says. "Florida is one of the states that seceded from the rest of the country. Their governor sent its National Guard in when the feds tried to erect the fence. They're playing by their own rules."

"These creatures appear to be heading toward Miami at the moment," Johar says.

"Tardigrade. They call themselves the Tardigrade," I say.

"Plain and simple, White Tower wants to help you stop them."

"And where does the money come in?" my father asks. "It's about money, right?"

Johar shifts in his seat. "We see a valuable business opportunity. This country is a mess. Local police departments are falling apart, schools are closed, millions are homeless, the military is crumbling, and more than a few major cities are underwater. Putting things back together is an excellent source of revenue."

"I knew it," my father grumbles.

"Leonard, I won't insult you by arguing. It's a cynical way to think, but yes, it's always about money. Capturing Alpha in an effort to make better soldiers was about money. Locking them up in a prison out of the sight of taxpayers was about money. Selling your daughter to the military was about money. Now, we can dither about the morality of it all, or we can decide to live in the real world, where that is never going to change. A company that wants to keep growing has to look for new profit streams—crisis management services sounds like a growth industry, and for once, it lines up nicely with what you and your daughter want as well. To get the peace everyone desires, we have to go to war, and we know a lot about war. We can provide you with nearly unlimited military and technical support, weapons, food, lodging, training, logistics, medical care, and computer technology that is more advanced than anything they have at the Pentagon. We also have hundreds of thousands of private military contractors at the ready.

"Lyric, business often makes for strange bedfellows. Companies join forces all the time, even companies that have spent years trying to destroy one another's market share. They do it to survive. We would be foolish not to do the same."

"Do you think we're stupid?" Bex says.

"No, let him finish," I argue.

"I've spoken to enough people on Capitol Hill, or rather, the bunker they now use to run this country, and reactions to your return, and the video you posted today, have put you back at the top of the most wanted list. They're digging in, Lyric. They aren't going to let the Alpha go, and if you show up on your own, even with your team of superfriends, they're going to put bullets into each and every one of you. You don't have to show up alone. This doesn't have to be a suicide mission."

"You're going to go to war with the government to help me?"

"We prefer to think of it as joining the Lyric Walker revolution. Ms. Conrad has done an excellent job at repairing your public image, and—"

Someone walks into the camera frame and whispers something into Johar's ear. His face tightens, and he sets down his drink.

"I'm afraid we have to continue this conversation at another time. Your location has been discovered, and Marines are on the way. It would be wise to leave now."

"What are you talking about?" Riley cries.

"Ms. Bachman is still causing trouble. I'm afraid White Tower is in the midst of its own civil war."

"Sit still," my father demands. "He's trying to flush us out into the open. If we go outside, a satellite will spot us, or one of those drones. They'll know exactly where we are."

"I could have sent a team to your location when I started calling hours ago. You're at 142 Eleventh Street in Wildwood, New Jersey, correct? Now take your family and go. Try to get to the Verrazano Bridge in two days, Lyric. We'll be waiting for you."

Bex closes the laptop, presses the power button on the side, and shuts it down.

"He might be lying," Riley says.

"He's not," my mother says as she enters the room. "I hear engines coming this way."

"You know what to do," my father says to Riley.

He obediently darts out of the room. I hear him race upstairs, kicking and pounding on doors, yelling for everyone to wake up. I expect panic, but instead I hear people bustling about, checking on one another.

Bex scoops up her computer and slips it into a backpack sitting next to her chair, then she straps it onto her back.

"All right, everyone, we've practiced this. You know what to do!" Riley shouts. Chloe and the others hurry up from the basement. They look sleepy but ready, and all at once, their gloves ignite. They break into two teams: one, led by Jane, runs out the back door, and the second charges out the front, with Riley taking the lead. My mother and father follow him, with me close behind. When I turn to make sure Bex is behind me, I find she has disappeared.

"Where's Bex?" I shout.

"She's got a job to do. Don't worry," my father says. "We're ready for this."

A spotlight invades the street, shooting down from the sky.

Trees sway back and forth as the air is churned into wind by helicopter blades. Two black airships descend from above, each equipped with guns. Missiles are mounted to their sides, and several armed soldiers are sitting with their legs hanging out of opened doors. A voice booms over the neighborhood.

"Get on the ground with your hands behind your back. We will be forced to open fire if you do not comply."

It wasn't a bluff. When we keep running, hot bullets zing through the air, crashing into the asphalt at my feet and turning it into dust and pebbles. I scream, but my clearheaded father drags me behind a parked car.

"Mom!" I see her and the children continue onward.

"Lyric, she knows what she's doing. We've trained for this many times," he says.

I poke my head over the hood and get a face full of sparks as bullets rip into the steel. When I look again, I can see her in the next yard. She hefts a propane grill off the ground and flings it at the first of the two helicopters. It smashes into the rotor, ripping the chopper's tail clean off, and igniting a fire onboard. The machine goes into a herky-jerky tailspin, and two soldiers fall out of the door, crashing to the street with painful thuds. If they survived, it's a miracle.

The helicopter smacks into a telephone pole and cracks in two. The rest of the soldiers leap out in a desperate effort to save their own lives, but debris rains down on them. Rotor blades snap and rocket in all directions, impaling the car we are using as cover. The jagged steel end crunches through to the other side, stopping just inches from my father's chest. There's a massive explosion when the chopper's rockets ignite and a wave of heat blasts the street.

My mother leaps behind the car, pressing her back to its side. Her face is calm and serious. So this is the warrior I've heard so much about.

"When I give the word, we run straight to the beach," my father commands, watching the second helicopter hover over the flames of its fallen twin. A man inside slides the door aside and swings a massive gun so that it's aimed at us.

"Now!"

There's no time to argue. He and Mom are on their feet and pulling me onto mine. We dash away just as the first bullet slams into the car and lifts it right off the ground. It crashes back down in an orchestra of crunching metal. If we had stayed one second longer, we'd all be dead.

Bullets as big as baseballs crash all around me, creating craters in my path. They spray everything, stop signs, trees, windows, everything. I watch one hit the side of a nearby house, cutting a hole in the wall as big as a pizza. If we're hit, there won't be anything left of us, yet I'm the only one who seems freaked out. My family is jogging along like they're in a charity race.

There's a massive explosion behind us, so loud and powerful that I fall forward and slam into the road. Debris and fire rain down from the sky. Katherine's house becomes a massive fireball. In the flames is a single figure holding a video camera aimed at the blaze.

"Not the best time to record right now, Rebecca," my father shouts at her.

"The world needs to see this," she argues.

"They're coming back around," my mother warns.

Bex joins us as we scamper to our feet. Together, we rush toward the beach as the chopper circles. When we hit the sand, I nearly tumble down the dune before my father grabs my arm to keep me upright.

I hear engines, and we are engulfed in the high beams of two fast-approaching jeeps. One of them has a gun turret mounted on top and a soldier taking aim. He fires at us, and the bullets whiz past like comets.

"We're out in the open here," I cry.

"So are they!" he says.

I brace for more gunshots, but suddenly, Riley and his team appear, their gloves lighting up the beach. Water rockets out of the ocean in massive flumes. I can't help but smile. My kids are about to bring the pain.

Chloe steps forward, the smallest of the bunch, yet she's got the most confidence. I barely recognize her in the shadows, with the glow of her glove turning her face into a bonfire. She's shouting something at the water, and it forms a spear. At the wave of her hand, it flings itself at the helicopter, piercing the metal skin the way I used to hunt fish. The chopper goes down, smashing violently into the sand. The pilot and the soldier manning the gun manage to crawl out just before it explodes around them.

Harrison turns his attention on the jeeps. The original two are now joined by eight more, all barreling toward us and firing wildly. His water becomes a battering ram that plunges right into their numbers, catching four of the vehicles and sending them flying. I'm stunned by what he and Chloe have managed to create. In the last three months, they have gotten better with their weapons than I ever was.

"They're incredible," I say.

"Your father makes them practice," my mother explains.

I feel a bullet snag the side of my hoodie, but it doesn't touch me.

"We're almost there," Bex shouts. "Keep running."

I hear a scream. It belongs to Harrison, and I turn just in time to see him crash onto his back. There is blood on his chest, face, and hands, but he doesn't cry out. He's very quiet, peaceful even. His glove dims and slides off his hand.

"No!" I scream, but my family won't let me stop.

"If you stop, they will kill us all," my father shouts, pulling me along against my will. When we reach the shore, my mother tells me to swim, but I can't seem to make myself do it. I'm too shocked, too full of despair. Harrison is dead. Two boats appear, shining their lights on us and blinding me.

"Get on your knees, now!" a voice booms from one of the boats.

"Dammit!" my father shouts. He's lifting his arms over his head.

Your Majesty, we are here.

"Husk?" His voice fills my head, but I don't see him anywhere. "I'm in trouble."

"Who are you talking to?" my mother asks.

Rusalka leap out of the waves like water snakes. Some cling to the sides of the ships. Others land on deck, their claws tearing at the soldiers who pilot them. Husk leads the assault and barks commands at his people. In the dark I can make out bodies falling overboard.

"There are six more vessels approaching, Your Majesty," Husk shouts to me. "We will engage them."

He growls something and dives back into the dark waves. The rest of his people finish their deadly work, then leap in after him. In the distance I hear screaming and gunshot, and see the flash of fires as others vainly fight. Soon, the attack is over. The ships are sinking offshore. The choppers lie dead in the sand. The jeeps are overturned and quiet.

Husk swims to shore with the rest of the Rusalka. When they come onto the beach, my mother gasps. Riley rushes to attack, and my father draws his gun. Husk ignores them all. He kneels at my feet and bows his head. The rest of the creatures do the same.

"The Tardigrade have come to the surface," he says.

"I know. You were right," I confess. "It's time to fight."

"Then we will," Husk says.

My father points his gun in Husk's face.

"Get away from my daughter," he shouts.

"Lyric, just come over here very slowly," Mom says, trying to sound calm.

"They're not going to hurt anyone," I promise.

"You can't know that!" my father shouts, cocking his gun.

"I do know it. They won't do anything unless I ask. I'm the prime."

"What?" my mother cries. She gazes at the bowing Rusalka, then moves to bow as well. I am by her side before she can, keeping her on her feet.

"No. Don't you dare," I say. "I technically still have one more year as a child, and I plan to be as irresponsible and bull-headed as ever. You aren't allowed to treat me any different. I'm having a hard enough time with these guys. Husk, please stand. All of you, get on your feet."

"It is a great honor," he says to my mother. "I am Husk."

My mother is slack-jawed. "You speak."

He nods. "I often saw you in hunting packs, before the city was built, and of course, every Alpha knows about your courage, as well as your family's proud warrior history. Please know I have taken a vow to protect your daughter, as have the rest of my people. She is the future of our Alpha nation."

"Do the rest of them talk too?" Bex asks.

"They all talk," I say to the crowd. "But Husk is the only one who speaks English. They are going to be a big help to us."

"You don't trust them, do you?" Riley asks as he steps closer to me. "They're killers."

"Yes, I trust them," I say. "Husk, this is my friend Riley. That's Bex, and the guy who won't lower his gun is my father. Dad?"

My father hesitates, but holsters his weapon. "Sorry."

Maggie and Finn step forward, cradling Harrison's body.

"We should go," Finn says, his face flush with tears.

My father takes Harrison from his brother.

"He's right. We have things we need to do," he says.

CHAPTER TWELVE

MY FATHER HAS A BOAT READY. IT IS ANCHORED A few yards off the beach and is big enough for our group, at least the humans. He hid three rafts in some brush near the dunes to help us get onboard. Riley, Bex, and I drag them down to the shore, help my mother into one, and then push it out into the whitecaps, careful not to let it capsize. She has to stay as dry as possible. I don't know what I'd do if she morphed while wearing the hobbler. I don't think anyone could handle any more tragedy today.

The Rusalka are still and obedient, aware that their presence puts my friends and family on edge. Husk directs them to be helpful, which they are, guiding the rafts along the silvery ocean surface and keeping them still while everyone climbs aboard the larger boat.

My father, with Finn walking beside him, carries Harrison's body in his arms the whole way, cradling him tenderly like a newborn baby. Leonard holds his tears so no one else can see them.

When everyone is aboard, they set Harrison down on a cushioned bench and wrap him in a blanket. The children gather around his body. Bex sits with him, eases his head onto her lap, and caresses his hair. My mother fights back sobs, bites her lips, and wanders around as if there are chores to be done but she doesn't know where to begin. Riley and my father go to the bridge, and soon the ship putters out to sea.

We sail up the coastline, drifting past silent cities. No one speaks except Finn, who sits on the floor beneath his brother. He holds his hands and sings "Across the Universe" by the Beatles. Behind the boat, the Rusalka follow; their heads pop up in the wake, then disappear, over and over again.

The sun is directly above us when my father points the boat toward shore. We've kept one raft tied to the back, and the children pull it in, help my mother onto it, then lower Harrison into her arms. The Rusalka push them toward a sandy beach with a backdrop of tall firs. Dad gets the ship as close as he can, still several yards away from the dry sand, and urges everyone to swim for it. He's going to turn the boat around, push down the accelerator, and send it out to sea. He doesn't want anyone to be able to find us from the air.

"Are you all right?" Bex asks me as we prepare to leap off the edge. My back is not going to like this activity, and the water looks frighteningly cold.

"I will assist you," Husk says, popping up in the choppy waves.

"Help the others," I insist.

Husk nods and reaches his hand out to Bex. She looks at it, then me, and her face curls up in nervous consternation.

"He's okay," I whisper. "I promise."

"Sorry if I don't trust you," she says to me. "You have terrible taste in guys."

She takes his hand and leaps into the water. Husk guides her toward shore, and I jump in next. Yes, it's cold. Yes, it's worse than I expected. It steals my breath, but the gills take over, and I start a slow trek toward the beach. In the water, I hear the boat's engine roaring higher and higher, and then the splash of my father's body leaping into the water.

When I climb onshore, soaked to the bone, I see a sign pounded into the sand that reads CATTUS ISLAND PARK, OCEAN COUNTY PARK SYSTEM.

"Where are we?" I ask as Riley turns on his glove and pulls the water out of my clothes.

"Toms River, New Jersey," my father says.

"Where?"

"Your grandfather brought me here a few times when he was having trouble with your grandma," my father admits. "We stayed a couple days, camping and fishing. The place always stuck with me. The town is on the other side of the park. There's a path right there that will take us. We have a house set up already."

"How did you know they would attack us?" I ask.

"To be honest, I thought it would happen sooner. We've

been lucky," he says, then looks down at Harrison's body in the bottom of the raft. "We were lucky."

Husk and his army join us on the beach. They seem solemn and quiet, like abandoned dogs.

"What's wrong?" I ask Husk.

"We lost two of our strongest," he says sadly. His despair hovers in the air, thick and heavy. "I believe it would be appropriate to say something."

"Me?"

Husk nods. "You are the prime."

I turn and look into their blank faces. Their friends' bodies are laid out on the sand. They are shockingly pale and rigid, each with a bullet wound in their chests.

"They don't want to hear from me," I argue.

"Lyric, it is my hope that you will do things differently than our previous leaders," he says, quietly.

"What does that mean?"

"In my lifetime, no prime has ever considered the loss of a Rusalka worth mentioning, while other members of the empire were publicly mourned, no matter how small their roles. We are few in numbers. Every loss is a strike against our survival, but there is also a loss that is not so pragmatic. There is a sadness you might ease."

Talking to anyone about death is not something I'm going to be great at, especially when the dead were trying to protect me. I hate him for not letting me hide.

"Lyric, we should get moving," my father says.

"No," I say. "Not yet. Everyone, please, join me."

As the Rusalka gather around their dead, holding hands in prayer, I take Harrison from my father and lay him next to the others. Then I join the circle, stepping between two of them, breaking their hands apart, and taking them in my own. Their hands are long and sandpapery, and the claws at the ends of their fingers are sharp. I squeeze their palms, and together we stare down at the dead. My mother joins us, then my father, then Riley. Bex gestures for the children, and soon we are all together, with our heads bowed.

"I don't really know what to say." I look up into each of their faces. "Tell me about our friends."

Husk raises his head. "Girod loved to talk about the sun. It amazed him. He often dreamed that he could fly into the sky so high that he could see the sun from every angle. He once told me it was as beautiful to him as his mother's eyes."

"Thank you, Husk," I say.

"Harrison loved hot dogs," Chloe says, between tears.

"He was funny," Renee says.

"Very funny," Riley adds.

"Our father loved basketball," Finn says. "Harrison was always working on his free throws. Dad taught us both a musical instrument. Harry loved the Beatles. He could play every song on *Abbey Road* on the piano," he adds, before tears take over and he can no longer speak.

One of the Rusalka looks up. When the words come out

of her mouth, I realize that she is female, and from how she describes her fallen friend, I get the sense that she had feelings for him. I ask her name, and she says something that sounds like Dahlia.

"She says his name was Bahl, and he was quiet and serious. He worked hard and listened well, but he longed to do work he wanted to do, rather than work he was forced to do. He and Girod were not friends. In fact, they often argued, not unusual for brothers, but even harder since they were both in love with her," I translate for the others.

I can't help but cry for all of them.

Husk lowers his head, as do all the Rusalka. He steps out of the circle and approaches me. He presses his forehead against mine.

"This is how my people give comfort to one another," he whispers.

I reach up and caress the back of his scalp, pressing my head into his as well, then much to his surprise, and mine, I give him a hug. He squirms a little, feeling constrained, but I hold him tight.

"This is how I do it," I whisper back.

When I release him, I approach Dahlia and do the same. She is stiff at first, like Husk, unused to physical contact with anyone but her own kind, but I feel like I need to do this even if she's uncomfortable. I think she might need it, too. I circle the group, giving everyone a hug, all the Rusalka, the children, and my parents, and before I know it, they are all hugging one another.

"Long live Prime Lyric," Husk says.

The Rusalka bark in agreement.

My father and Riley take the path, leaving us behind on the beach, but promise to return soon. There's a hardware store not far from the park. We need shovels to bury our friends. An hour later, they return. Everyone takes a turn shoveling the three graves. My back screams in protest, but it feels wrong to let others do the work. Harrison, Girod, and Bahl lost their lives trying to help me.

When our friends are buried, Finn gives me Harrison's glove. He scooped it up before we left and thinks it might be helpful.

"He believed in this," Finn says.

The glove is such a small, almost flimsy thing. How has it caused so much trouble? I thank him and watch as he follows the others along the path.

"Is the house far?"

My father shakes his head.

We walk up a grassy embankment, then under a canopy of evergreens. Gray and brown needles carpet the ground, and the morning sun fires daggers of golden light through the thin branches above, down onto a crunchy path littered with brittle twigs and acorns. I take a deep breath and let the clean air zing around my lungs. It helps take my mind off my sadness.

"It's a miracle we weren't all killed," I say to Bex, who hovers at my side. Riley is on the other side, holding my hand.

"Do you think Johar ordered the attack?" Bex asks.

"He warned us they were coming," I remind them.

"I don't think anyone who works for White Tower is capable of being honest," Riley says bitterly. He knew Harrison for years. It's obvious to me the boy's death has hit him hard. "I'm sure it was a setup."

"He's definitely got an agenda," Bex says.

"Sure, but maybe it's an agenda we can take advantage of," I say.

Riley stops in his tracks. "I can't believe what I'm hearing."

"People are dying," I say. "It's my fault. There are too many bad guys and too few of us. We need help if we're going to have a chance."

"He's playing a game with us."

"What if he's not? What if he really will help? Who cares why they're helping. It doesn't matter to me, and to be honest, that's someone else's headache," Bex says.

"So you believe this crap, too?" Riley cries.

I squeeze his hand to calm him.

"We're just trying to keep everyone alive. We have to get the Alpha out of that camp and somehow convince this country to fight for its survival. If Johar can make that easier, I really think we should consider his offer."

When we finally make it through the park, we find ourselves on a quiet suburban street with tiny one-story houses lining the road. Their windows are black and grimy from rainstorms, some so filthy that I can't see through them. Unlike the Jersey Shore, Toms River looks as if it has suffered a hurricane. There are a couple of homes missing their roofs and cars pushed onto their sides. Trash is everywhere, piled by nature into heaping clumps. Birds are circling everything, desperate for scraps of food. I don't see a soul anywhere.

"All right, we all know the plan. Renee, Brady, get to the house as soon as you can and start getting things set up," Bex says. "Check the fuel on the generators and make sure the food hasn't been invaded by raccoons and rodents."

"I'll take Finn," Renee says. "It might be good to keep him busy."

Bex nods. "Start boiling water for drinking and baths. Riley, I'm giving you the laptop and the camera. Once you have the generator going, plug them in. The cold eats the battery, so they're probably dead. Might as well double-check the cameras we stashed in the foldout bed. Can you post something about the attack? Tell them what happened to . . ." She trails off for a moment, sounding defeated and exhausted, then hands over the backpack with the laptop.

"Maggie, can you and Jane make a run to that Walmart we found last time we were here? We need everything. Load up some shopping carts and wheel them over. In fact, everyone else go with them, too. They could use the help."

"Make a list," I say.

"Don't worry. I've heard all the stories about Texas. We'll only get what we need," Maggie says, before racing off with the others. Chloe wants to linger behind with us, but Bex shoos her off to join her friends. "They'll forget your coloring books if you don't go with them."

The little girl chases after the others, shouting for them to wait.

"They needed something to keep them busy," Bex explains as we watch them disappear down the street.

"Maybe you need something, too," I say. I take her hand, and she automatically tries to take it back.

"It's just . . . He was such a good kid. He was really goofy and . . ." She takes several very deep breaths to hold back tears.

"So you told everyone about our crime spree?"

"I told her we were a couple of beautiful criminals."

"No point ruining the story with how little we bathed."

She nods, and a weak smile sprouts on her face.

"Let's get off the streets," my father says. There's a hard edge in his voice. He's struggling with Harrison's death, too.

"What would you have us do?" Husk asks me.

I'm at a loss. I look out on his crowd and feel stupid.

"Follow us?"

"Everyone must be freezing," my mother says. Everyone is in their pajamas. Only my mother has warm clothes. She takes off her jacket and wraps it around me, then hands Bex her mittens.

"You're going to get frostbite," I warn her.

"I don't think I can," she admits. "You probably can't either."

"Now you tell me." I sigh, then take off the jacket and hand it to Bex as well.

Dad steers us through the neighborhood, leaving the road and cutting through lawns. The grass is crunchy with frost, and there is a brisk breeze slapping us in the face. We wander in and out of backyards filled with gas grills and rusty lawn chairs.

"How are you feeling?" my dad asks.

"Queasy," I admit. "I threw up at the other house and haven't felt right since."

"You might have gone too fast with the carbohydrates," my dad says. "I wish there was something healthy to feed you."

"You can lie down when we get to the house," my mother promises. "How's your back?"

"It hurts. It always hurts."

"I'm sorry. I'm babying you," she says.

I grab her by the hand. "That's your job."

The house looks like the house on every sitcom I have ever

seen. It's a flat, one-story ranch with a cobblestone path leading from the front porch to the street. There's a NY Mets flag fluttering on a pole out front and a matching doormat.

"You picked this one, didn't you?" I ask my father. In New York there are two baseball teams to choose from, the Yankees and the Mets, and when you make your choice, you are expected to be a fanatic. My dad chose the Mets when he was seven, way late according to him. He swears it broke up friendships when a few of his buddies *settled* on the Yankees. He used to love to talk about the heated arguments at the precinct every time April rolled around. We never had the kind of money you need to go see a game, even before we were locked into the Zone, but he watched a lot of highlights on ESPN and caught as many games as he could on the radio. He grins at my accusation. He's guilty as charged.

The inside of the house is locked in a time warp — 1960s shag carpeting, plastic furniture, Formica kitchen counters, and wood paneling as far as the eye can see — but it's warm, which is all that matters right now. Bex opens a closet and hands me a sweatshirt that reads I'D RATHER BE FISHING and an oversize pair of sweatpants with a paw print on the rump.

"Sorry, but they're warm," she says.

"Thank you," I say, and give her a hug. "Let's find Riley."

"He's in the back bedroom on the computer." She points me down the hall to a closed doorway. I hesitate to enter, wondering if he needs time to think about Harrison, but maybe he could use someone to talk to, if that's the case. I tap on the door and open it slowly. Riley is sitting on a full-size bed with a big oak headboard. The laptop is open in front of him. When he sees me, his face turns red, and he slams it closed.

"I'm sorry," he says.

"Are you watching porn or something?" I say, with a little laugh.

"I didn't think it was private," he says, flustered. "I thought it was for the site."

I close the door. "What are you talking about?"

"There's an email for you from someone named Dr. Lima. I opened it thinking it was a video or something for the site."

"Okay, it's cool. Lima was the doctor on the airplane," I explain. "What does she want?"

"You should read it yourself," he says.

I cross the room and sit down next to him, but he leaps up like I have a deadly contagion. When that doesn't put enough space between us, he backs toward the door.

"What's wrong with you?"

"I'm sorry," Riley says again. "I swear I wasn't snooping."

I open the laptop and the mail application. I see Lima's email right away. It has a little red "important" flag next to it. I scan through several paragraphs wondering what about this email is making Riley treat me like I have the plague. I don't catch much of what she's saying or what it means or even how she found me, but I do spot a word that locks my eyes in place.

Pregnant.

"I'll get Bex," Riley says. He must realize by my face that I've gotten to the important part of the message.

"No. Riley—"

"I'll go get her," he says, opening the door a sliver and slipping through as if he's trying to keep the news inside the room.

I sit by myself, completely baffled by what I'm supposed to do or say. Should I write a reply to her? Tell her she's made a mistake? Should I get my mother? This is an emergency. It feels like an emergency, but I can't seem to move. I'm numb. I turn and look at the space that Riley just inhabited. His face burns in my vision, the sadness on his lips, the betrayal in his eyes. He didn't just need physical space from me, he wanted emotional space. His heart is broken because I'm . . .

Pregnant.

I'm seventeen years old. The world is about to end. I laugh. This is ludicrous. I can't be pregnant.

"Fathom," I whisper, then slide off the bed to the floor. "It was only one time!"

One time is all it takes, dummy.

Bex enters.

"Riley is having a weird panic attack out there," she says, closing the door behind her. "Did you show him your boobs?

I know he's our age, but he's really not ready for that kind of excitement."

"I'm pregnant."

She screams, causing me to leap up and clamp my hand on her mouth.

"Shut up!" I whisper.

"Sorry," she says. "It's just . . . I always expected to be the first one to have to say that. How do you know?"

"There was a doctor on the plane that brought me here. She did tests. She sent an email to the site. Riley thought it was something else and read it."

"Oh," she says. "Fathom?"

I nod.

Bex sits down next to me on the floor. She takes my hand in hers. "I'm just going to say that I feel somewhat vindicated. Everyone, and I mean EVERYONE, thought I was the slut."

I growl. "I'm a moron! Bex, I know better than this. I'm a smart girl. Why wasn't I careful? I know how all the stuff works. Why didn't I stop him? Why didn't you stop me? Why don't I understand by now that if my life can get harder, it will?"

"This is going to be all right, Lyric."

"Bex, don't bullshit me. This is not going to be all right."

I have never been the kind of person who thought much about the future. The present was either too much fun or too much to handle. College was a moth flitting toward a distant star. I never really thought I'd get there, but now I know it's at the top of a list of never evers. Jobs? Marriage? Kids? All of them were vague notions that required none of my mental energy. When the Alpha came, they put everything that might have been for me on hold. I was too busy keeping my head down to look toward the future, even though, I realize now, almost everyone else was trying to get ready for it. Mr. Ervin asked me what I had planned hundreds of times, and I blew him off. While kids like Samuel were busting their asses with academics or athletics, hoping to find someway out of the Zone, I was sneaking into bars and flirting. I thought everything would take care of itself. Even after the attacks, even in Trident, I always assumed that there would be a time when things would settle down and return to normal. When that happened, a door would open for me, some opportunity —maybe I'd open a clothing store or design dresses. I didn't know. But something was going to happen, right?

"Your father is going to have a coronary, but he'll get over it. No . . . no he won't. We may have to drug him."

I drop my head into my hands.

"Riley will be all right with this eventually," she whispers.

I shake my head. "You saw his face."

The door flies open. Bex and I scream from the surprise. My mother charges into the room, then closes the door behind her.

"Whose is it?" she says, sitting on the floor beside us.

"How do you know? Is Riley talking?" I ask.

"No," she says, pointing to her ears. "Alpha hearing."

"It's Fathom's," Bex says. "Duh!"

"Don't tell Dad," I beg her.

"You're kidding, right?" my mother says. "Lyric, you can't hide that from him. He will be crushed if we lie."

"He's going to hate me."

"No, Lyric, he's not," she says.

"He'll just ground you until your baby graduates from high school," Bex says, reaching over to rub my belly.

My father opens the door and pokes his head inside.

"What's wrong? Why is everyone slamming doors and screaming?"

"Nothing," my mother says. "Girl stuff."

"Tampons," Bex adds.

My father cringes, clearly remembering our last conversation. He's not eager to repeat it. He closes the door behind him.

"I guess that explains all the barfing. We should get you a pregnancy test just to be sure," my mother says.

Bex and I hoof it over to a pharmacy a few blocks from the house. Getting out without being noticed was nearly impossible. I'm sure the whole crew is still chattering away about how mysterious and awkward our exit was and why we were so tightlipped about where we were going. Riley was nowhere in sight when we left. I didn't see him outside, either. He's found a place to hide, and he's staying there.

"The evacuations happened in the middle of a workday," Bex explains when she forces the automatic door to the store open. "People didn't have time to lock up. Everything is pretty much wide open. We've stocked up on everything—well, almost everything."

I squeeze through the door.

"Follow me," she says as she leads me down the aisles like she's been in this store a million times. She finds the pregnancy tests right away.

"I am not going to bring up that you found these very quickly," I tease.

"They're in the same place in every store," she says, giving me the sideways eye. She snatches a test off the shelf, and we head back down the aisle. On the way, she snatches a bottle from the vitamin aisle and stuffs it into my hands. They're pre-natal vitamins.

"Just in case. What are you going to do about Riley? Want to get him a card?" she says, gesturing to the Hallmark section.

"You're not funny."

"No, I'm not."

All the way back to the house, the test is a burning coal in my pocket. I can't keep my mind on anything else. When we arrive, all I want to do is take it and get it done, but my father wants to brag about the work they did to get our secret head-quarters ready. Chloe wants me to work on her coloring books with her. I am not even on this planet, and it's obvious.

"Are you all right?" Brady asks. "You look pale."

"I'm fine," I stammer. I can't even fake it. He knows I'm not. I might as well have a sign on me that flashes the words TEEN IN CRISIS.

The house doesn't have any working toilets, so Bex leads me into the backyard behind the garage. I can see my breath, and my fingers go numb, so she has to open the package and take out the test for me. It's sealed inside a thick foil bag that fights against tearing. Once it's out, she throws all the evidence over a fence into the neighbor's yard. With the amount of trash floating around town, no one in our camp is going to notice.

"I don't know how to use this," I confess.

"I do."

"Bex!"

"Tammy had to take one at least every other month. It's pretty simple. You just pee on it and wait."

It's so damn awkward and weird. I've peed in front of Bex a zillion times, but never did it hold such importance. I do my best not to make a mess, and when the stream is over, I place the stick on a cinderblock leaning against the back of the garage. Bex and I stare at it in silence, watching the little window that promises answers.

"If it turns blue, it's yes. If not, then you aren't. What are we hoping for?"

"I can't be pregnant, Bex."

The window hypnotizes me, swallows me whole, like I have fallen into it and can't crawl out.

"I'm nervous," she admits.

"You're nervous?"

Bex pulls me into a hug. "Of course I'm nervous. I'm your best friend, Walker."

"Bex, what am I going to do?"

"Whatever happens, you're going to be fine. I will help you do whatever you need to do, and I will take care of you no matter what, so stop acting like you're alone."

"I can't look at it anymore," I say, and turn my back to the test.

"I know. This sucks," she says. It's followed by a long, unusual silence from a normally talkative person.

"It's blue, isn't it?" I say.

She hugs me tighter than usual.

I don't know if I can cry about this. I can't say I'm numb, but the feelings are spinning so fast I can't hang on to one long enough to feel it completely. I have never wanted to be a mother, but I don't even know if I could get an abortion the way the world is right now. It's not like there's a clinic around the corner, and even if there was one, I have no idea if I could get myself through the door.

Husk steps around the side of the garage and scares the two of us, so we scream again.

"I didn't mean to frighten you, Your Majesty," he

apologizes. "Is it safe to assume that you know you carry the heir?"

"Husk, you know too?"

He nods. "There is a smell—"

"Okay, let's stop the conversations about my smells," I beg.

"The others are pleased. They have vowed to protect him."

"Oh, good, you're all discussing my pregnancy," I grumble. "Husk, I don't know if I can keep this baby. The Tardigrade are coming. We're going to war."

"Then we have another reason to win," he says, and leaves us alone.

"I guess he's pro-life," Bex says.

We sit behind the garage for a long time, comfortable with the silence around us. I stare at the test until all I can see are blue crosses when I close my eyes. When it gets too cold to stay outside, I cup my hands and dig a small hole in the soil. I bury the test, pressing the earth into place so that it looks undisturbed. Maybe someday the people who own this house will come back here and find it. They'll wonder about the girl who hid it while they were away. They might worry for me. I hope so. I need all the good thoughts I can get.

Thomas Johar is on the computer when we go back inside the house. He's sitting in his office, staring at my father.

"Ms. Walker, so glad to see you again," he says.

I contemplate the dark circles under his eyes, then his corneas and pupils, hoping I'll find something I can trust about him, but there's just no way to know. I've run out of options. I need the Alpha to save the world. I need Fathom. I guess I need White Tower to make it happen, especially with a baby growing inside me.

"All right, Johar. This is how it's going to work."

The rest of the evening, we study maps of the roads and highways that will take us to the Verrazano Bridge, one of the main paths from New Jersey into Brooklyn. Johar promised that White Tower would meet us there and escort us the rest of the way to the detention center.

He also sent satellite images of Coney Island. There are tens of thousands of soldiers stationed there, fully ready to fight with tanks and rocket launchers. There's a battleship sitting off the coast, watching the sea for another invasion. Scattered along the beach are tiny buildings used for storing weapons and keeping the camp's electrical grid safe. There are also twenty long buildings open to the elements, which he claims are used for housing the Alpha.

There's a makeshift fence that surrounds most of the neighborhood. It's assembled from whatever junk the soldiers could scavenge, built in a hurry after protestors stormed through the original fence built five miles away. Guns are trained on it twenty-four hours a day and have been known to fire on people who have attempted to climb it. Fifty-seven people have been injured doing just that this month. Ten of them are dead.

It's late afternoon when I send everyone to bed.

"We have two days to get to Brooklyn. We're traveling slow and at night, so you need to get as much sleep as you can before we leave."

The littlest ones drift off to bed. I suspect they have a sleepless night ahead of them after Harrison's death and all the worries that we're making a mistake with White Tower. I won't be sleeping, either. I hover, hoping to get Riley alone. I don't know what to say to him, but I feel like I need to try. Unfortunately, the first opportunity I get, he stands and offers to read Chloe to sleep.

"Give him some time," Bex says before cuddling up next to Finn.

Eventually, it's just Husk and me, watching the videos Johar sent us of the Tardigrade. They're now in South Carolina, but luckily they came ashore at an evacuated town. Sadly, there was a small group of National Guardsmen stationed there. They were no match for the beasts.

"I can feel them getting closer," Husk says.

I nod. They're a nagging poke in my thoughts that I try to ignore. Their voices are like low murmurs under everything.

"We will be ready," he says confidently. "The best we can."

"I abandoned you," I say. "I feel like I need to explain why."

"You are the prime. Your choices do not have to be explained to me," he says.

"I think you deserve better than that, Husk. All of you do. I want to say I was afraid you and the others would get killed if you came onshore with me. The truth is I was a coward who planned on running."

"You overcame your fear. That is what matters," he says. "Just as we did when we walked onshore. All of us are aware that our presence causes hostility. We know we could be killed despite our intentions to help."

"But you came anyway?"

"The other clans may say terrible things about the Rusalka, but they can never say we aren't loyal."

"Maybe a little too loyal, Husk. You got pushed around a lot."

"That is the life of a Rusalka."

"No," I say. "That's no way to think. There is no difference between you or a Ceto or a Feige, or a Triton. You deserve to be treated as well as the rest."

"Well, you are the prime. If you wish it, then it will be."

"I do wish it," I say.

"Perhaps I will live to see these changes. I tried so hard to make them happen for my brothers and sisters and failed over and over again. The rest of the nation knows me as the agitator, the one who urged the Rusalka to rebel. Little did I know how it all would end. Change asks a heavy price, Your Majesty."

"Well, chances are the Tardigrade will kill us all and I won't have to pay it," I say.

"When I was small, my father used to tell me the story of a lost Alpha clan called the First Men."

"I've heard Fathom call himself one."

Husk shakes his head. "The Triton stole the name and made it their own. The story challenges their superiority, and that can't be tolerated. No, the First Men were the original tribe, the ones that gave birth to us all. The story says they spawned everyone—the Nix, the Ceto, the Sirena, the Triton, even humans."

"Humans?"

"Like I said, it was a story for a child," he says. "But I always loved it. I begged my father to tell it to me over and over again."

"Because in it all the Alpha were equals," I say.

He nods. "All of us were brothers and sisters."

"So what happens in the story?"

"The children of the First Men flourished and spread throughout the oceans. The darkest depths and the most horrible dangers did not stop them, because they were connected to one another. Together they were strong, and their parents watched with wonder and admiration."

"Connected," I say.

His face darkens. "Yes, connected."

"You think this story has some truth to it?"

"I believe the Tardigrade are the First Men. They talk of links and connections. They refer to us as their children. You can feel their anger, correct? They are enraged that we are separated from them. For some reason, it threatens them."

"They fear it."

"I sense that, too," Husk admits.

"They're going to kill everyone who isn't linked," I say. For a long time, the room is silent. "We're going to have to kick our parents' ass, Husk. I just have no idea how we're going to do it."

"The Nix have a saying. 'The day offers problems. The night provides solutions.'"

"You're sending me to bed."

"Good night, Your Majesty," he says, then wanders out of the room and outside to join the rest of his people. It's cold out there, and I'm tempted to call him back, but if they welcome him, then that is where he should be.

I find a quiet room at the back of the house that has a twin-size bed with a railing on the side. There's a sewing machine in the corner and an antique dresser. The floral wallpaper is peeling slightly at the seams, and there's a faint hint of mothballs circulating in the air. I am too tired to look at all the photos on the wall, but there is an oval picture frame made of porcelain resting on a side table. Inside it is a black-and-white photo of a tall, handsome man in a Navy uniform. He's smiling in that vague way people do when they are proud of themselves but trying to hide it.

I kick off my shoes and crawl under the blankets, feeling the plastic sheet beneath me. Whoever lived here might have been sick, a person who would be difficult to move in an emergency. I wonder if he or she survived the evacuation.

The door creaks open, and my mother enters, kicking off her shoes as well.

"Make some room," she whispers.

She nestles in until we are so close we are sharing the same air, then runs her fingers through my clumpy locks, trying to tame an unruly patch, over and over again, until finally giving up.

"I don't know if I can take care of it," I confess. The words rattle around the room, slamming into things, looking for an escape.

"No one knows," she says. "I didn't know. I found out pretty fast, though, kind of the second you were in my arms. We had you in the bathtub, you know. I couldn't go to a hospital for fear someone would figure out what I am. Your dad told everyone it was a yoga thing."

"Yeah, how did that work with the tail and everything?"

"Oh, we didn't fill the tub," she says. "I can't actually give birth in my other form. Sirena find land when their babies come. It's safer that way—no predators."

"But why the tub, then?" I ask. "Wasn't it uncomfortable?"

She shrugs. "Our apartment was tiny, Lyric. The bathroom had the most space," she says, then laughs. "It was over fast. You were eager to see the world. One second I was trying to catch my breath and focus on what was about to happen, the next you were out, with no instruction manual in sight. I figured it out, and so will you. The first couple years, there's not a lot to know, really—one cry means the baby is hungry, another means they are tired, and the third means uh-oh, boom-boom."

"Uh-oh, boom boom."

"That's what your dad's mom called it. Sounded right," she explains. "Listen, I have no worries about you. You have a mothering personality. You take care of Bex. You take care of your dad and me. You took care of that mangy cat you found by the waffle place for two weeks."

"It died."

"You were five years old, and that cat was going to die anyway. You gave it the best two weeks of its life. You'll be fine, and your dad and I will help, and you've got Bex and the kids."

"Can I say something terrible without being judged?"

She nods.

"I want it out of me," I whisper, the guilt tripping me up before I can even finish. "I'm afraid it's not normal."

"Honey, why wouldn't it be normal?"

"You know what I mean. What if it has flippers or a

blowhole, or what if there are a million of them in there? What if it has blades in its arms and opens them inside me?"

"Because he is Triton and—"

"Not just Triton. This kid is, like, a million different things. Grandma is Sirena, and Grandpa is human, and I'm a freak."

"Lyric, I happen to love the person you're insulting," my mother scolds. "You are not a freak. You are beautiful and unique. Your child will be the same, and it will not have flippers or a blowhole. I promise. There aren't any Alpha that have blowholes."

"And this world! Is it fair to bring a baby into this chaos? People are so terrible. It will never have a normal life. People will hate it wherever it goes."

My mother is quiet for a very long time, so long that I worry she's backed out of her promise not to judge me.

"The tide washes everything away," she finally says.

"And that means what?"

"Nothing is permanent. The waves destroy everything we build. Right now a lot of people are building hate, but it can't last. Little by little, it all breaks apart until there's nothing left. You know there was a time in this country when a black person could not marry a white person. Not long ago, a gay person couldn't marry their true love. By the time your child is old enough to recognize a hateful person, there might not be many left. But I suspect, if he's anything like his family, he'll be a fighter. The world won't destroy him. It will make him strong, and if you raise him well, he'll grow up to make it easier for his children."

"Why do we keep referring to him as a boy?"

"It's a strong, healthy boy. I know."

"Please don't tell me you can smell it," I groan. "I can't believe you're not disappointed in me. I'm disappointed in me! Don't you think if I can let something like this happen that maybe I'm not ready to be responsible for another person? Maybe I need to do something about it."

"You are entitled to make choices for your future, Lyric. You're old enough, and I will support you. Your father may have a problem because of his beliefs, but maybe he won't. It's hard to tell sometimes. But there is only one thing you have to consider. You are the prime. The baby is not only your child, he's the heir to a struggling empire who may need him. For the Rusalka, and I assume, the Alpha, he represents the future of our people. The empire has never had a prime who refused to have a child."

"Why not?"

"That is just how it has always been. The prime continues the bloodline. The heir takes the throne," she says.

"What if he doesn't want to be the prime? I don't even want to be the prime."

"You will teach him about his responsibilities—"

"You mean brainwash him?"

"That's a harsh word for tradition," she says.

Something about what she says makes me cry. Maybe it's the responsibility heaped on my shoulders. Maybe it's because I know I'm not equipped to handle any of it.

"Nothing has to be decided today," she says.

My belly rolls. I fight the nausea by taking deep breaths. It helps a little.

"What am I going to tell Dad?"

My mother lies on her back and looks up at the ceiling. "We'll tell him together. Bex can help us. He can't stay mad when she's around." She pats at my loose locks again, but they still won't stay in place. "Sleep, honey," she says, then wraps herself around me.

CHAPTER THIRTEEN

THE CHILDREN PACK FOOD AND WATER, FIRST AID KITS and warm clothing. They make second trips to the Walmart and the pharmacy to get shoes and socks, pocketknives, sleeping bags, and tents. Jane is kind enough to bring me some extra-strength pain medicine for my back. The pills have all the potency of a couple M&M's, but I appreciate the thought.

My mother makes peanut butter and jelly sandwiches on rice cakes because the only bread they can find is green. There are Fig Newtons and granola bars and single-serving applesauce containers with their own collapsible spoons. In at least one way, our mission is a little kid's dream come true. Mom would never have let me eat this crap when I was their age. Now, we're having junk food for breakfast, lunch, and dinner.

Riley avoids me by trying to organize. He unpacks and repacks whatever the kids have finished. I still feel terrible that he is hurt, but I'm irritated at how complicated he's making things. When he's nearby, everything has a sharp corner; everything might hurt if I bump into it. We need to talk, but really, everything sounds stupid. *Hey, I know we've got this thing between us, but sorry, I'm pregs. Oh, yeah, I need you to risk your life to help me rescue my baby's daddy.* I should be grateful he's giving me the Typhoid Mary treatment. I can't think of a single thing to say that will make either of us feel better. Though I know exactly what I want him to say to me. In my fantasy world, it doesn't matter to him. He says he's going to be here for me. He's going to be sweet and charming and, oh, he wants to run off for half an hour and make out. I know there's nothing quite as fun as a girlfriend carrying someone else's baby, but it's my fantasy, and that's how I want him in it. He should swoop me up in a kiss and then help me pick out baby names.

He should be everything Fathom would never be.

I suppose if I were in his shoes, I'd keep running off to Walmart for Fruit Roll-Ups rather than face me, too.

Getting to Brooklyn is not as simple as it sounds. The boat is gone, and Dad is convinced we'd be spotted if we stole another one and took it up the coastline. I'm not too excited about going into the water anyway. The Tardigrade voice gets louder by the hour.

"FIND THE BROKEN ONES. MAKE ROOM FOR THE NEW FAMILY."

My head aches every time they speak.

Driving will not be easy, either. The plan is to go at night without using our headlights. That means Bex and I are on car acquisition duty, otherwise known as teen girl grand theft auto. She and I have a bit of experience in stealing cars, not that I'm bragging. Actually, I am.

Unlike Texas, there aren't a lot of options out here in Toms River, New Jersey. When the evacuation was ordered, people must have taken everything they could with them, including their automobiles. We find several motorcycles and a handful of Vespas, but they're pointless. We walk blocks and blocks for every car we spot. We thought we'd try to focus on SUVs because they have room for lots of people and our packs, but soon we're considering everything we come across, including a Mini. Sadly, we can't get it started.

Eventually, we stumble across a used car lot packed with choices. The words *Deal!* and *Near Mint!* are painted on the windows. Bex tosses a brick through a window in the office door and finds a drawer full of keys. With a little trial and error, we manage to unlock a few SUVs on steroids that I swear seat eighty people comfortably. Bex takes one and I take another, and we drive them back to the house.

"Not even a scratch!" she cries when we park them at the curb. She gives me a high-five, then we hoof it back for one more. We're going off to war in style.

Dinner is a hodgepodge of packaged foods—cheese crackers, ramen noodles with "artificial chicken flavor and other natural flavors," breakfast cereals eaten with cans of Yoo-hoo, and more applesauce. There's lots of pasta smothered in Prego and Ragú. I have no appetite. It's mostly nerves for what we're about to do, mixed with a self-conscious worry that my morning sickness (which seems to be happening all damn day) is going to become obvious to the others. I don't need them worrying about me. I need them focused and confident.

"You feeling all right, L?" my dad asks.

I nod my head a little too vigorously. I'm lucky I don't give myself whiplash.

Bex tries to divert his attention by telling him he needs to triple-check the batteries on the cameras and find a room with some decent light to make today's video message. Much to my disbelief, he does what she wants.

"I've got the Big Guy right where I want him," she brags.

Coney Island is approximately eighty miles from Toms River. Husk promises he and the other Rusalka will meet us there, coming in quietly from the water. I wish them luck and tell them to be careful. They stare at me like I'm crazy.

"A prime has never cared about their safety," Husk explains.

"Oh, brother," I sigh. "If we survive this, I'm putting all of you into therapy."

The rest of us leave shortly after sunset, when the colors in the streets are consumed by the hungry night. We move at a turtle's pace, rarely breaking twenty-five miles an hour. We can't use our headlights for fear of being spotted, but the roads are clear. I drive the first car with Finn, Renee, and Chloe. My father is in the second, with Riley, Brady, and Maggie. Bex drives the third car with my mom, Sienna, Jane and most of our gear. I can't see a thing without lights, which only adds to my anxiety. Luckily, we have walkie-talkies from Walmart, along with the laptop.

"So, Husk? Is he single?" Bex says over the radio.

"I don't think you're his type," I respond.

"I'm gonna try not to be insulted by that. How is he going to find us?"

"He can sense me," I confess. "I can do the same to him."

"So, like, you can read his mind?" Sienna says, joining the conversation.

"No, I mean, not really. We can send each other short messages and images of things. We have access to each other's memories."

"So he knows you made out with Anna Bowman at the ninth-grade dance?" she jokes.

"It was a tiny kiss, and it was a dare!"

"Can we use the walkie-talkies for emergencies only?" my father's voice growls.

Bex chuckles on her end.

We travel at a stressful crawl. The drive is unsettling, not only due to how deeply dark it can get when there are no streetlights to guide you, but also how lonely it feels out here on the roads. I wasn't underwater so long that I've forgotten what a night drive is supposed to feel like, the low rumble of cars passing on either side, the honks, the sudden whine of tires braking on asphalt.

But it's more than the empty houses and deserted streets that are disquieting. This might be one of the last days of our lives. This trek could end right at death's door. It shouldn't be so quiet and anxious. As many times as I have faced my ending, I've grown accustomed to the bang and shock that preceded each near-death scenario. I guess I'm just not used to taking the scenic route.

We stop for gas in a place called Old Bridge Township. It's as sad as the miles of road that brought us here. Ranch homes and cars on blocks are how they roll here. Old Bridge didn't get hit by the storm that slammed Toms River, maybe because even a hurricane feels bad about kicking a town when it's already down. It's like one of the dusty dots on the map that Arcade, Bex, and I drove through in Texas, sans the signs on the door reminding intruders that the Second Amendment is alive and well in the Lone Star State.

We decide to crash in the cars rather than find another house. Mom keeps a group of kids busy with yoga. Chloe works on her coloring books.

"Riley is upset," she whispers.

"I know. He's mad at me," I say when I step out of the car

to stretch my legs the next morning. I inhale a huge crispy-cold breath of Jersey air and blink into the brutal sun.

Riley is repacking his car. He loads with calculated detail, making the most out of the space. It's exhausting to watch. I'm tired of his pouting. I'm going to fix this right now.

"Stop it," I say. I know. It's very profound, but it's a start.

He looks at me, then turns back to his work. I guess he needs more.

"I'm scared," I continue. "I know that's not how you start a conversation like this."

"It's kind of unfair, too," he says.

I realize it was a little manipulative, but it's true. He gives me a few seconds, waiting for me to say something else, but the hinge on my jaw is jammed, so he gives up and turns back to loading.

"Riley."

"No," he says, and for a while I wonder if that's all he's going to say. Then he turns to face me. "I won't be your plan B."

"You're so not," I say, reaching for his hand. He pulls it away, denying it to me.

"'Cause you're my plan A. You're the one I want. There's no one else I'm thinking about. I'm not hanging on to you because I'm trying to figure something out and don't want to lose you if I take too long."

I'm so embarrassed my scales rise up on my arms. They're as red as tomatoes.

"That's not what you are," I say, but my voice has no conviction. I might as well have given him a teddy bear for guessing correctly.

"I'm not stupid like he is," Riley says, firing a shot at Fathom. "I was actually okay with giving you some time to figure it out, because I thought if you could just see me and not him, everything would fall into place. I was sure you'd see he's not right for you, but now, well, I can't . . ."

"Riley?"

"You don't know how important parents are until you don't know where they are. A kid needs his mom and dad. How can I get in the way of that relationship?"

"Whoa! Fathom and I aren't going to be a family."

"But you love him," he says. "And whether or not the two of you end up together, you will always wonder what that would be like. You tried to hide that from me 'cause you are hiding it from yourself."

I'm a garbage person. I'm Gabriel. Hell, I'm as cold as Fathom. I might as well be a full-blooded Alpha the way I smash through lives like a wrecking ball.

He nods as if having some internal conversation. There's a debate going on inside his head, and I wonder if he's trying to find a way to keep trying with me. Could he really be that great? Wouldn't it be amazing if he was really that great?

"Do you love him, Lyric?"

"I don't want to love him, so I'm not going to," I say.

"That's the most honest thing you've said to me," he says. "But it's not the answer to my question. Or maybe it is."

He takes a step back, then looks around him as if trying to find a place he can run, somewhere to hide.

"I didn't plan this," I cry. I need to sit down. I feel hot and tired.

He gives me one of those smiles you give a child who has fallen and scraped her knee. He bites his lip, and turns and walks down the street. I call after him.

"What?" he says, turning to face me. His voice is irritated and stung, but it's so full of hope. He's giving me a last chance to say something that will make him stay, but I have no idea what it would be.

"I really care about you."

I don't need to be able to read his mind to know what he's thinking. *I really care about you* is a kick to the groin. I know that as well as anyone. I've had to say it a few times, and I always knew what it meant. It's relationship-ese for "you have no mojo." I am not attracted to you. You are like my brother. You are better off in the friend zone. I want something else, someone else. You will never have me.

"Great," he whispers.

"Riley, you have to give me some time to figure this out."

"You've got a day," he says over his shoulder. "Tomorrow we're probably all going to die."

I spot my pack in the car. The zipper is open, and Harrison's glove is poking out. I take it and slip it onto my hand. If I had some power, maybe I could make things right, but it won't click shut. The gloves are done with me, just like Riley. I slip it back into the bag, only to cause his neat stack to tumble onto the ground. I messed it all up. I mess everything up.

I'm too exhausted to drive, so Bex takes over for me. My mother slides behind the wheel in the other car. Dad tells me he has been teaching her to drive over the last three months and she'll be fine, but I keep checking my rearview mirror, sure she's going to steer the SUV into a ditch. Everyone is quiet but wide-eyed, anxious about what will happen when we arrive in Brooklyn. We've been on the road for hours, and I'm exhausted. I put my head against the window and close my eyes. I just need a little sleep.

"We should have made some mix CDs." Shadow appears in the driver's seat. He smiles at me, then turns his attention back to the radio, stabbing the buttons in hopes of finding something to listen to, but static is the only option on every station.

"I have an idea I'd like to run past you. Let's not do the mysterious, vague-advice thing anymore. I saw it in *Star Wars*, and you're plagiarizing Yoda something fierce. Let's try clear, precise answers to my questions," I say.

He chuckles. "You know, you really suck the fun out of everything. How did the real Shadow put up with you?"

"What happened to my upgrade?"

He points to my belly.

"Oh, I get it," I cry. "The baby is the blessing, right? Thanks for nothing!"

"No, Lyric. Think about it."

I look down at my belly as if I'll find a clue written there for me. What does the baby have to do with anything? Oh. Dammit!

"The baby got the upgrade."

"Plot twist," he says. "My work here is done, Walker. I won't be bothering you anymore. This is our last visit."

"Where are you going?"

He winks and points to my belly. "He needs me more than you."

"What if I don't survive?"

He taps the steering wheel. "Find a way, Walker."

"WHY DO YOU RUN FROM US?" The voice comes out of his mouth. It's so loud my head is thrown against my window. "YOU HEAR THE VOICE. YOU ARE CONNECTED TO THE FAMILY. YOU WILL SURVIVE THE PURGE."

Shadow's body inflates. His skin turns white. Every aspect of him is twisted and engorged, then rewritten until he is a Tardigrade. It studies me, tilting its head from left to right, like a curious dog.

"You want to kill people I love," I cry.

"THE CHILDREN ARE BROKEN, LYRIC WALKER. THEY MUST BE DESTROYED TO MAKE ROOM FOR A NEW FAMILY."

I can feel it trying to rationalize murder to me, pushing its twisted philosophy into my mind. Why do I feel so inclined to listen? I push back, but when it looks into my eyes, I can see its point of view. I understand its intentions. *People should be linked to one another. It would end so much pain and suffering. There would be no more prejudice, no more bigotry. There would be no more wars, no more hostility.* There's a frantic tone to its thoughts, an insecurity about how its children have gone wrong. *Disconnection should not be possible. Are we broken as well? Must we be destroyed?* There is an insane, neurotic itch in the voices.

"WITHOUT CONNECTION, THERE IS ONLY EMPTINESS, THE TERRIBLE BLACK NOTHING," it rages. "THOSE THAT CANNOT HEAR THE VOICE ARE BROKEN. NEW OFFSPRING MUST BE CREATED TO REPLACE THE BROKEN ONES. ROOM MUST BE MADE. THIS TIME WE DARE NOT SLUMBER. WE WILL WATCH OUR CHILDREN. WE WILL ENSURE THE CONNECTION PREVAILS."

I agree with their intentions. Room must be made.

Someone shoves me hard, and my head slams into my window. I'm back in the real world. The car is stalled on the side of the road. Everyone is rushing to see if we're okay. Chloe whimpers when she looks at me.

"What happened?" I ask.

"You were freaking out," Bex says.

"You were raving about killing children," Sienna adds.

I rub my temples. They feel hot. My pulse taps against my fingertips. A fresh headache is biting into my skull.

"I'm sorry. Where are we?"

"We're here," my father says. "Or at least as close as we're going to get."

I have to shield my eyes from the glare of headlights ahead of us. The on-ramp to the Verrazano Bridge is crowded with cars, and the line goes back for what looks like miles. People have abandoned their vehicles, going by foot toward Brooklyn. They pass us, hefting huge packs and rifles strapped across their backs.

"Who are all these people?" I ask.

"I think they're my fans," Bex quietly cheers. "They're here because I asked them to come."

"I wasn't expecting this many," my mother says when she approaches our car.

"I'm sort of a big deal," Bex says.

"Johar said he'd be waiting on the other side," Maggie says, craning her neck to look over the crowd.

"We can't drive through that. We have to go the rest of the way by foot," Riley says. "What do we do if this turns out to be a huge setup?"

"Make them regret it," I say.

"The big shots will be recognized the second we step into that mob," my dad says, gesturing to Bex and me. He removes his hat and tucks it down over my head. Riley gives Bex his jacket and adjusts the hood so it covers part of her face. "Spread out a little. Don't make eye contact with anyone, but don't be unfriendly either. Just try to blend in for the first time in your lives."

"And keep an eye on one another," my mother urges the rest of the group as we grab our things out of the SUVs.

"I hate this plan," my father growls as he hefts a pack onto his shoulders. He turns to me and takes my hand. "Keep your head down. You're carrying my grandson."

"How?" I say, surprised that he knows the truth.

"The pregnancy test package blew back into the yard."

"You're not mad at me?"

"I'm furious with you," he admits. "I also love you with all my heart. We're going to be okay, you know. We're going to rescue his father. Just keep your head down."

"I'm sorry," I say.

He lets me out of his bear hug but keeps his hands on my forearms. "No, Lyric. Don't do that. Just stay alive."

"I will if you will," I say.

We drift into the crowd slowly and confidently, acting like we're supposed to be there, just like everyone else. We nod at strangers as they pass by, avoiding the snares of their frantic energy. There is a vibration, a mix of anger and eagerness and fear coming off everyone, but there's also a feeling of patriotism and justice and a sense that they are crossing this bridge to do something important. People push through the mob, loaded down with their supplies, blinking into the rising sun. It turns the guns they have in their hands into white-hot diamonds.

Chloe tries to stick close to me, but Riley pulls her away with him. Mom walks with Brady. My father teams up with Finn. Maggie and Sienna and the rest form teams of two. Bex and I stay together. It's probably not wise. She draws attention without any help from me, but I want her near.

"So, what are we going to find on the other side?" I say.

Bex waves her tiny video camera in every direction to capture the scene around us. "Some people have sent in drones, but they get shot out of the sky. The government does not want the public to see what they are doing on the beach. There were some shots from a couple miles in the sky, but it's hard to see anything but the outline of things. Johar's pics were the best I've seen."

"This just gets better and better," I say as we continue onward.

We move through the crowds, zigging and zagging to make our way. People are climbing on top of abandoned cars, being general ass-hats and showoffs, but we pay them no mind. Others have set up tents, right here on the bridge. Another has a keg set up in the back of a pickup truck. He's selling plastic cups of mostly foam for twenty dollars. People are actually buying them. The farther we go, the more unusual the crowd gets. People in mermaid costumes hold signs that say FREEDOM. I spot a man, clearly on drugs, wandering around dressed only in an American flag. My heart sinks with every step. These are the people we asked to join us. They aren't fighters. They're not ready for the Tardigrade. This is a house party. This is Coachella.

A kid walks past us. He's a white boy with dreads and cargo shorts. He looks like he's on his way to an Ultimate Frisbee tournament rather than a fight to save the world. He gives Bex a once-over and grins.

"Hey," he offers.

She gives him a noncommittal head tilt, and he drops back, rejected.

"This plan has only one ending. We're doomed," I say.

"No, we give the Tardigrade the Brooklyn beat-down, just like we do every time," Bex says.

"When did you get so brave?"

"You didn't just say that. I've always been the badass of this duo," she preaches.

I can't argue. She's right.

We put our heads down and push forward. The farther we go, the tighter the crowds. I start to worry if we'll be able to get to the other side. The bridge is a massive structure, probably a mile of concrete and steel and cable. Two colossal archways rise up toward the clouds. Tethers run along their crowns, connecting one end to the other and supporting the whole thing hundreds of feet above the river. Below is the Narrows, a perpetually brown waterway that keeps Jersey from ever attaining the effortless cool of its neighbor. I catch glimpses of it through the crowd as the sun bounces off its surface, turning the world into a disco ball. I can't help but worry about how many people are up here, how many cars have been abandoned, how much weight this bridge was designed to hold. It's windy as hell, and I can feel its bullying force, causing the bridge to sway back and forth. There are walkways on either side of us, but they are largely ignored. The main road is where everyone wants to be, thousands of people forming one gigantic organism.

"What's that noise?" Bex says, scanning the sky.

I look up and see a helicopter hovering overhead. It slowly descends, careful to stay away from the cables. White Tower's logo is painted on the belly.

"It's Johar," Bex says. "He actually showed!"

"No! Look!" I point to the open door on the side of the chopper. Leaning out of it is Samuel Lir.

The crowd noise morphs to a scream, and there's a mad push to get away from either side of the bridge. There are two waterspouts, one to the left and one to the right, rising and churning like tornadoes. They sail high above and meet just beneath the helicopter. Samuel leaps out and lands on his strange creation and it lowers him to the bridge.

The tornadoes fall from the sky and crash down on the crowd, washing hundreds over the side. Screams fill the air as survivors race in both directions. A stampede of panic pushes everyone away, so that when Samuel's feet touch the concrete only a few yards away, there are only Bex and myself to greet him.

"Samuel, what have you done?"

"They were traitors. All of you are traitors. This stupid revolution of yours has to be stopped," he cries.

"You just killed all those people," Bex rages. "They're dead because of you."

Dread fills me as I worry that my family and friends were among those swept off the side.

"They made their choice," he says, unapologetically.

He's so angry. He's had a long time to get bitter, and now that he's healthy again and with power he never imagined, he's eager to make people pay. Reasoning with him is pointless. I tried it before. He's not going to listen to me, not anymore, and the rest of my team is locked in a human cage. I can't let him hurt Bex.

"Samuel, you have to let us go," I say.

He frowns. "You are a wanted criminal, and I've come to take you into custody. Please just surrender. You brought little kids with you, and I'd hate to see this escalate."

"Samuel, there are monsters you haven't seen yet, and they are on the way here. They're planning to kill everything in their path, and I believe they can do it. If we are going to have any chance, I need the Alpha. I need you, too. I need everyone, these soldiers, civilians, the entire world has to get ready to fight. Please, help us."

"You lie," he says. "I'm going to give you one last chance, Lyric, and then I'm going to put you down. Give up now!"

"I don't know what she's done to you, Samuel. Your father is in one of these cages on the beach. How can you turn your back on him?"

"My mother and father are dead, Lyric. Everyone from Trident is dead. Ms. Bachman hated to do it, but she didn't have any choice. They wanted to close the camp. She couldn't let the sickness infecting my mom spread, and she couldn't let the Alpha continue their war on humanity."

"She killed our parents?" a voice says from the crowd. Riley pushes through, his face frantic and broken.

"What about the other hybrid kids?" I demand.

"She did the right thing," Samuel says.

Riley's glove burns brighter than any I've seen. Before I can tell him to stop, a flume of seawater lifts him off the ground, shoots him like a cannonball at Samuel. The attack is brutal, fists out, fast as hell. Samuel's reactions are slow. He's still not able to use his powers to their fullest potential, and his body, though miraculous, is not what it used to be. He throws up a wall of liquid, but Riley slams through it and crashes into the boy. Samuel flies backward, five, ten, maybe even fifteen feet. I've never seen anyone get hit that hard.

Riley lands effortlessly. He stomps across the bridge, stalking my old friend. He's crying, his face streaming tears. His mouth is ugly and broken.

"They never did anything wrong," he shouts.

Samuel staggers to his feet. He's wounded and off balance, but his hand is as white-hot as Riley's. He throws a wave so vicious that Riley is swept to the side of the bridge and tumbles off.

"NO!" I scream. I race to the side, hoping he's found some handhold to keep him alive, but even before I get there, his body rises above on a spout that sets him back on safe ground.

He creates missiles out of the liquid and fires them one after another, like a rocket launcher. Each crashes into Samuel's chest, forcing him backward foot by foot.

Samuel fires a string of water like a whip. It crashes into Riley and slams him onto his back. Samuel stalks toward him, hovering overhead with his serpentine weapon.

"We are freaks," he rages at Riley. "We should never have been born. Our Alpha parents planned to use us in their war. How can you mourn someone who uses you like a weapon? They would have thrown us into the fight. That was why they had children, Riley."

"You know what? When you got hurt, everyone felt bad for

you. It was hard to see you in that wheelchair, especially since you were gonna be a big star, play college ball, and get out of the Zone. But I never thought that. You were always arrogant. Being in a wheelchair only gave you time to perfect what an asshole you are."

Riley fires a watery fist into Samuel, who topples. He stands over Samuel as he recovers, and turns off his glove. He grabs Samuel by the shirt collar, drags him to his feet, and slugs him. Blood shoots out of his mouth, and he groans. Before Samuel can defend himself, Riley punches him again.

Bex races to my side. "I guess this is going old school."

Samuel scampers back, trying to avoid Riley's punches, only to suffer his kicks. He's beaten, bleeding from his mouth and his nose, scared like a cornered animal. He's been here before, the last time at the brutal hands of a paranoid street gang called the Niners; this time it's a kid who is just like him. There's fear in his face as Riley takes him down one punch at a time. He's seeing another wheelchair in his future.

"Where is she, Samuel?" Riley demands. "Where is she hiding? Why didn't she wheel herself out here? Is she up in that helicopter?"

His glove glows. Water races skyward like a spear. It impales the chopper hovering just to the side of the bridge. Like a fish, it flops around, trying to free itself, but it's caught.

Whoever was inside it is probably dead. I watch it fall out of the air, drop below the bridge; a few seconds later, we hear the crash as it slams into the Narrows. Black smoke rises on both sides of us.

Samuel stands, then laughs. "She's not here, Riley boy. She's somewhere safe where no one will find her, and when she's ready, she'll come back better than ever. I'll still be here to help her rid the world of the monsters, but you'll just have to take my word for it. You won't be around."

The whip returns and flies through the air. It ties itself around Riley's throat. He reaches up, trying to pull it free, but it's water. He can't get a handhold, and it's strangling the life out of him.

"Samuel, let him go!" I shout.

If he can hear me, he doesn't let on. He's consumed with his anger and shaking with raw power.

"He's going to kill him!" Bex gasps.

I have to stop him, but I've got nothing. If only I had my glove. Putting on the second one robbed me of all that power.

"Damn!" I shout, pulling my pack from my back and tossing it on the ground. I manage the zipper and open it wide, digging inside until I find what I need—Harrison's glove.

"What are you doing?" Bex says.

"Something stupid," I say over my shoulder. I'm already running, straight at Samuel. His back is to me. He's taken me for granted again. Maybe when he gets his reboot, he'll get some brains like Husk.

Before he can stop me, I've clamped the glove onto his free hand. He looks down at it and then at me. His eyes glow like there's a star behind them. He has the power to kill us all now. When it happened to me, I could fly. I felt like there was nothing I couldn't do, but he's too confused to take advantage of what he's feeling.

The gloves open and slide off his hands. His stranglehold on Riley ends, and the boy takes desperate gasps for air. Samuel falls to his knees and looks up at me.

"I can hear them," he says.

I nod. "Welcome to the family, Samuel. Those voices belong to the Tardigrade. They're coming to kill everyone, Alpha and human. No one will survive. You have to stop fighting us. We have important things to do."

I help Riley to his feet, then gesture for Bex. "C'mon."

We point ourselves toward Brooklyn and start walking. The crowd of petrified people stares at us, then move aside to let us pass. I hear my name in whispers. I see people watching Bex in awe, but they don't stop us. Along the way, my parents join me, then the other kids, and when I look back, I see that the space they gave us is filled with people, all following us across the bridge. I have my army.

When we get to the other side, there is another black helicopter waiting. It has a White Tower logo on the side too.

Soldiers stand by with AK-47s. The door opens, and Thomas Johar steps out in a suit. He smiles.

"I assume everything went smoothly."

I have to hold my father back from punching him in the nose.

CHAPTER FOURTEEN

Y**OUR CALL TO ACTION PROVED SUCCESSFUL,**" JOHAR shouts over the chopper blades as we fly above Brooklyn. The streets below are flooded with people, all walking to Coney Island. "The crowd is so huge outside the detention facility the government has reached out to Canada for military assistance. Canada respectfully declined. Ms. Conrad, you may have a bright future in public relations."

"How many are out there?" my father says.

"We've estimated five hundred thousand," Johar says. "But there are more on the way according to satellite images. We're expecting close to a million by sunset. There should be more, but there have been a number of problems at the state borders. A dozen people were shot and killed in Texas trying to get through. Tear gas was released in Tennessee, but the good news is that most of the states with fences have opened them rather than face a standoff."

Bex looks at me with huge eyes.

"It might not make a difference if they shoot us out of the sky," my father shouts.

Johar nods. "Yes, we're working on that."

I lean over and grab his hand. Fishing with a spear for three months has given me serious strength. I could break his fingers if I want.

"Bachman killed the parents and the rest of my team," I say, as low as I can. He squirms trying to free himself, but I hold tight. "And you knew."

"The kids needed to have their heads in the game. You have my apologies, but what good was it going to do to break their hearts with so much on the line?"

I let him go. He's making sense. It still sucks. I look back at the team I have left. My mother has Chloe's hand in hers. The little girl looks drained. She is officially alone in this world. Both of her parents killed in Trident. The others stare out the window, listless. Renee's eyes are still swollen and puffy from crying as we marched across the bridge. Samuel hurt us in a way he never expected. He used the truth.

I lean forward again. "When this is over, you're going to do me a few favors."

He nods. He's smart not to fight me.

Riley sits next to me, his face turned to the window. Every few moments, his body trembles. His poor hand is bloodied and bruised from fighting. I feel helpless. I'm so tired of feeling helpless, so exhausted by limitations and roadblocks. I'm just so over things getting in my way. I reach for his hand, slowly intertwining my fingers in his, fully ready to get a grenade in the face, but he lets it happen. He doesn't look at me, but he lets it happen.

The helicopter circles the camp, swooping over the grid of cages and temporary buildings. The gun towers do not fire on us, but their sights stay locked onto every turn we make. At any moment, they could shoot us down, but for some reason, no trigger has been pulled. That's good, because we've been up here almost forty minutes.

Johar shouts at someone in his headset. He's demanding that we be allowed to land, threatening whoever is on the other end with an open attack on the camp by White Tower. It's a surprising change in attitude. So far he's seemed a little soft to me, but now he's dropping f bombs between each word. If it's all an act, he probably could win an Oscar.

"Oh, you think so? All right, look on the other side of your fence. That little crowd out there is two hundred thousand strong. By nightfall, it will be more than a million. You've got satellite access. If you don't believe me, take a look, but when you do, please keep in mind that with a single word, Ms. Walker can light the fuse on that crowd. Is your camp ready? Very good, sir. Very smart!" he shouts, then pulls the headset off his ears. He leans forward and taps the pilot on the shoulder. "We have clearance to land. Put her down right away."

I look over to him, stunned by what he's accomplished.

"What just happened?" my father says.

"Someone pulled rank and gave us permission," Johar explains.

"Who do we thank?"

"The president," he says. "He's waiting for us down there."

The chopper lands in a clearing near the beach. The propeller is still spinning when I spot fifty soldiers sprinting in our direction. They surround us, but unlike most of the soldiers we've met lately, they don't have their guns drawn and aimed at my face.

"Ms. Walker?" one of them shouts over the whir of the engine. He's wearing dark sunglasses that hide his eyes. He reminds me of Doyle. If he had a cup of coffee to sip on, I'd swear he was his twin brother. "I've been asked to escort you to meet the president. Will you come with me?"

I look to my parents, then Johar.

"We're all going," I say. It's not a request. It's just a fact.

The soldier doesn't argue. He helps everyone out of the helicopters, then leads us across the sand. Soon, we come across the cages I have heard so much about. They're frighteningly familiar, the same tiny little boxes Bex and I were forced into when we were in Trident. The whole layout is nearly identical too.

"Do you guys have some creepy manual on how to set up and design these camps? Like an evil IKEA instruction book?" I ask Johar.

He's not as chatty as before. His eyes are wide and glassy as we follow the soldier down rows and rows of the cages. There are Alpha in each one, and Johar is getting to see their actual faces peering out at him. I guess the board members never tour the camps. I suppose that would challenge their business strategy. It's probably not a good thing for the bottom line if your staff questions the moral nature of their jobs.

Nix, Sirena, and Ceto are everywhere in this section, and the next aisle over is where they keep the larger Alpha—the Triton and the Selkies. Their cages are a little bigger, but not much. None are big enough for the occupant to stand or stretch out. The prisoners in each are on their knees or curled up and trying to sleep.

"I want to see Fathom and Arcade," I shout to our escort.

"I've been instructed to take you to the president without delay. He asks for only a few minutes of your time," he says. "Afterward, arrangements can be made, depending on the outcome of the meeting."

"Outcome?" my father presses.

"Certain things are above my pay grade. I'm sure it will all be clear very soon."

We hurry through the grid. As we go, our sudden appearance surprises the captives. Those who can rise to their feet cling to the chain-link fence that makes their habitat. They press their faces to the steel and watch me in amazement. My name starts as a whisper, but as we go farther, it is spoken in a rousing chorus.

"I promise we will get all of you out soon," I say.

"Lyric Walker," a voice shouts. It's one I know. I turn to find Ghost poking a long white finger through the openings in his cage. His huge, melon-size head leans against the fence as if he is too tired to hold it up any longer. Even for a Nix he looks thin and pale.

"I'm getting you out of here," I say.

"You weren't exactly in a hurry," he hisses. It's nice to see that captivity hasn't changed him.

"Why didn't you use your glove to fight?" I ask him. Ghost, like his lost love, Luna, could use the machines as well as the Rusalka. They were only a handful of Alpha members that weren't rejected by the glove. Why wouldn't he turn it on the guards? Was it a massive EMP like they had at Trident? The answer brings bile into my throat. He raises his hand, or rather, where his hand should be. What remains is a stump wrapped in a dirty bandage.

I turn to Johar. His eyes tremble while the rest of his body fights for composure. "I didn't authorize that," he stammers. "That's not our policy."

"Ghost, I'm getting you out," I promise, but I'm seeing something I didn't prepare for when we planned this fight. The Alpha are exhausted and sick. Most of them are starving. I don't think I've seen a single one that doesn't need medical care, and I know how sending in doctors will go over. This is no fighting force. It's a hospital for invalids.

We approach one of the long buildings Bex showed me on the computer. Johar called it a detention building. The soldier opens a door, then gestures with his head for us to enter. I step through to find a room just beyond, with a sand floor. There are pallets stacked up in a corner and cement blocks lining the base of each wall. A generator feeds electricity to the room's sole fluorescent light hanging from the ceiling. I look up at it as it pops in and out, flickering as if the energy to stay on is just more than it can handle. In the center of the room is a man sitting in a folding metal chair. He wears a blue suit and tie, with a little steel flag pin on his lapel. He looks tired. His shoulders are hunched with the weight of some unseen burden, but when he sees us, he sits up straight and smiles. I can tell this version is for the voters. The real president is barely keeping it together.

"Mr. President, I have brought Ms. Walker and Ms. Conrad, as well as the members of her organization."

"Thank you, Sergeant," he says. "You can wait outside."

"Sir, I have been instructed not to leave you alone," the soldier insists.

"I'm pulling rank, son," he says, and gestures toward the door.

The soldier grimaces, but leaves as he was instructed, closing the door behind him.

The president stares at us for a long time. He examines each one of us, as if we are sculptures in an art museum. I'm expecting him to stand and get a peek from different angles.

"There are thirteen of you," he says, wearily. "Thirteen people. Ten of you are children. How did you do this?"

"Do what?"

"No, it's not you. I've bungled this," he admits, running his hand through his gray hair. "I broke this country apart."

Johar steps forward. "Sir, you have the opportunity to turn things around—"

"Shut up, Johar," he says, shaking his head. "I hate you White Tower people. Every last one of you has a stink like rotting garbage. I know all about my opportunities. I'm not here to talk to you. I'm here to talk to Ms. Walker and Ms. Conrad."

Bex reaches over and takes my hand.

"You've caused an awful lot of trouble," he says.

I look to Bex, half expecting her to say something hilarious, but she seems dumbstruck, or maybe it's starstruck. He is, after all, the president. Even I'm having a hard time remembering to breathe. Despite everything that's happened, Bex and I are a couple of kids from the ghetto.

"I have a question, and I'm hoping you will be completely honest with me," he says.

Bex nods.

"All right," I say.

"Are you behind the things that are coming onshore?"

We both shake our heads.

"We weren't behind anything that happened," Bex says. "Neither of us is responsible. Lyric tried to stop the invasions.

I'll admit we stole a few cars and some candy bars, but sea monster attacks are not our fault."

"We came here to try to stop this one," I say. "Just like we tried to stop the previous two."

The president stands and steps toward me. "This afternoon they landed in Newark, Delaware, and attacked a naval compound. I just got a casualty report. The National Guard has stopped counting dead soldiers. What do they want from us?"

I shake my head. "They want you to die."

"And this is where you plan to fight them? What happens if you can't stop them?"

"I think that's a question for you," my father says.

The president's face grows dark with worry. "What do you need to win?"

"You can start by taking down the fence," Bex says.

"Actually, sir, I have a very thorough list of actions that will ensure our success," Johar interrupts.

"I have no doubt you do," the president says with a grimace, then turns his attention back to me. "I should have met with you sooner."

"It has actually been difficult to get on my calendar lately," I whisper. I look to my friends and family, then back to him. "Aside from Mr. Johar's list, I have a few things I need from you —assurances, really, that will determine whether we stay or get back on the chopper."

"And what would they be, Ms. Walker?"

"Hold up." Bex reaches into her pocket and removes her digital video camera. She flicks it on, and the red light glows. She points it into the president's face.

"Ms. Conrad, you don't need the camera. You can trust my word," the president promises.

Bex shrugs. "Maybe. All I know is that when I post this, I'm going to get at least a billion hits on the site."

CHAPTER FIFTEEN

I RUN THROUGH THE CAMP, SEARCHING EACH AISLE FOR ROW nine, section two.

"Where is it, Johar?" I shout over my shoulder. He's behind me with a clipboard, flipping through a massive list of detainees and where they are being held.

"There," he says, pointing to a handful of cages closest to the biggest detention building. My legs fight me. They know what I'm going to see, and they are trying to stop me. I almost fall. The best I can do is a slow, deliberate shuffle until I am there.

In the first cage I find Flyer, Fathom's cousin. He is dirty and haggard. Even the smile he has worn every time I have seen him is gone. His head hangs off his shoulders like it is no longer connected to his spine. It takes him considerable effort to raise it and look at me. When he does, he whispers a name.

"Arcade."

At first I think he's asking me where she might be, but

then I realize he's calling to her. Arcade is in the next cage, cross-legged, her eyes closed, her hands in her lap. She's much thinner than I remember. She opens her eyes and looks at me. There's no surprise, no flash of confusion or urgency. I can't help but smile at how unemotional she is at my appearance.

"Your Majesty," she says, bowing her head slightly.

"You know?"

"There is no other possible conclusion I could make. You are here, returned to the surface. Minerva must be dead. How did the little minnow find the strength to fight her?"

"I had a good coach. We're letting everyone out," I promise, then look at the cage next to hers. It's empty. "Where is Fathom?"

"He spends his days inside the building," Flyer says. There's foreboding in his voice.

"They're torturing him?" I say, turning to eye the evil structure. It looks a lot like a barn, but painted gray. It's just one of many. A buzzer sounds, and I hear a click. The president promised to release all the Alpha, and he's lived up to his word. The doors on the cages swing open. I rush into Arcade's cage and help her to stand. Flyer staggers to his feet to join her, and they wrap around each other.

I sprint around more rows of cages and into the detention buildings. The interior is divided into huge stalls, almost like a horse barn. When I peer into one, I see a dozen or so metal cots without mattresses. I also see dried blood on the ground.

"Fathom!" My voice echoes off the walls and back into my ears, so I can hear the panic twice. It startles a few pigeons who have built a nest in the rafters. Their flapping wings compete with my cry.

I move along the stalls, some so dark I have to step inside them to make sure they're empty. I quicken my pace, searching willy-nilly, racing from one pen to the next. When I'm almost certain Arcade has the wrong building, I race out the other side and around the back. There, I find him, his hands tied with a rope strung to a post on the roof. His back has been savaged by fresh wounds. His chest is no better. Someone has been whipping him, mercilessly. Whatever decisions I made about my future with this kid are temporarily forgotten.

"Fathom, I'm here," I cry, trying to get him on his feet so I can untie the ropes. They are too tight with him hanging from them, but the boy is as solid and heavy as a tree.

His eyes peek open, but it's several moments before they focus on me. There's no smile, only sorrow.

"Lyric Walker. They captured you, too," he says. He sounds defeated.

"No, I came here to rescue you." Damn, that feels good to say.

"No," he argues. "Do not dishonor me."

"Shut up," I say.

He tries to balance himself while I manage to get him untied, then I drape his arm around my shoulders, even though the pain from my own wounds is still intense. I bite my lip and guide him back around the building.

Take notes, buddy. This is how you love someone.

I wait outside the Red Cross tent and try to pump myself up for what I'm about to say. I have no idea how Fathom will react, a frustrating fact about our relationship rearing its head once again. I just can't predict what he will say, and it's exhausting. How are we going to raise a child together?

A nurse steps out and gestures to me. "He's finally calmed down. You can see him."

"Calmed down?"

"He fought everything we tried to do. If there's any silver lining to how bad his condition is, it's that he was too exhausted to stop the treatment."

Inside, Fathom sits in a chair. He has an IV inserted into his arm and a drip bag on a post is leaking fluids into his body. His eyes are clearer than before. He even looks stronger. When he turns to me, I can see he is angry about the doctors. I'm too swept up in his face. This boy—he knocks me out.

There's a doctor standing over him listening to his heart rate.

"It's high," I say. "That's normal. We all have it."

The doctor makes a note and smiles before ducking out to give us some privacy. Fathom nearly pulls his tubes out of his arm when he notices me.

"Sit, please," I beg. "I don't want you to hurt yourself more. I need you healthy."

He does, but reluctantly.

"You are changed," he says.

"Yes." I can feel myself playing self-consciously with my hair, so I force my hand back to my side.

"You are the warrior I always knew you could be, Lyric Walker." He reaches up to run a finger along the back of my neck. "You even have trophies. Now we can be together. The others will recognize you as an Alpha."

He doesn't know I'm the prime. I'm tempted to tell him, but I don't want him to go into "loyal subject" mode like Husk. I need him to be real with me.

"That's what you wanted?" I ask.

He peers up at me, confused. "Of course."

I snatch a folding chair leaning against the tent wall and sit down next to him. He takes my hand and smiles. It feels rationed, like he only has so many. Now that I'm deserving, I guess they're free. A rush of anger bubbles up, but I tamp it down. This is not the time.

"Funny, back in the day, the boys seemed to love me the way I was."

I can't help but think of Riley and what he said outside the SUV. Wow, did I ruin it.

"You are angry," he says, and he looks genuinely surprised.

"Another time. I have to tell you something important."

He reaches for my hand, but I take it back. I can't get drunk on his touch; that'll cause me to make bad decisions. "I don't want you to freak out, because it's going to be okay. I think it's going to be okay. I really don't know, but it is what it is, and we'll be fine."

"What does 'freak out' mean?" he wonders.

"We're going to have a baby," I say.

He stares at me for a long time. I automatically start to find another human word to explain, then realize there's a good one in Triton. I manage to say it despite being on the surface. He seems surprised by the news and my tongue.

"At the camp," he whispers.

I nod. "How do you feel about this?"

It's his turn to nod.

"Okay, I'm hoping for a little more acknowledgment than a head bob. Maybe something more like a genuine emotion —happiness, anxiety, anger? Are you crapping your pants? Just tell me. I'm ready."

"We will marry," he says.

I'm not ready for that. "Fathom, no."

"But we love each other."

I'm speechless. It's not what he said, exactly. I know he loves me. It's more how he says it that takes me aback. This is all predetermined to him. *Of course we'll get married. We'll defy the odds. Our love is star-crossed. It can't be stopped. Happily ever after is right there for the taking.*

"I pick me," I say.

He's confused again. This time, I take his hands in mine.

"I had a choice to make," I say. He doesn't need to know he's been one corner of a love triangle. He doesn't need to know that I was flipping Riley and him over in my head, trying to see them from every side, so I could decide which one to buy. He doesn't need to know that Riley helped me understand something that right now makes sense. "And I picked me."

I tell him that I love him and that I probably always will, and then I tell him all the reasons why it's not a good enough reason for us to be together. He doesn't argue or try to manipulate me. He doesn't go on and on about how if we want it, we can have it. He just sits and listens. For the first time since he came into my life, he is exactly what I need him to be.

The cages are opened, and the Alpha who can walk gather on the beach, close to the shoreline. Some sit in the waves, too tired to move, or maybe it's some desire to be close to the sea.

Soldiers move through their numbers, disconnecting the hobblers. Fights break out. A soldier's leg is broken.

Those who can't walk are carried to a medical tent by soldiers, some of whom have played a part in their suffering. The victims refuse to let doctors see them. Some attack the nurses who offer ice packs. It's a complete mess.

"This is a waste of time," my mother tells me. "Alpha do not accept medicine or medical care."

"They're going to have to change," I say.

"You're going to have to tell them."

I have feared this moment since we arrived. None of the Alpha know I'm prime, other than Flyer and Arcade, and it's not going to go over very well. I've had visions of Selkies charging at me, challenging me for my title. I've worried that all three thousand of these creatures will rise up to tear me apart.

"I suppose you should stand on something when you speak to them," Bex says as she scans the beach for a proper setting.

"Yes, it's important to get me up high so everyone will have a better target."

My mother and father approach, with Johar close behind. Bex explains the plan to them.

"Are you ready for this?" my mother asks.

"Nope. Does it matter?"

"What are you going to tell them?" my father says.

"How it is," Bex crows.

Johar, despite his creepy worldview, is incredibly helpful. He has a small stage constructed for me to stand on, then sets up a microphone and a sound system. One of the men helps me on top, and once I'm up there, I look out at the gathering. There are a few thousand Alpha watching me. White Tower guards and soldiers alike are looking on as well. My kids and Bex sit up front. Fathom, Arcade, Flyer, and his father, Braken, join them, as well as Ghost. But there is little intermingling. The Nix sit with the Nix, the Selkies are with the Selkies, Triton with Triton. All the groups carefully gathering with faces that look like their own.

I raise my hand to speak, but the crowd ignores me. I try again, but it's no good. No one respects me, for a myriad of reasons. If you're a soldier, I'm just a kid. If you're a White Tower guard, I'm a dangerous terrorist. If you're an Alpha, I am a filthy human.

Bex smiles at me and mouths, "You're the boss." It's as good a place as any to start.

"I killed Minerva!" I shout. The words bounce off the waves and come back at me. There's a feedback loop that whines so loud it's shaking the fillings in my back teeth. But I have their attention. Fathom stares up at me in disbelief.

"What did you say, human?" Arcade shouts. She sounds aggressive, but she's trying to help. Her people respect strength, and she's lending me some of hers.

"I said I killed Minerva."

I don't have to wait long. The crowd breaks into a rumbling chatter that rises and rises, until it threatens to turn into chaos. I raise my hand again. "I fought her inside the Great Abyss. She's dead, and I have claimed her title as mine. I am the prime."

"You lie!" a Selkie shouts at me. He stands as if he's preparing to attack. Arcade notices and steps in his way.

"I lived in the hunting grounds for three months. I saw your temples and art. I saw your homes. I was imprisoned in Tarooh's lab, the very person who gave the Alpha the power to build its city."

The arguing explodes. I wait patiently, hoping they will quiet down and let me speak, but they are enraged. They shout and bark at me. Before I would have shrunk at all the noise, but now I know their language. I know what ugly words they're shouting at me. My calls for attention are ignored.

Their noise is suddenly suffocated by a thrum. It sweeps across the beach and covers the crowd like a blanket. After all this time, it still startles me, even though I know it's a sound I can trust. The crowd turns to see Husk and the Rusalka rise out of the surf. They walk through the crowd of screaming Alpha, all shouting threats at them. Even the soldiers spring into action, cocking weapons, but Johar hops onto the stage and demands they stand down.

They don't lower their weapons, but they don't fire them either.

Husk stops in front of me and bends his knee. The others do the same.

"Your Majesty," he says.

The crowd roars at him. They call him an agitator and a traitor. He is a mutant and devil and a heretic. He and his people are obscene.

"The abomination returns," a Ceto shouts. "You and your cowardly bottom feeders come to fight when we are at our weakest. There is no honor in a thing like you."

Husk waits patiently before he speaks again.

"I witnessed the challenge. Minerva fought Lyric Walker with her bare hands. It was a foolish choice, and on that day the Daughter of Human and Sirena was the stronger of the two. I have witnessed her bravery. I have seen the warrior inside of her. She has my respect. She has the respect of the Sons and Daughters of Rusalka. We have pledged our loyalty to her and her vision of the Alpha empire.

A Nix stands. "I will not follow a human, even one that has Alpha blood! She is not of our people."

A Triton woman pushes her way toward the front of the crowd. "I will not bow down to the former prince's harlot."

I jump down off the box and land in front of her. She's surprised. I want to keep her that way.

"Say it again!" I shout so everyone can hear. "Say it to my face!"

She releases her blades, and the crowd grows quiet.

"Are you presenting a challenge?" I ask, fighting down my fear.

The Triton girl's eyes narrow. "I am."

"Step back," Fathom says, rising to his feet. He places himself between the Triton and me. "Ancient law allows for another to fight in her place. I will fight for her."

Arcade steps forward and releases the blade in her good arm. "I will fight for her."

My mother stands and walks through the crowd. "I will fight for her."

Dahlia the Rusalka grunts and flashes her talons. She will fight for me.

Chloe joins the growing list, her glove ignited and burning bright. Riley, Maggie, and all the children join her.

My father is next. "I will fight for her."

Flyer, Braken, even Ghost stand with me, all pledging to defend me.

Johar takes the mic off the stand and hands it down to me.

"These are your rules," I say to the Triton girl. "The person who kills the prime becomes the prime. I'm in charge, so go find your seat before I put you in it."

The Triton girl snarls, but she's no dummy. She backs away to her original spot in the crowd.

"Anyone else want to come up here and get embarrassed?" I ask, looking out at the crowd. I don't see any takers. It's good, because as tough as I sound, I'm pretty sure I'm going to wet my pants. "So, listen up because this is what is happening. We're going to war. Husk will explain. He's going to be my adviser."

"Adviser?" a Feige cries. "Rusalka are untouchable. They cannot council the prime."

"Oh, really? Well, I'm the prime, and I say they can," I shout. "No one is untouchable in my empire. None of you is superior to any other. None of you are better. You are equals."

"It has never been done!" someone shouts.

"You can cry about it later, if you survive, because if you can't put your stupid rules aside, you won't. That's right. Something in the water is coming to kill us, all of us, human and Alpha alike. It isn't picking sides. It hates us all the same. They're called the Tardigrade, and they will be here tomorrow. I need you to prepare."

Johar shouts to the crowd. "We have a team of nurses from the Red Cross coming to look at your injuries—"

The crowd erupts in anger again.

"I need all of you healthy," I cry. "Being hurt and sick on purpose is stupid. You'll be killed first, and trust me, you don't want to die the way a Tardigrade kills you. Are you really going to let yourself be killed because you are too tough for a Band-Aid?"

Husk's voice is in my head. He wants me to use the word *dishonorable*.

"It is dishonorable," I shout. "If you can be strong and fierce but choose to limp into a fight, you turn your back on your empire. So, here's another new rule to add to your list. You are going to let the nurses and doctors help you feel better, or you will be labeled a traitor."

The crowd is silent.

"We've got a lot of work to do, and if we're to have any chance of success, you're going to have to work together with the humans, and before you start whining about it, I'm—"

Before I can finish, my attention is stolen by a crowd of people trickling onto the beach. They are armed with guns and bats and machetes. They are tentative when they see the Alpha, and their presence causes another angry stir. I look to Johar, and he gives me a nod. The president delivered again. The fence is down. My army, for what they're worth, has joined the fight.

"Welcome to the party," I say to them as more and more people gather to watch. "I'm telling my friends here that we have to fight together. We have to look after one another. This is about the end of the world, and we have to put aside our hate and fear of one another. If we can't learn to stand together by tomorrow, we'll all be lying together dead."

Alpha and humans stare at one another. Their eyes are full of suspicion, but at least they are not attacking.

"All right. I think I've said enough. We've got work to do."

I turn and see Riley. For the first time in days, he doesn't tear his eyes away from me.

"So that went well," I groan.

He laughs despite himself. "Next time let me write your speech."

CHAPTER SIXTEEN

DESPITE MY ORDERS, THE ALPHA FIGHT WITH THE medical staff. A few of the arguments turn violent. My rule isn't going to change things overnight. Their wounds are their trophies, and they are desperately proud of them. The ones they have now show the world that they could not be broken, even when caged and starved for three months. I sympathize, but they're just going to have to tell stories about this day rather than show off their wounds around a campfire.

They resist the food as well, though this I understand. Suddenly, I'm asking them to trust that there are people interested in their well-being, when they are the same people who have been abusing them for months. In desperation, I ask Finn and the other children to use their gloves to pull fresh fish out of the ocean for the Alpha to eat. God help them. The water in Coney Island is full of garbage, even more so after two tidal waves destroyed everything and dragged it out to sea. Some of the fish might very well have three eyes.

It's just another layer of worry to add to my growing teenage ulcer.

"They're eating," Husk says. "That's all that matters. It will make them strong again."

"It doesn't mean they'll fight."

"There is still time to persuade them," Husk promises.

"Time is something we are running out of," I say.

We both feel the Tardigrade out there, approaching fast. It's hard to say when they will come onshore, but it's almost certain to be too soon.

I'm heartened to meet a few Alpha who are strong and willing to train groups of humans in hand-to-hand combat. Unfortunately, many of the people have come here from far away, and they are nearly as exhausted as the Alpha. Riley and the kids help, coaching people in the techniques Doyle taught them at Trident. I watch with hidden pessimism. Hand-to-hand combat is not going to stop a Tardigrade. Luckily, someone higher up, maybe Mr. Johar himself, realizes it's pointless, and as the sun begins to set, a line of trucks arrive, delivering hand grenades and rocket launchers. I hear a rumor that more tanks will be here by morning.

Bulldozers push massive mounds of sand together, some two and three stories high. On top of each one is a soldier assembling a giant gun. There must be fifty mounds. The closest to me is already finished with an artilleryman working on his assembly. When it's finished, he stands and peers out at the ocean through binoculars.

When the sun has finally given up on this day, I find a spot on the beach and watch the activity around me. I'm approached every few minutes with questions and concerns. I've found that it's better to pretend like I know what I'm doing than admit that I have no idea. For the most part, the soldiers are listening to someone else, and they don't bother me. The Alpha line up behind Fathom and Flyer, but the humans wander around without a clue. They're not fighters, and three of them have accidentally shot themselves in the foot. I suspect a majority of them have never even been in a fistfight, but there are some who are starting to stand out—the survivalists and militia members and paranoid people who have been living off the grid. They know how to shoot rifles and build camps and fires. They build "tiger pits" on the beach—deep holes lined with wooden spikes they cover with leaves. It's as good an idea as any.

"So you're the kid running this show?" an older woman asks me. She's in a black T-shirt with long gray hair tied in a ponytail. She's got an AK-47 strapped onto her back. I can see she's not taking me seriously, but then she shrugs. "My sons and I pushed a wheelbarrow of ammo all the way from Paramus. Where do you want us to put it?"

My father works with some of the White Tower guards to create a perimeter. He feels the Alpha should be in front, assuming they are healthy enough, followed by the soldiers and guards. Humans, everyone agrees, should guard the rear. Hopefully, the Tardigrade will never get to them, but if they do, they'll have to fight.

"The surface is theirs," my mother says. "It's only right that they are the last stand."

Arcade and Flyer approach.

"May we join you, Your Majesty?" Arcade asks.

I groan. "How do I get you guys to just call me by my name?"

"I don't understand?" Flyer admits.

"How is your father?" I ask him. I've met Braken a handful of times. He was the prime's brother, but the reasonable and mature one of the two. Sadly, he was one of the worst injured we found in the cages.

"He is tired," Flyer responds. "The nurses have sewn some of his wounds together with a string. He is unconscious, so he has not been able to stop them. I would think they might consider themselves lucky."

"I fear more for your hybrids, Lyric Walker."

I look back to the children. Arcade's right. All of them have been quiet, except Riley, who is putting on a brave face.

"I hear that the demon in the rolling chair killed their families and friends," Arcade hisses. "Cowardly and dishonorable filth. If she shows her face here, I will slice it right off."

"You don't have to worry about that," I say. "One of the promises that was made to me before we started this fight was that Pauline Bachman would get what she deserves."

"The loss of parents in such a tragic way is a terrible thing to deal with before a battle," Flyer says. "I fear they have lost the fight Arcade tells me they once possessed."

I can see Chloe leaning her head on Brady's shoulder. They aren't speaking to each other. They just stare out at the sea like they are castaways, lost and forgotten.

"The humans have the passion, but they are fearful and dumb," Arcade says. "And my people are broken. Do you have a plan you are not discussing with the rest of us that ensures success?"

My head falls between my knees. "No. I don't have a plan. There isn't a plan for something like this. We're going to get ready. When the time comes, we will fight. It's the only choice we have."

"Many will die," Arcade says.

"I know. I know."

"You lack confidence in those assembled before you?" Flyer asks.

"I've got fighters who can't fight and regular people who don't know how."

"For most, it is the loss of everything that teaches us to fight," Flyer says as he looks to Arcade.

"When the battle begins, the warriors emerge," Arcade

promises. "Perhaps your news might light a fire in their bellies."

"What?"

"When an Alpha is with child, it is a call for celebration."

"You know?"

"There is a smell—"

"You people and your noses. It's gross."

"If you were to announce it to the others, the empire would rise to fight for you. Your place as the prime would go unchallenged. Fathom's royal blood gives the child validity as a future ruler."

"Were we at the same meeting? Someone called me a half-breed. No one is accepting me as the prime. If you hadn't threatened to kill that Triton girl, you'd have her running this show and I'd be cut into a million pieces. I think most of the empire would be just fine with that."

"You must tell them," Arcade says.

I wander through the tents, past the fires where the Selkies and Ceto and Nix gather. The Sirena watch me warily. When I move through the Triton, they turn their eyes to the ground. They mutter words in their own languages. I'm a failure and human filth. They don't know that I understand every word now. Their insults scare me, not because I can't handle some shade, but because I know these people. Insulting a prime to her face is an open challenge that in the past would have resulted in a fight to the death. The Alpha don't respect me. I'm weak and unproven.

A call is made for them to gather once more, and by the time I stand on the little stage, it is well past midnight. Johar has set up some lights, but they just make me feel like a target. I'm afraid that Flyer and Arcade are wrong. I'm more afraid of how the humans will take it.

My mother and father squeeze my hands and promise me it will be all right, but my dad has one of his hands on the hilt of his pistol. Husk escorts me through the crowd.

"I am most pleased with your announcement and quite honored that you are planning to name the child after me."

I laugh. "Husk, you told a joke."

"I have heard that humor can relieve tension and stress in humans," he says, then steps aside. "Perhaps you could use some of it at the beginning of this address."

"Do you know any Alpha jokes?"

He thinks. "There are no Alpha jokes. Mine are serious people. Perhaps you should avoid humor."

Johar waits for me at the stage. He looks pleased with himself.

"White Tower just signed a fifty-billion-dollar government contract to help rebuild vital infrastructure, train police and teachers, as well as take care of trash removal. It looks like the feds might turn over the entire electrical grid, too."

"Congratulations. I hope we win."

"That would help. Oh, and I heard the good news."

"He's not a business opportunity," I say.

He laughs uncomfortably. I think he knows I'm not joking.

"If you, or anyone at White Tower, ever think he's a profit opportunity, I will kill you first," I promise.

He hands me the microphone, and I turn to the people once more. I tell them that I have an heir growing inside me and that their empire's future is secure. I urge them to fight for that future with everything they have.

For a long moment, there is only silence, and then a roar of approval. I'm going to go out on a limb and say that it might be the only time in the history of the world that an unwed, underage girl has ever received a standing ovation for getting pregnant from unprotected sex.

I can't sleep. No one can. I'm restless and listless at the same time, drowning in responsibility and lack of confidence. I can feel these monsters getting closer. I can sense their numbers. I shudder at their strength and how they callously use it. More videos spread around the camp throughout the day. The images are grotesque and blood soaked. The Tardigrade have murdered entire towns. They've turned rivers and streets into blood. I know that when they are done here, they will go back and kill the towns next to them, until there are no towns, no cities, no people, but they can't resist coming here first. They seem attracted to Husk and me, pulled toward the last connections they sense on this planet. He and I are the chum that lures the shark.

When the Rusalka attacked, I never feared for the whole world. I just fought for Coney Island. When Minerva sent the Undine and its horde of tentacled babies, I never thought it would get all the way across the country. I drew a line, and we stopped it within ten blocks of the beach. But this time I worry for people in other places, other countries. Being inside of their minds, I know what a Tardigrade is capable of doing. I can feel the determination and the strength to accomplish the bloody work. Running was never an option.

I climb up one of the mounds, slipping on sand until I get to the top. The same soldier I watched earlier in the day is up here. He's young, thin, serious. He's lying on his belly with his eye glued to the scope on his rifle.

"I hope you don't mind," I say. "I just wanted to get a better look."

He shrugs. "It's fine," he says. His accent is a mix of French and something else.

"Where are you from?"

"Baton Rouge, or at least what used to be Baton Rouge before the killing started."

"Were you there?"

He shakes his head. "I was on Louisiana Border Patrol. Stupid waste of time, obviously. The fight always comes from the water."

"Did you lose anybody?" I hold my breath for the answer.

"Yeah." It's all he's able to say.

"I've lost a few too."

"You sound tired," he says.

"Tired of fighting."

I train my eyes on the beach. The Triton have picked up the militiamen's strategy and are digging ditches to line with spikes. The Nix carve spears by the dozens. Everyone is working to the endless pounding soundtrack of the Atlantic Ocean. Funny, I once thought of this place as peaceful, especially at this time of night, when I would sneak out and plant myself in the sand to calm my achy head. My mother and I sat on that stretch of beach below and meditated, and talked, and made fun of my father.

"Good luck," I tell the soldier, then scurry back down the mound.

I walk through the camp toward a little tent White Tower set up for me. It's near the Red Cross tent, which, much to my surprise, is overwhelmed with Alpha waiting for treatment. Husk approaches. He's brought fish for someone.

"You should be sleeping," he says.

"So should you."

"They grow closer. They will be here sooner than expected. They will be onshore before dawn."

"I know."

"I must confess something to you," he says. "They invaded

my thoughts this morning. I was swimming along the curve of the shore, looking for ways we might slow the Tardigrade when they approach. They reached out to my mind. They told me terrible things. For a brief moment, I felt sympathetic to their cause. I wanted to help them kill. It made perfect sense to me that everyone needed to die. I believe that I might jeopardize our fight tomorrow. I worry they are capable of making me turn against our army."

"It happened to me, too," I confess.

"So our link may be used against us in the fight."

"When you have your visions, you see your father, correct?"

He nods.

"Mine looks like an old friend of mine. We called him Shadow. He told me that if they can invade our minds, we can do the same. Think about the time I went into your memories. You couldn't get rid of me for a while. Do you think we can do that to the Tardigrade? You know, mess with their heads?"

"We will have to try," he says.

CHAPTER SEVENTEEN

JUST BEFORE DAWN, I HEAR THEM. THEIR PRESENCE LIGHTS A slow fuse in my thoughts that snakes around my skull, popping and crackling, until their voices explode in the center of my brain.

"WE HAVE FOUND THE BROKEN ONES. CLEANSE THE OFFSPRING. MAKE ROOM FOR THE NEW FAMILY."

I try to stand, but I'm overcome with dizziness and pain, and fall back to the ground.

"Lyric? What's wrong?" Bex asks. She stayed with me last night.

"They're here," I whisper.

Bex looks out of the tent flaps, straining her eyes against the rising sun. There's nothing out there, but she doesn't need evidence.

"What do we do?"

Husk. I reach out to his thoughts.

I know is his response. A moment later, I hear the Rusalka thrum conquer the sky of Coney Island.

I grab Bex by the arm. "You know where to go?"

"I do." She reaches into her hoodie pocket and takes out a pistol.

"Where did you get that?" I ask.

"The Big Guy gave it to me. I was hoping for a dress," she confesses.

We crawl out of the tent and see that activity is already underway. Soldiers are running in every direction. Alpha are rousing one another and beating on their chests. Behind us, the human army is waking and loading guns.

I point to the top of one of the mounds where Baton Rouge is waiting and watching. "Get up there and don't move unless he tells you something else—and try not to shoot yourself."

She takes off at a sprint.

Maggie races to my side with the children in tow: Finn, Sienna, Brady, Renee, and Jane. My parents are right behind them. Chloe's hand is tucked into my mother's.

"Are they here?" Maggie asks. "We don't see them."

"They're here. Light them up, kids."

They all race in single file down the beach in both directions, spreading out as far as they can, a thin line of defense, but I have more faith in them than the rest of the army combined. The children ignite their gloves and lift them toward the sky.

Husk and the Rusalka hurry to join us. Each one holds a spear. They know what they are supposed to do. They line up next to the children and watch the water. Husk stays by my side.

"I think I asked you to join the others," I shout at him.

"My place is with you," he says. There's no arguing with him.

I look up and down the beach, watching tanks roll into position and soldiers charging forward with rocket launchers on their shoulders. Infantry march into position with guns in hand. And the Alpha rush forward to fill in the gaps. Fathom raises his arm, and in one fluid motion, the Triton's blades pop from their forearms. The Nix allow their bodies to morph so their hands become long, spindly claws. The Selkies roar and dig into their positions; the Sirena stand guard, many with bats and pieces of lumber. The tiny Ceto crackle with electricity.

Riley is suddenly to the left of me. Fathom appears on my right.

"Look what you did, Lyric Walker," Fathom says.

I glance back, beyond the tanks and mounds. There are hundreds of thousands of people with makeshift weapons and firearms. Johar said we'd get two million by morning. I think he underestimated. I have never seen this many people gathered in one place in my life.

I look over to Riley. He rolls his eyes and gives me his oh-brother expression. "Let us take the lead, all right? You need to think about the baby."

Something massive hurtles itself out of the water. It lands with a crash only a few yards away, spraying sand and soil in every direction. The rising sun shines on its bloated body, illuminating its deathly white skin so that it radiates in my eyes. The creature shakes itself off, turns its head back and forth, and eyes those who stand against it. It sniffs the air and stomps a foot so hard I feel the thump in my feet, then it shoots its cone of teeth in and out of its horrible mouth. It blasts a huff of air at us. It smells like death and rot.

"YOU STAND WITH THE BROKEN ONES."

The voice is directed at Husk and me. It's so horrible and loud, made up of a hundred thousand individuals, each of them is angry and offended. The noise is pounding. Husk lowers his head, clearly suffering as much as I am.

"We do," I answer.

"THE OFFSPRING ARE FLAWED. THEY MUST BE ELIMINATED TO MAKE WAY FOR A MORE PERFECT FAMILY."

"It's you that are flawed," Husk argues. "The nature of your children is to be individuals, free to make their own decisions and have their own feelings. We are not broken. We have rejected your voice."

"TO REJECT THE VOICE IS TO BE ADRIFT IN LONE-LINESS."

It's trying to reason with us, again. I feel it tugging at my mind and manipulating my feelings. I can see the logic in what they are saying—connection to one another is not an ideal, it is necessary. Without it, there is only sorrow. No! I push them out of my head.

"TO DISCONNECT IS NOT WHAT WE INTENDED."

"Yeah, well, kids have a way of disappointing their parents," I shout. "Go back to your volcano. There is no reason why we have to fight."

"YOU HEAR THE VOICE! YOU KNOW ITS BEAUTY! MOVE ASIDE FOR YOUR CREATORS. THE BROKEN CHILDREN MUST BE ELIMINATED."

The words hit me harder than a punch. I almost fall, but Fathom keeps me standing.

"What's happening, Lyric Walker?"

"They're not leaving. Fight."

The Alpha let loose a ferocious cheer. The Rusalka's thrum rises high into the air. The soldiers let loose bullets and rockets in a thunderstorm of artillery. The Nix leap forward like frogs and slash the beast's flesh. The Triton join in, then the Selkies, pounding on the Tardigrade with their massive fists. I'm stunned when it falls over. I never expected it to be so easy to kill. The bullets stop, the shouting quiets, and everyone turns to me.

"This is the terror you warned us about?" Arcade asks.

Tardigrade leap out of the water in the hundreds. They crash around us, sometimes on top of people, crushing them dead. Bullets burn through the air. I see a rocket slam into one, leaving a trail of black smoke behind it. The first hundred are joined by a hundred more, then another hundred. With their gigantic size and numbers, the beach gets crowded very fast, and their quick, bulky bodies crash into our lines and make massive holes.

One monster races right at us. Fathom leaps off the ground, his blades extended from his arms, and he slices its head off. The carcass collapses, sending a spray of sand and blood right at us. It doesn't dissuade the others. Another Tardigrade charges, only to have Riley command the ocean to snatch it off the ground. He throws it so far out to sea I can't see it anymore.

My father rushes to join us, loading and reloading his pistol, emptying bullet after bullet into the approaching horde. He manages to blast one in the face, and the beast falls dead.

"Where's Mom?" I cry.

"With Chloe," he shouts, pointing down the beach. I can see the little girl's creations pulverizing the beasts as they stomp out of the water. My mother uses her bare hands to knock one off its feet. All the while the Tardigrade direct their numbers, managing them with one single voice that sends them into different attacks. I shout to the soldiers, ordering them to rush different parts of the beach, then calling others back. Husk does the same to the Alpha.

"Lyric!" Riley cries. "I can hear them too."

"You can?"

I look down the beach at the kids. Maybe they can all hear them.

"Riley, you need to tell the others to listen. The Tardigrade announce every attack. We can stop them!"

Riley nods and takes off running down the beach.

A Tardigrade gets too close to me, and a soldier I don't know opens fire. His weapon jams and the creature pounces, trapping him beneath his weight. The Tardigrade's mouth curls open, and its circular jaw shoots out like a whip. I saw this in the videos, but it's so much worse in person. The spike stabs the soldier's chest for a split second, then recoils. A moment later, it lumbers off the man to attack someone else. Dumbfounded, the soldier gets to his feet, seemingly unharmed, but it's only a second before he and I know something is terribly wrong. His body swells. He screams in agony, dying long before the metamorphosis is complete. When he is nearly three times his original size, his chest splits open and a grotesque white crea-ture, a mixture of a tadpole and a maggot, slithers out onto the sand. Before anyone can attack, it hops into the air and crashes back down into the sand, burrowing with such lightning speed there's nothing left but a hole.

My father fires his gun into the ground. "It's crawling around down there."

"Everyone, get off the sand!" I shout, but I have no idea where they would even go. There is nothing but sand. This is a beach!

We scatter, but not before there's an explosion of earth to my right. I watch the Tardigrade's creation shoot out of it and swallow a Nix whole. His friends claw at the baby Tardigrade's side. It screams and tries to burrow to safety, but the Nix are all over it, cutting it to pieces.

"What the hell is that?" a soldier shouts.

I think that's our baby brother.

Another wave of Tardigrade charges out of the water; this time a thousand take the beach. The sudden arrival of so many overwhelms our forces.

"Push forward!" a soldier shouts, as another row of military personnel rush forward with flamethrowers strapped onto their backs. They roast whatever gets close, but it seems only to anger the monsters. They tear into the men, stomping and ripping them apart, spiking their chests and causing nightmares to come out of the bloated victims.

We run for the mounds, scampering up the sandy sides, struggling with every step. There, the kids can fire on the creatures from safety. They target their attacks according to what they hear in their heads, but there are far too many monsters to stop them completely. They use their numbers to rush between the mounds like cattle. Baton Rouge and fifty other soldiers like him fire viciously into the mutants. Many are killed, but there are so many more. They crawl over their fallen brothers. Tanks blast them with their guns, but the Tardigrade slam into them, knocking them on their sides. They've broken the last line of defense. There's nothing between them and the humans.

Husk barks at his Rusalka, and they race after the horrible beasts as they crash into the enormous crowd of people. Guns fire in every direction. A mass of thousands scream and trample one another. People are dying everywhere I look. Soldiers are in retreat. Ceto and Selkie lie face-down in the surf. Brady falls off one of the mounds into the mass of monsters. He's gone. We failed. We failed.

A terrible sting bites my side, and I turn to find a Tardigrade behind me, his tooth-covered spike retracting into his mouth. I look down, feeling a terrible pain growing inside, a searing expansion of every muscle and organ. Riley races to my side. He's screaming, but I can't hear him. Fathom attacks the monster, but it's pointless. I'm already dead.

CHAPTER EIGHTEEN

A LIGHT SWALLOWS ME. IT'S BLUE AND BRIGHT AND CALM. It comes with the loveliest sensation. Every part of me feels warm and awake. All my pain is gone. Every worry melts away. I am safe for the first time in many years.

"Lyric?" Bex is hovering over me. I've fallen, and she's trying to get me back on my feet. "Can you hear me, Lyric?"

Lyric?

"Shadow, is that you?"

Yeah. Guess what?

Husk stands over me. "Lyric, stay with us!"

Fathom stands over me. Riley is here, too. My mom and dad are here. My mother is holding my hand.

No Lyric, no games. I'm really out of here this time. Don't worry, the baby is going to be fine.

"But I'm not," I say.

I hear him laugh. *Plot twist.*

Suddenly, my friends and family melt away. Shadow is gone, and I am somewhere else on the battlefield, but I am not alone. I feel my son inside me, and the power coming from him.

I stand over the Tardigrade Fathom attacked. She lies on her side, staring up to the sky, leaking black blood onto the sand. I peer into her hideous face, and suddenly I'm inside her. I am in her mind. I am her.

"STOP!" I shout.

The Tardigrade shudder at my presence. Across the beach, they stumble. Some cry out in pain. My words hurt their minds.

"WHY DO YOU HURT US?" they ask.

"GO BACK TO THE GREAT ABYSS. YOUR CHILDREN REJECT YOU," I threaten.

"NO! THE BROKEN ONES MUST BE DESTROYED. ROOM MUST BE MADE FOR A NEW FAMILY."

"THERE ARE NO BROKEN ONES!" I shout. The baby's power explodes out of my consciousness. It's nothing more than a seed, but when it splits open it sprouts a vine that twists and turns around the voice, choking it and pulling it apart. The Tardigrade scream for mercy, then threaten to kill me, then weep at their own ending.

I can feel every one of them. I can see through all of their eyes. I can walk through thousands and thousand of years of their collected memories. My vine burrows into them, finds the connection they all share, that they believe we need, and strangles it. The voice is gone. I am no longer linked to them, or Husk. I stand and watch the monsters fall.

• • •

The White Tower trucks arrived quickly, filled with food and water and blankets for anyone who needed them.

"I'm surprised they didn't get here sooner," I say to Johar.

He smiles. "Opportunity knocks. We'll be in touch, Ms. Walker."

"No, let's not."

I watch him walk off to join several other men and women in business suits. I suppose they're the board of directors.

My mother and father look tired. Chloe hovers at my mom's leg.

"I guess I have a baby sister now?" I say, smiling into her little face. She smiles back.

"You know, I come with the deal," Bex tells her.

Husk and Fathom stand together. They wait for me to give them orders.

"I'm abdicating," I say. "One of you has to be the prime."

"That is not allowed," Husk says.

"Wait, Fathom quit. Why can't I?"

"Fathom was a prince, not a prime."

"Well, I'm in charge. I can change the rules," I argue.

"I'm afraid there are some rules that cannot be broken," Fathom says.

"I'm not going back into the water. Fathom rules in my place. Husk is your adviser. Arcade gets to be whatever she wants to be. Fix your people. Together."

Fathom's hurricane eyes lock onto mine. "I will not abandon you and the baby," he says.

"You have no other choice," I say.

There are a million things left to say, but I can't imagine one of them that should be said. He and Husk shout to their people, and I watch them lead the Alpha back into the ocean.

Arcade and Flyer stop in the progression and turn to me. Arcade bends her knee and bows. I think it's the closest thing I will ever get to a goodbye hug from her.

I take Flyer by the hand. "Take good care of this girl," I whisper. "The prime commands you."

He smiles and nods respectfully, and soon they are gone along with the others. There is a tap on my shoulder, and when I turn, I find Dahlia the Rusalka, along with the rest of her clan.

"Yes?" I say.

She wraps me into a hug, then steps aside for the others to do the same. I watch them follow the rest, and soon they are gone, back to the sea.

The kids gather around me, Riley included. Brady's death is another blow, but their uncertain future seems to be troubling them more. They look to me for an answer, some kind of direction I can point toward.

"We stick together," I say. It's vague, but it seems to satisfy them.

Bex puts her hand in mine. I look at her, and she smiles. She is my bestie, my BFF, my sister from another mister. I chose me. She's part of the deal.

"Where to now, Walker?" she says.

I look out at the crashing waves. "Somewhere boring, Conrad."

My family and I stay in the camp for several days while arrangements are made for something permanent. It's going to take time. There are a lot of problems the country is facing at once. Some of the states are refusing to rejoin the union. There's talk of war.

On one afternoon, the president fulfills his last promise to me and a helicopter arrives to pick me up.

The prison isn't far, perhaps an hour and a half. We touch down behind its huge fence, lined with barbed wire, and the pilot helps me step out onto the ground. He points to a door in the side of the building and gives me a thumbs-up. He promises to wait.

There is a guard standing at the desk. I don't know her, but she smiles at me like we are friends. People have been doing that since the battle. It's nice.

"She's ready," the guard says, then leads me through several locked doors that open only when she calls out to some unknown person. We descend a flight of stairs to a door with the words *solitary confinement* painted in black.

The guard opens the door and gestures for me to enter. "I'll be right outside," she says.

She closes the door, leaving me inside, but I am not alone.

Pauline Bachman sits in her wheelchair. Her once-perfect hair is flat and dry. Her ever-present blue business suit has been replaced by an orange jumper with her prisoner number stitched on the front. Her face, however, is as twisted and mangled as ever.

There is a chair sitting across from her, so I sit in it. She eyes me up and down, then snarls. I have imagined this moment many times. I have considered shouting at her, threatening her, demanding answers, even trying to reason with her, but as I sit across from her, I'm not sure any of those things will make me feel better. She knows I put her here. She knows this is the payment I demanded to save the world. She knows that she will never leave this room again. Really, what am I going to say to her that is worse than what is unsaid? I sit back in the chair, look around the room, and then sigh.

"So, how's the food?"

EPILOGUE

I HAVEN'T BEEN BACK TO CONEY ISLAND IN THREE YEARS. I'M told things have changed, but when we roll down the new Neptune Street, it looks a lot like it used to back in the day. There are still mom-and-pop pizza shops, and video game arcades, and raucous bars. The lights are still gaudy, and the people gaudier. They rebuilt the Cyclone, but it's a bit too fancy for me. It's not a real roller coaster if it's built to safety codes.

We park the car in a lot and hand a man with an orange flag twenty bucks.

"How long do you plan to stay?" he asks.

"Hard to say, really," I answer. He shrugs and gives us a ticket for the window.

"Can we get ice cream?" Max asks. He's all about ice cream, and the flavor doesn't matter. I suppose that's what I was into when I was three.

"Maybe," I say. "Did you brush your teeth this morning?"

He opens his mouth wide to show me he did.

"All right, but later. We don't want to keep him waiting."

"Are you nervous?" Riley asks as we cross the street and head for the boardwalk. I can already hear the waves, and in a few more steps, I'll see the whitecaps curling in on themselves as they hammer the beach. It's a miracle I can hear anything over all the construction. There must be at least three hotels going up on the same block. I guess some things do change. The closest thing we had to a hotel was a homeless shelter.

"Of course she is," Bex says, giving my shoulder a little squeeze.

"Why are we here?" Max asks. He's forgetful, but again, he's three.

I kneel down on the wooden planks so that we are eye to eye. He listens better when I am on his level. "I told you, Pickle. We're here to meet your daddy."

"Are you sure he'll come?" Bex asks.

I nod.

"What does my daddy look like?"

"He's hot," Bex says. Riley gives her a little scowl. She giggles and wraps him up in her arms. "Not like you."

She tries to kiss him, but he playfully pulls away. "Nope, you blew it."

"C'mon, baby, you know you can't resist me," she says, laughing.

It used to hurt a little to see their love. Bex offered to end it, but it was pretty obvious they were built for one another. He's given her a place where she feels safe to feel things. I love him for being her hot nerd with potential.

Max giggles and blushes, then hides behind my leg. Bex notices and scoops him up.

"If I can't get a kiss from my fiancé, I'll get one from you," she says.

My son squeals when she plants a wet one on his cheek. Riley and Bex laugh and laugh. I suppose it won't be long before the two of them have a Max of their own. It's fine. There's plenty of room in Denver. Maggie has already found her own place, and Sienna will be next. I'm losing my kids one by one.

"Tell him we said hello," Bex offers.

She and Riley hang back as I take Max's hand and walk him down onto the beach. We get as far as the surf, then stop. He stares out at the vast ocean and blinks into the sunshine. A wave rolls in and nearly gets his sneaker. He's got such an easy laugh.

"Mommy, tell me where you got my name again."

"Again?"

"Please!"

"A long time ago, a princess from Brooklyn met a prince who could not read. She gave him a book called *Where the Wild Things Are.*"

"Max!" he cries.

"Yes, it was about a boy named Max who went to an island where monsters lived, and he became their king."

"So I'm the king of the wild things?"

"Yes, honey, you are."

There's a splash, and a crowd of people rise from the water. Husk and Fathom lead the others until they are standing before me. All of them kneel and bow. Max giggles, nervously, then looks up at me. I wink at him, then bend down.

"I'm the queen of the wild things," I whisper.

Fathom is still the same beautiful creature I met years ago, with eyes like hurricanes and golden skin. His hair is a bit longer, but he still takes my breath away. Ghost and Flyer are by his side. Arcade follows, along with a few Alpha I don't know.

Husk gives me a hug.

"Your Majesty," he says.

"You know I hate that," I say.

"I do," he says.

Fathom smiles at me. There are a lot of things going on in it, things I am surprised I am eager to see, surprised I still feel myself, but we say nothing. We never had to say anything. Today is not a day to talk about messy entanglements and romantic impossibilities, anyway. Today is about our son.

Fathom kneels to Max's height. He stares at the boy with glassy, amazed eyes.

"Max this is your daddy."

"Hello, Max."

"Are you a wild thing?" he asks.

"Of course. Where do you think I learned to do the wild rumpus?"

Fathom stands tall and does a silly, awkward dance. It's forced, but it's the most unguarded thing I have ever seen him do. It makes his son laugh. It makes me fall in love, again.

"Do it with me," Fathom pleads, and Max apes his ridiculous movements.

I look around at the beach where I grew up. This is where everything changed for me. I was just a girl who happened to witness the arrival of a strange race of people from under the sea. One of them was the most beautiful person I ever met. He walked out of the ocean and changed my life forever.

Funny how history has a way of repeating itself.

ACKNOWLEDGMENTS

Sarah Landis gave me the greatest gift an editor can give a writer—more time. Thank you for your patience and understanding as I swam through murky waters. This book wouldn't exist if not for two women, Betsy Groban, who always believed in it, and Alison Fargis, who always believed in me. I'd like to thank Rachel Wasdyke, Hayley Gonnason, Lisa DiSarro, and the rest of the sirens who worked so hard to lure sailors and readers to this series. Thanks to everyone at Houghton Mifflin Harcourt for all your passion and hard work. Thanks to everyone at Stonesong for uncountable favors and support. Thanks to friends and family, who hopefully know that when I disappear, it's into an imaginary world I can't wait to share with them. And thanks to Finn, my wild thing.